All that Shines and Whispers

Advanced Praise for
All That Shines and Whispers

*****

"I finished this novel in only two days because I couldn't leave the characters alone."

"WOW! The suspense truly kept me turning page after page. I loved the amazing foreshadowing weaved throughout with the unsuspecting twists and turns!"

"All That Shines and Whispers is a page turner with just the right amount of mystery. Great read!"

"A perfect little read about a not-so-little (or perfect) family who escaped Nazi Germany but couldn't escape their big secret!"

"Great read. Craven does it all in this book. Portraying just how far one will go for those they love. A page turner until the end!"

"An amazing story. The Weiss family reminds us all that families are strongest when they stick together."

For the two Nancys
When I think of you, I think of music.

Mother Protecting Her Child

Jean-Baptiste-Camille Corot, French, 1796 - 1875

ALL THAT SHINES AND WHISPERS

ONE

February 1940

The coins hit the bottom of the mason jar with a tight series of clinks. Lara held the thick glass at eye level: three little circles—two silver, one bronze—lay inside, their emblems and prominent profiles staring up through the jar's opening. She jiggled it in her hand, listening to the coins clang against each other.

They sounded like freedom.

Two francs. It was far from what she needed, but it was a start.

Biting her bottom lip, Lara replaced the lid and shoved the jar under her mattress for safe keeping. The act felt deceptive. The money wasn't hers. In that moment, she'd become a common thief.

She sat back on the floor and stared at her bed, second-guessing her decision. It wasn't too late. She could return the money and continue with a clean conscience.

Who am I kidding, she thought. *There's nothing clean about any of this.*

They certainly couldn't judge her. After all, they'd hardly given her a choice.

Lara stood, pleased. If they thought secrets were so important, she ought to be allowed a few of her own.

* * *

"Come along, girls," Marlene called to Miriam and Gloria. "This wind will send a chill right to our bones."

Her voice, firm but kind, echoed off the brick buildings on the busy main street. The sisters held hands and they followed step by step behind their mother's stride, so brisk that their ankles would have formed blisters had their leather boots not been broken in by years of wear from their older siblings.

Hand-me-downs—a new consequence of their mother's frugality.

From a distance, they looked like an ordinary family: mother and three children, on their way to the market. Two youngsters, barely waist-tall, following their mother's footsteps, and a baby propped on the woman's hip. A common sight, especially in one of the most populated cities in Switzerland.

But this was no ordinary family. This was a prominent family. A wanted family.

Braving the blustery conditions of a particularly chilly February morning, Marlene glanced over her shoulder and hustled her daughters across the street toward the grocers. The hood of Gloria's cape fought against angry wind for its place on the girl's head. She reached up with her free hand to hold it in place, keeping her ears from the cool air.

Ahead, in Marlene's arms and wrapped in a heavy blanket, baby Erich peeked out from behind the hem of a thick stocking cap. The heavy knit drooped lower over his eyes with each step his mother took, leaving him to simply hold on and trust her course.

A car whizzed past, and Marlene paused to adjust the empty produce bags on her shoulder. Her neck was tight. Shopping with three small children in tow took patience and dexterity—things she was learning to master in her new role as Mother.

At times, she had to remind herself: *You're a mother of eight now.* Her past life seemed like a distant memory. One day a single, young woman, and the next—*bam!*—seven (eight, once Erich was born) children to raise.

She regretted nothing.

Having lived in Zürich for just under two years, Marlene was still acclimating to her new home. The children's adjustment was easy—they readily adapted to their new surroundings and seemed quite content to start a new life so long as they were together. Marlene had never experienced such a bond between siblings before entering the Weiss' lives. They were devoted to one another.

The children were closer than close. They'd been each other's only playmates, spending full days without seeing another soul outside their brood. That type of connection can fuel one of two things: annoyance or affinity. For the Weiss children, it was the latter.

Adjustment for Marlene and her husband, Doctor Gerald Weiss, on the other hand, didn't come quite as readily. They

3

needed time, feeling very much like they'd left a piece of their hearts in Austria. They'd left so suddenly—less by choice than by force—when Gerald was ordered to serve as the private doctor to the top level of government officials. The Nazis wanted him. His vocal opposition only made them want him more.

"I won't do it," he'd said. "I'd rather lose my license than care for those bastards."

In the end, with a threat of direct escort looming over his head, he'd gathered the family and fled into the mountains, where they'd made their way across the border to freedom.

Now, despite its geographical proximity to her homeland and the similarities between the countries, Marlene still felt like a visitor in Switzerland.

Everywhere she went, she scrutinized her surroundings. Were people staring at her? Did they *know?*

Reaching the other side of the street now, Marlene stepped up onto the curb and hoisted Erich higher on her hip, repositioning her arms under his chunky thighs. She turned to make sure the girls were close behind. Her bright eyes rested on their wind-flushed faces.

"We're here, Mother," Gloria answered the unspoken question with a smile that revealed two missing front teeth. Her cherubic face melted Marlene's heart every time the girl spoke. She'd been the youngest for so long that despite Erich's arrival, Gloria still acted like the baby of a family. So sweet, with full cheeks and long flowing hair, their youngest daughter had her parents tightly wrapped around her stubby, little finger.

"Alright," Marlene said, ushering them through the wide double doors. The warmth of the store thawed their bones, and the girls removed their hoods. Marlene plucked Erich's hat from his head, and as she did the acrylic sparked static electricity that made his fine, baby hair stand on end.

The girls giggled.

Already overheated from her heavy wool coat and the twenty-pound human on her side, Marlene focused. "Let's pick out what we need for dinner." She grabbed a basket with one hand and strode toward the produce stands.

The sisters helped hand items to Marlene, while she balanced the baby in one arm and the basket in the other. When the string beans started to spill over the edge of the woven metal rim, the girls took turns carrying a second.

They didn't need much, as grocery trips were something that kept Marlene busy during the week. She liked shopping for the family's food. Back in Austria, before they were forced to flee the lives they knew and the home they loved, they'd had the luxury of a housekeeper. Frau Schuster did the grocery shopping then, and kept a kitchen full of crisp produce, soft breads and the best cuts of meat. The children had become accustomed to luxuries like a freshly-frosted cake on the counter, or a perfectly layered trifle proudly displayed under a glass dome. To them, the origin of these treats was a mystery. But it didn't matter. They just appeared and sat there begging to be eaten.

Spoiled with a life of privilege, the Weiss children had lived comfortably. More than comfortably, in fact—at least in the material sense. In terms of attention and affection, they'd been sorely lacking for years before Marlene revived their father's affection.

Now, the idea of their family gathering around the grand dining table and welcoming meals prepared and served by staff was nothing but a distant memory.

Marlene shook the thought from her mind. Things were different here. And while it took Gerald longer to adjust to their decline in affluence (a proud man never receives a demotion gladly), Marlene welcomed the change. Now, buying and preparing her own meals gave Marlene a sense of pride and utility. Living with such extravagance was never something she warmed to fully anyway, during the brief time following their wedding, particularly having come from an unpretentious life at the abbey. A spacious mansion? Grand parties? She preferred simplicity. Who needs the newest fashions when you can make your own perfectly suitable clothing from scraps of fabric around the house?

"Marlene?" A silvery voice made her turn from the rows of green and red apples. "Oh yes, it is you. I wasn't sure from behind. Your hair is longer!" The woman, short and stocky with a spotted complexion—Marlene couldn't tell whether they were freckles or age spots—flapped a hand in Marlene's direction. Her headscarf was tied so tightly around her face, it made Marlene think of the wimples worn by the nuns she once called roommates.

Nora Huber was a teacher at the secondary school where Marlene's middle children attended. When the family inquired about admitting two of their older children, Lena and Felix, after settling in the new town, Frau Huber was kind and welcoming. She gave Marlene and Gerald a tour of the facility and explained to Lena and Felix what a typical day's schedule would entail. The looks on their faces said it all: pure intimidation. So the generous woman went out of her way to make the Weisses as comfortable as possible, seeing it was the first time the children had ever attended a public school. And for that, Marlene was eternally grateful.

"Oh, good morning, Nora," Marlene replied warmly. "How are you?"

"Well, thanks. Aside from this bitter cold, that is. You?"

"We're fine. Just grabbing a few things for dinner." She gestured to the handfuls of apples Miriam and Gloria were dropping happily into their basket. "I told them we could make apple strudel," she laughed. Marlene licked her lips and grinned at the girls, whose basket was nearly overflowing. "Hey now, that's plenty, you two."

Nora chuckled. "So sweet, your girls, Marlene. I hope to have them in my class someday!" She crouched to come eye level with the children. "I imagine you're as much of a delight as your older siblings." Miriam nodded politely, while Gloria grabbed onto her mother's leg for security, sure the woman's massive smile would bust the seam of her scarf along her jaw. Marlene rubbed the girl's shoulder for reassurance.

"And look at this strapping lad!" Nora returned stood and reached out to stroke Erich's tiny hand. "My, you're getting so big! He's adorable, Marlene. Really just the perfect combination of you and your husband."

"Thank you." Erich rested his head in the hollow of Marlene's neck, and she gave him a squeeze. "He was the perfect addition to our brood."

"Yes. You have a beautiful family. You're truly blessed, Marlene." She articulated each syllable—Mar-lay-na—in that eloquent way teachers do.

"We are."

She swallowed the words down. They tasted bitter. *That's not a lie,* she told herself.

"Listen," Nora said, flicking her outstretched fingers, "we're celebrating Clair's eighteenth birthday next Friday evening. A big bash. You should send your girls over! She'd love to see them! The more the merrier."

"How kind, Nora. I'll certainly let them know."

Gloria tugged on Marlene's skirt.

"Okay, okay, we'll keep going."

"Oh yes, please don't let me keep you," Nora said, taking a step backward. "So nice running into you, Marlene! Give my best to the rest of the family. And tell Felix and Lena I'll see them bright and early in class on Monday!"

She wiggled her cupped hand at the girls—a gesture one only does when saying goodbye to young children—then turned the other direction. Marlene led her gang further into the stands of vegetables, running through her mental list. They grabbed what they needed for dinner—veal, cabbage, and more than enough apples—paid the teller, and began their six-block walk home. The girls skipped ahead, a bag in each hand.

* * *

Upon arriving in Switzerland, Marlene and Gerald agreed that living in the city, rather than the countryside, was a much-needed reprieve. Their lives in Austria had been secluded in a way, and Marlene worried about the children becoming terribly lonely if they were forced to live in a remote place once again. They chose Zürich for not only its location but also its bustling, dense population: big enough to blend in. Marlene was determined to give the children a new life—one that she'd first introduced when she began her role as their tutor—which included dissolving their father's impossibly strict rules.

From the moment she'd stepped a scuffed boot into the foyer of their sprawling home, she'd set the family on another course.

It was the Reverend Mother who had suggested Marlene apply for the tutor position with the Weiss family. After spending only two years working in the convent classroom, Marlene and the Abbess had grown close, Marlene often turning to the woman for guidance.

At first keen to meet and help mold new young minds, Marlene was unprepared for the tenseness she encountered. Still, after time, her presence softened Gerald, bringing a renewed joy back to his soul, and the children relished in this gentler, sweeter family dynamic.

In Zürich, they immersed themselves into the general public of their fresh city, leaving behind much of the isolation the children had been used to. It proved to be a smart decision—the kids were thriving in Switzerland. They had friends—real ones, outside of each other!—and even engaged in extracurriculars. In all, each of the Weisses had become more outgoing, and overall more comfortable both in and outside the house.

Marlene's magic touch had worked.

Their two-story home sat at the end of a dead-end street adjacent to the main drag. Being so close to town meant the family could walk most places, which Marlene enjoyed, and it gave the children an opportunity to breathe fresh air every day. She'd always loved the crisp smell of nature and using her legs to get her to where she needed to go. It was as if her limbs had a mind of their own—her muscles itched to explore, to take her new places. Marlene would start out walking and before long, she'd be skipping, dancing—and often singing—with the merriment of one without a care in the world.

Of course, she had cares now. Plenty of them. They lived in one of the largest cities in Switzerland, surrounded more by brick and shingles than grass and streams. Instead of frolicking in lush meadows, she now fought the clock to get homework done before dinner. Still, Marlene often found herself daydreaming of the times, when after she'd finished the lessons with her pupils in the little classroom adjacent to the convent, she would slip from its cold, stark walls and get lost in the green hills.

A soft voice brought her back.

"Mother, can we go to the park today?" Gloria asked, as they rounded the corner of their street.

"No, darling. It's far too cold today. Plus, we need to get home because your brother is getting heavy." She rearranged the boy in her arms again. Miriam and Gloria, having learned manners above all else, kept their disappointment to themselves, but dragged the canvas bags of food along behind them.

When they reached the wrought iron gate in front of their home, Marlene used her key to unlock and swing it open. The girls rushed through, galloping as quickly as they could while carrying the groceries, and bounded up the front steps, disappearing through the door. Marlene followed, trudging slowly under the weight of the baby and the full sack of food on her shoulder. From behind the white swiss curtain framed by two gray shutters, Marlene caught a glimpse of a child's face. She suspected it was Karl, anxious for her return.

Once inside, Marlene placed Erich on the floor and dropped the groceries to the counter. Her biceps tingled from the baby's heaviness, and she shook her arms to bring feeling back to her fingers.

"We're back!" she called. Erich promptly crawled out of the room, his hands slapping against the linoleum. A loud pounding of footsteps followed, and soon four more Weiss children stood in the kitchen.

"Hello, dear. Help me unload these?" she asked Bettina, fifth oldest with thick raven hair and a wise look in her eyes. She was a reclusive child, more likely to spend the day reading than engaging with other eleven-year-olds.

"Yes, Mother."

"What did you get today?" Lena asked, peeking into one of the bags. Tall for fourteen, her height—along with her steady nature—often deceived people. With gangly limbs and butterscotch bangs cut blunt across her forehead, Lena lived in the gray area between girlhood and ripeness. She worshiped Lara, her older sister.

Or at least, she used to. But that was another time.

Before Lena could get a glimpse, little Gloria answered her question. "Apples!" she exclaimed. "Mother said we can make strudels tonight." She hopped off, clutching a ruby red orb in each hand.

"Yum," Felix said. "I hope you got enough for Karl and me!" The two boys of the family, aside from baby Erich, ate more than their fair share of food and Marlene continued to be amazed at their bottomless stomachs. At sixteen and twelve, the boys were sprouting fast, constantly outgrowing clothes. For that, at least, Karl was never in short supply of hand-me-downs from his older brother.

Felix was practically a man—evident by not only his stature, but also the deepening of his voice a year earlier and the blond whisker shavings Marlene wiped from the bowl of the sink (a much lighter shade than her husband's dark five o'clock shadow).

Marlene watched the children put the food in the pantry. Lena folded the muslin bags and placed them in the small crate by the door, ready for the next shopping trip. Their father had

11

instilled a firm expectation of obedience in his children, and even with Marlene's more relaxed approach, the children still displayed a sense of responsibility that made her proud.

"Where's Lara?" Marlene asked, heaving a sack of flour into the upper cupboard. The oldest of the children, Lara was a beautiful girl on the brink of womanhood, with shoulder-length dark hair and blue eyes as clear as a tropical sea.

The teen hadn't quickly warmed to Marlene. "I'm too old for a tutor," she'd insisted. "I'm practically finished with my schooling anyway." Her attitude had changed, though, once she discovered Marlene's most generous heart and fierce loyalty. When the relationship between Marlene and Gerald turned from business to pleasure, Lara's openness grew. Soon, Lara and her stepmother were close.

At seventeen, Lara was the only one of the children who didn't attend public school, instead reasoning with her parents to concede in allowing her to complete her high school education with an instructor who would come to the house regularly.

It was the least they could do.

"Upstairs, I think," Lena answered her mother's question casually. "Haven't seen her much today."

"Do we ever?" Bettina echoed.

Marlene frowned. It was no secret that Lara had struggled with their new life in Zürich. Since their arrival, she'd become withdrawn and somber, quite the opposite of her once genial self. Her siblings chalked it up to teenage heartbreak, after Lara's boyfriend, Rubin, had turned out to be far from the person Lara thought he was.

And that was true—at least partly.

"Would you mind telling her to come down?" Marlene asked Karl, who was standing closest to the edge of the room and the one of the group contributing least to unloading the groceries. He spun in place and leaned his upper body around the edge of the doorframe.

"LARA! MOTHER WANTS YOU!" His high-pitched scream made Marlene wince.

"I meant could you go upstairs and get her." She shook her head at the wide grin that spread across his round face. He smiled, clearly amused, baring all his teeth for display. Karl was once described as incorrigible by a great-aunt, but Marlene knew he was simply playful and young. The middle child certainly kept everyone on their toes.

Near her feet, baby Erich pulled up to stand, holding onto a drawer handle for balance. Bettina plopped down on the floor on the other side of the kitchen, spreading her legs in a wide "V." She stretched her arms out in front of her and clapped her hands together.

"Come on, Erich," she urged. "Walk to me. You can do it!"

Erich gave her a smile, four little teeth poking out of his pink gums. He glanced up at Marlene as he bounced in place with eagerness.

"Go ahead, little one. Walk to your sister," Marlene encouraged.

He slid a foot out, still holding onto the handle with one hand.

"You have to let go, silly," Bettina said. "Come on, come to me." She wiggled her fingers out in front of her.

Erich wavered, then let go. His unstable body tilted from side to side as he attempted to gain balance. Taking two small steps forward, he quickened his pace, before falling to his bottom not far from where he began.

"Good try, buddy," Bettina said with a chuckle. Marlene swooped down and gave him a peck on the cheek.

"You'll be walking soon enough, my love," she said. Then, turning to Lena, "Can you watch him for me for a couple minutes?"

She needed to find Lara. It was time for another talk. Her patience was wearing thin.

But, mother and daughter were wound tight—twisted together like the intricate tapestry of an abstract canvas. Push a girl too far, and everything could unravel.

TWO

Marlene climbed the stairs up to the second floor, passing both the boys' bedroom and the little girls' bedroom on the left. On the right, the door to her own room stood open. Centered along the back wall, was her neatly-made bed, its pale coverlet tucked and folded just so—an accurate representation of their picture-perfect life.

Only it was a lie. And every time she looked at the bed, it taunted her.

I know what happened here, it warned. No amount of ruffled pillows could hide the truth of those sheets. Marlene shut her eyes, but the images found her regardless.

Flesh. Blood. Fraud.

She closed the door, against the memories. The bedroom at the end of the hall belonged to the two eldest girls, Lara and Lena. A teen girl's oasis: the room was crowded with heavily perfumed wardrobes and makeup samples they didn't dare wear around their father.

Marlene knocked softly on the door.

"Lara?"

No response. She tried again, but the other side of the door remained silent. Marlene twisted the glass knob and cracked the door open, peering in through the tiny sliver. On the far side of the room, she saw a figure, sitting on the window bench, knees pulled up to her chest. Marlene opened the door further, its creaking hinges announcing her presence, but the girl didn't acknowledge her.

"Lara? May I come in?"

Lara stared out the window to the small garden patio at the back of the house. A swing hung suspended between two trees and rows of rainbow flowers lined the stone pavers. The small refuge brought a sense of country to their little lot in the city, and Lara often found herself drawn there for peace and quiet.

Marlene approached her daughter and placed a tentative hand on her shoulder. Lara retracted without a word, pulling her body away from her mother's touch. With a sigh, Marlene dropped her head.

"Lara. You've got to come out of this room more. It's not healthy to stay cooped up like this."

A single tear rolled down Lara's face. Marlene felt a pinch in her heart at the girl's sadness. She gazed around the room, thinking of what to say next.

"Clair Huber is having a party this weekend for her birthday. I ran into her mother at the market this morning. She said you ought to come. Why don't you tag along with Lena? And hey, maybe that handsome boy from down the street will be there." Marlene cocked her head and lifted an eyebrow, attempting to rouse Lara with a bit of lighthearted teasing.

Lara was in no mood.

16

"Handsome or not, my heart belongs elsewhere," she said with enough melodrama to force Marlene's eyes closed.

"Come on, darling. Things could be much worse, you know. We're safe here. We can finally be a happy family."

Lara whipped her head around to face Marlene. Her eyes were bloodshot.

"Happy?" she said as her chin quivered. "How can I be happy?" Before Marlene had a chance to respond, Lara turned sharply, folding her arms across her chest and refusing to budge. "Just leave me alone."

"Lara."

"I've done enough of what you've asked of me. I'm done."

Defeated, Marlene left the room. Lara's temperament wasn't new—it had been a rough year in many ways, for more than just Lara. There were days when their reality felt too much to bear, but she and Gerald had an image to withhold: one of a lively, healthy, secure family. A moping teenager didn't fit the mold, and the family was growing restless with Lara's doom-and-gloom attitude.

Downstairs, Marlene returned to the kitchen and swept Erich into her arms.

"Hello, little one," she whispered in his ear.

"Ma ma ma ma," he babbled.

The front door closed, and familiar footsteps approached.

"Father!" the children yelled. They swarmed him, wrapping their arms around whatever appendage they could reach. Tall and handsome with slicked back hair and military posture, the only hint of imperfection on his impeccably groomed exterior was a small vertical scar under his bottom lip. He was Adonis incarnate.

Gloria slid down Gerald's leg until she sat atop his shiny, patent boot. She hugged his shin happily.

"Hi everyone," he chuckled. "I'll never get tired of these warm welcomes." Gerald shuffled to Marlene, dragging Gloria along on his foot.

"Hello, my love," he said. They kissed, and Erich, still in Marlene's arms, patted Gerald's cheek. He nuzzled noses with the little boy, who squealed with delight. The children watched him, captivated by his very presence. To them, Gerald was larger than life—a figure to be not only loved, but admired.

He looked around to each of their adoring faces. One was missing.

"Lara?" he asked Marlene under this breath.

"In her room."

His jaw tensed.

"Gerald, she barely comes out anymore," Marlene lamented. "This can't go on. I'm getting concerned. We've got to do something."

"Like what? We're damned either way." Pulling her into the side room away from the curious ears of the children, Gerald continued. "I'm doing everything possible to establish myself here, Marlene. It's not easy, especially after the way we left. It's taken a lot of work and a great deal of convincing. We can't afford any mistakes."

"I know, I know. But Lara. I'm worried."

"I am too."

In her arms, Erich squirmed.

"Come here, you," Gerald reached out and took the baby from his wife's hands. "You're so loved, do you know that little boy? We didn't think we'd have you, but here you are." He stroked the boy's dark hair and stared into his crystal blue eyes.

The resemblance between Erich and Gerald was uncanny. And Marlene's heart swelled seeing the tenderness the baby brought out of her husband.

"Let me try to talk to her," he said, "I'm her father. She'll listen to me."

THREE

The talk was no use. Lara regarded her father with the same cold irreverence she'd shown Marlene.

"How can you expect me to just go on as before? Nothing is the same." Her face flushed with emotion. "I just want to go back."

"Lara, you must understand," he'd tried. "We're all doing our best." But she'd stared right through him as if he didn't exist.

That evening, Marlene prepared tafelspitz, the children's favorite. She pounded the veal with her wooden mallet, transferring all her angst into the poor chops, before boiling the thin cuts of meat until tender. If only strife could evaporate as easily as water from a bubbling pot. She drizzled a homemade horseradish sauce atop each piece, and then scooped a serving of potatoes onto each plate. A savory aroma filled the house.

It smelled like Austria.

The children gobbled the meal. Miriam exclaimed as she nearly choked on her last bite, "Can we make strudels now?"

"Chew and swallow, dear," Marlene said, patting Miriam's hand. The girl gulped a far-too-big bite and then more clearly repeated her question.

"Now can we?"

"Yes, sweetheart. We'll make strudels, just as soon as everyone is finished."

Gerald rolled his eyes playfully from the other end of the long oak table at his daughter's fervor. Lara sat silent. She poked at the thin slice of veal sliding down the heap of potatoes like a car down an icy hill.

The stubborn girl had begrudgingly agreed to join dinner— only at the most insistent request of her empty stomach. The pangs of her hunger won over, Marlene figured, enticed by the smells coming from the large kitchen below.

"I'm supposed to bring my favorite book to school tomorrow," Miriam said, rather suddenly. "But I don't know which to choose."

"You can borrow one of mine," Bettina offered. The bookworm of the family, Bettina was always nose deep in worn, white pages. Her siblings knew they could go to her for any of their literature needs, but also felt slightly intimidated by her brains. They joked that of anyone, she'd be the one to have an important job someday. Bettina got high marks in all her classes, and never having received letter grades from a teacher before, she found it quite satisfying.

"What about you, Felix? What do you have going on this week?" Marlene asked, turning to the eldest boy. She liked these newly regular family check-ins.

"Well, now that football is done, I suppose I should start focusing on my schoolwork." He winked at his father. Gerald took academics seriously and insisted the children did too. For a

21

long time, their intense focus on proper appearances had bordered on regimented. Marlene, though, inspired a sense of carefree wonder. She encouraged the children to explore other interests, which is why Felix had felt comfortable trying out for the football team at school. Gerald, initially hesitant, had loosened a little and allowed it. His wife's appetite for life rubbed off on him.

Felix was surprisingly inclined for athletics. With an arm for throwing, he played an unusual number of games for a rookie. Before long, he'd caught the eye of not only the coach but several members of the cheer squad.

"You should try football next year," Felix said, now, to his younger brother. Lena stifled a giggle behind her napkin.

"Nah, too much running," Karl replied. Gerald laughed at his son's blunt honesty. On the chubbier side ("Fleshy," the doctor had called him), Karl didn't show an ounce of the sporting chops Felix did, instead developing a keen interest in business, and showing early signs of an entrepreneurial spirit. He was no jock—that was no secret—but he did love to dance. Marlene often caught glimpses of him twirling and leaping when he thought no one was watching.

She'd even once taught him the Laendler.

"You could be one of those pom-pom shakers on the sidelines then," Felix said. Karl gave him a playful punch.

"How are your studies going, Lara?" Gerald changed the subject, turning to his daughter who stared down at her plate.

"Fine."

"Frau Zimmermann still satisfied with your work?"

"Yes."

"Are you planning to give one-word answers to every question I ask?"

"Yes."

Gerald gave up. He shrugged at Marlene.

Next to her Erich cooed in his highchair. Marlene cut a small sliver of meat and put it on the boy's tray. He wolfed it down and banged his hands on his tray, demanding more.

"Patience, Erich," Gloria mimicked her mother's tone, clearly proud of her display of good breeding. *Tsk tsk.* "Mother is feeding you as quickly as she can." No longer the baby of the family, Gloria took on a performance of maturity, as if she were seventeen and not seven.

Marlene peered up through her eyelashes and met the gaze of her husband. *Would the lying ever get easier?* She glanced around the table. The other children happily finished their remaining food, unaware of the unspoken signals passing between their parents. Marlene looked to Felix. His head was bowed, as was Lara's.

"May I be excused?" Lara asked in a near-whisper.

"Yes." Gerald reached for her hand to give it a squeeze, but she pulled from his grasp before their palms met. She left swiftly, and Gerald looked to the ceiling as the sound of feet climbing the stairs reverberated through the room.

Attempting to lighten the tension, Marlene clapped her hands. "Who's ready for strudels?" she asked with a false, but effective, enthusiasm.

"Hooray!" the children cheered, pushing back from the table and carrying their plates to the kitchen in a single file line.

Marlene dragged Erich's highchair near the sink so he could watch. He danced in his seat, unsure what all the excitement was about, but feeding off the energy of his siblings nonetheless. When he saw the apples, he smacked his lips and excitedly flapped his wrists back and forth as if revving a motorcycle.

Their baking was a well-oiled machine. Marlene and the three youngest girls mixed and kneaded the dough while Lena and Karl—who didn't yet find matters of the kitchen too feminine—peeled and sliced apples into a bowl.

An hour later the timer dinged, and the children ran to the oven. Atop the baking sheet sat a dozen perfectly folded lumps, golden brown with heat and sugar. Marlene cut into the flaky pastry and watched the gooey filling spill from the center. Gloria reached her finger in to swipe at the little butter-brown puddle.

"I don't think so, sneaky girl." Marlene shooed the girl's hand away. She dished a piece for everyone. It came with a scoop of vanilla ice cream, a Sunday night treat. The house was heavy with the distinctive smell of apples and cinnamon.

It was heavenly. But it wasn't enough to pull Lara from her room.

FOUR

Lara finished her lessons with Frau Zimmermann around two. The middle-aged woman rewarded her pupil's gains with an early close for the day—a gesture Lara wasn't sure could be attributed to the tutor's uncharacteristically good mood, or Lara's actual progress in arithmetic.

Lara didn't love math; she struggled with visualizing the complex calculations, and the numbers themselves, as she advanced through her schooling. Frau Zimmermann was tough but fair. Her glasses sat at the tip of her nose, and every time she leaned over Lara's shoulder to check her work, Lara waited for the frames to fall off onto the table. When the woman moved in extra close, Lara cringed at the smell of garlic on her breath. What could she possibly have eaten at nine o'clock in the morning that left such a horrid stench?

Aside from her strict manner and unfortunate breath, Frau Zimmermann was a good teacher. She'd insisted they spend extra time learning formulas, which by show of the girl's headway, had paid off. "I think you might show promise for university after all," she'd said, sounding pleased.

Lara managed a smile. The woman didn't know that attending university was the last thing on Lara's mind.

"We're done for today," Frau Zimmermann said to Marlene, who was mending a hole in Karl's pants, as the crotchety woman passed through the kitchen to the side door, with a leather tote slung over her shoulder.

"Oh!" Marlene said, surprised. "Wonderful, thank you." She glanced at her watch, noting she'd have to leave to fetch the youngest children from primary school soon. She usually took these walks alone, but today a thought occurred to her: perhaps she could convince Lara to join her and Erich for the short jaunt to the children's school.

Marlene put a pause on the pants, placing her needle and thread on the counter. She entered the front room where Lara's small desk sat in the corner near a window with thick, floral drapes.

"You finished early today," Marlene said, conjuring cheerfulness she hoped would rub off on her daughter. "Want to walk with us to get the kids from school?"

Lara parted the curtain panel. The sky was bright with sunshine, and though it was deceiving—it was quite chilly outside—the optimistic weather tempted her away from the house's stale air. She'd been inside for nearly four days. Her body itched for a fresh breeze, her legs longed to move.

She turned to face her mother. "Okay."

Surprised, Marlene rushed to grab their coats before Lara changed her mind. Then, the threesome headed down the sidewalk, Marlene pushing Erich in a gray, metal pram with a canopy to shield his fair skin from the sun.

A few houses down, a woman in a houndstooth coat stood on her porch pulling a stack of envelopes from the mailbox. She waved as Marlene, Lara and Erich passed.

"Hello Marlene!"

"Hi Clara!" Marlene called in her typical buoyant manner. Lara marveled at her mother's never-ending gaiety. *How can she be so happy all the time?* It was borderline unnerving.

Further down the street, another neighbor walked a small, white poodle. Lush fur trimmed the collar of her heavy swing coat, and she wore T-strap heels that clicked against the pavement with each step. Lara considered the outfit and found it strangely formal for an afternoon walk. The dog lunged excitedly at Lara's leg, tail wagging.

"Afternoon, Marlene," Elin said, both groups slowing as they neared each other. "Hi Lara, nice to see you!"

The red-haired woman peered into the buggy. "Your brother is an absolute doll," she purred, standing next to Lara.

Another flash behind Marlene's eyelids: Sweat. Screams. Whispers.

"Yes, he is."

"So sorry, Elin," Marlene placed a hand on Lara's back, "but we must be going. Can't be late to get the children from school!"

"Oh, of course! Don't let me hold you up. I hope to see you at the ladies' neighborhood luncheon next week," Elin called as Marlene pushed Lara onward.

"I wouldn't miss it!" Marlene shouted over her shoulder.

Lara stared at the ground as they continued, counting the cracks in the sidewalk, and stepping over larger holes as if they'd swallow her whole should she step in them.

"I know it's hard for you," Marlene said, gently. "To be here, I mean." Lara only nodded. The three walked a few more beats in silence before Lara finally spoke.

"You know so many people."

"The folks are nice here, Lara. It's a friendly neighborhood. I know you could make more friends if you tried. But sulking all day isn't going to do it."

"I don't want friends. That's not what this is about, and you know it."

Marlene pursed her lips and looked ahead to the school coming into focus. Of course she knew.

When they reached the small patch of grass, Marlene and Lara waited amongst the handful of other mothers before children poured out through the front doors. Miriam and Gloria came first, as the younger classes dismissed early to give their little legs a head start out of the building. The girls ran toward Marlene, their hair swinging behind them like horses' manes. They wrapped their mother in a tight hug.

"Hello dears. How was your day?"

"Good," they said in unison.

Karl and Bettina followed within minutes, descending the concrete steps with a group of friends. Bettina intertwined her arm with another girl's, the two deeply engaged in the chit chat considered sacred to eleven year olds. Marlene tilted her head, surprised. Bettina wasn't the most social of her children. In fact, Marlene would have gone as far as to consider the girl an introvert. To see her cheerfully engaged with a classmate was a pleasant surprise. *Perhaps she'll come out of her shell after all*, Marlene thought. Erich squealed in the pram at the sight of the siblings he so much adored.

"Hi Mother! This is my friend, Anna," Bettina said as the girls approached.

"Hello Anna. Very nice to meet you."

"Hello," the girl replied. Then to Bettina, "Is this your baby brother? He's so cute."

Marlene's mind drifted. *The smell of blood—metallic and raw.*

Erich pulled up on the side of the buggy and rocked back and forth with excitement. His ability to draw attention wherever he went didn't go unnoticed by Marlene—his perfect features, porcelain skin and chubby cheeks made him irresistible to friends and strangers alike.

"Yes," Bettina answered. She reached into the buggy to rub Erich's head. "Hi, bud! And this is my oldest sister, Lara." She wrapped an arm around Lara's waist. The oldest had served as a role model, and even a mother figure, for the younger children before Marlene entered their lives. They admired her beauty and poise, and even on occasion, styled their hair to replicate Lara. The youngest snuck into her makeup bag to try on their sister's precious lipstick and rouge.

"Mother, can Anna come over and play?"

"Of course, but not today, dear. Soon, okay?" Marlene loved the sound of children's voices filling her home—and that joy multiplied when her children began welcoming friends into the mix.

"Okay," Bettina said. "See you tomorrow, Anna!" The girl skipped away toward the far side of the yard where a woman stood with a toddler at her side. Marlene raised a hand and acknowledged the mother with warmth.

The group reversed the course they'd just taken, only this time they split in three pairs to accommodate the narrow sidewalk. The children jabbered on about their day: Gloria was learning subtraction, Bettina perfecting her cursive handwriting. Miriam gushed about being chosen first for a game in the schoolyard during recess. ("They must have known I was a fast runner!").

They relayed to their mother the day's activities, and in Karl's case, how he'd gotten out of any physical activity—once again—in gym class.("I'd get blisters for sure if I had to jump around in these shoes!").

Over the fifteen-minute walk, Erich dozed in the buggy, the bumps beneath the tires along with his siblings' endless chatter having lulled him, rocked him, to sleep. When they reached the house—deep blue with gray trim, the color of wood smoke—the children dashed past Marlene and Lara. They ran through the gate and into the house, kicking off their shoes and leaving a trail of mis-matched footwear in the entryway.

Marlene peered into the buggy to where Erich slept, his head drooped to his shoulder, his arms limp at his sides. Oh, to sleep like a baby.

"I'll take him to his crib," Lara said. It was a statement more than a question.

Marlene hesitated for a moment. "Okay."

She watched as Lara reached down and gently cradled Erich in her arms, pressing his tiny body against her chest. His cheek squished against her arm, in a pout that made the girl smile. Swaying in place, she gazed adoringly at the sleeping boy. It looked so natural. A familiar knot twisted in Marlene's gut.

Lara entered the house and tip-toed up the stairs, careful not to wake Erich. She pushed open the door to her parents' bedroom and went to the small white crib along the far wall next to the double bed, whose pillows were propped in the perfect arrangement.

Leaning over the rail, she lowered Erich onto the mattress. His tiny form melted into the cushion and he turned over to lay on his belly, pulling his knees in and lifting his little bottom up in the air. He smacked his lips in his sleep and shifted a few times, until finding a comfortable position and becoming still.

Lara beamed. She dropped a hand into the crib and placed it on his back, gently stroking the length of his body. Peeking at the door behind her to make sure no one was there, she spoke the words she had only ever uttered in her mind.

"Mama's here," she whispered. "I love you, my little boy."

She sank to the ground coming to her knees in front of the crib. Her hands gripped firmly on the wood slats, like an inmate begging to be released. Only Erich wasn't the one in jail—it was her. Trapped in a web of lies from which she couldn't break free.

She watched her son's ribs rise and fall with each breath. And as hot tears slid down her face, she lowered her head and let them collect in a puddle on the floor.

FIVE

One year earlier

I t was about eight weeks after their arrival in Zürich that Lara first became concerned. Not only had she missed her monthly menstruation (or was it two?), but also, she just didn't feel right. Crippling fatigue took over her body. She wasn't tired—she was utterly exhausted. Her body felt like it had been hit by a freight train and the lethargy consumed her from head to toe.

The buttery hue of morning light was no longer a welcome sight. Instead, she struggled to get out of bed, praying for the sun to stay down for just an hour longer. Beneath the buttons running down the neckline of her nightgown, her breasts were sore and swollen. They pulsed with an odd tingling, one that she couldn't quite decide felt good or terrible.

The first morning she had to run to the bathroom to vomit, she knew something was wrong. Had she caught some sort of nasty stomach bug? The degree of debility told her this was something different—but what, she didn't know.

Marlene, having noticed recent uncharacteristic behavior in her daughter, initially attributed it to the family's grueling escape from Austria. Climbing the Swiss Alps was a daunting feat in itself, not to mention that Lara had taken turns carrying her youngest siblings for long stretches over rough terrain. Could the girl still be reeling from physical exertion two months later? It seemed unlikely, but who was Marlene to say?

Soon, however, Lara's demeanor became too noticeable to ignore. When Marlene overheard her in the bathroom one morning, she crept out of bed, careful not to wake her sleeping husband. She opened the door and saw Lara hovered over the toilet, hands white-knuckled on the rim and head aimed directly at the water below.

Dread fixed her bones. *Tired all the time, lacking energy, and now getting sick repeatedly. Could she be? No, it's not possible.*

Marlene let it go for another few days—wishing desperately to be proven wrong—but Lara's symptoms were clear. When the girl continued to be ill each day, Marlene felt the truth to her core. It was categorically obvious. The next morning, before the rest of the house awoke, she snuck into Lara's room and pried the girl from her bed.

"Come," she whispered, "we need to talk."

"Hmm? What?" Lara mumbled, still in the depths of sleep.

"Just come."

Lara summoned the energy to roll from bed. The two padded down the hardwood stairs to the lower level and out of earshot.

"Lara, tell me what's going on," Marlene pleaded. "You're not yourself. And I've heard you in the bathroom in the mornings."

"You have?"

"Yes. Are you sick?"

"I don't know, Mother." She was now fully awake. The line of questioning brought an unpleasant feeling that stimulated her emotions. Lara's eyes brimmed with tears. "I'm so tired all the time. And my body feels weird. It's like it's changing every day. My dresses don't fit anymore, but I'm hardly eating anything."

Marlene's stomach dropped. Her intuition was right.

"Oh, Lara, you didn't."

"Didn't what?"

"Was it Rubin?"

All color drained from Lara's face.

"What do you mean? What about Rubin?"

"Lara, I think you're pregnant."

"Pregnant? What? No!"

"Yes. I think so. These are all the classic signs."

The girl started to heave. Short, violent breaths seized her lungs. Marlene put a hand on her daughter's back to calm her down.

"Take a deep breath, darling. That's it. Slow down."

When her breathing regulated, Lara stared into her mother's eyes. Marlene took a deep breath.

"Were you and Rubin...intimate?" Marlene hardly knew how to address this topic. She herself was utterly naïve before her romance with Gerald took her by surprise and bloomed so suddenly. So freshly hatched, she'd barely had a chance to even contemplate the passion taking over her very being. Who was she to interrogate another about such a private matter? She may not have been promiscuous as a young woman, but she knew teenage sex existed—she just didn't expect it to live in her own home.

Marlene felt her motherly instinct kick in. Lara wasn't her blood, but the love she felt for each of the children far surpassed this fact. She was disappointed, but more than that, she felt an innate need to protect her, much like a lioness shielding her cub from danger.

"Lara, you have to tell me."

Shame shadowed Lara's face. Her cheeks flushed, and she ringed the hem of her nightgown with agitated fingers.

"It happened so quickly. I didn't know what I was doing."

"When?"

"Shortly before we fled. When you and Father were on your honeymoon, actually."

"Oh Lara." Marlene dipped her head and cast her gaze to her lap.

"I'm so sorry, Mother. I didn't know this would happen. But I loved him. I still love him."

"Still love him? Lara, do you hear what you're saying?" Her voice loud and sharp. "Rubin betrayed us. He betrayed you."

"No! He was coerced, I know it. He's not a bad person, Mother. I know he loved me too. He told me."

"Of course he told you that." Frustration soured in her mouth. Lara's jaw dropped, stunned, hurt. She looked away, as a giant lump formed in her throat. Bile churned behind her ribs and she felt as if she might be sick again.

Marlene's face softened. She remembered those early days of young love, the butterflies that tickled her stomach. Lara was just seventeen. It was a mistake. One with a serious consequence. But she didn't want to place any more guilt on her daughter's shoulders.

"Okay," Marlene said, sitting up straighter. "What's done is done. There's no sense trying to erase the past. We're here now and we need to figure out what to do."

"What do you mean?"

"You're pregnant, Lara. You're going to have a baby."

The girl's eyes widened and her mouth fell open.

"But you can't," Marlene continued straight-faced. "Your father. He's trying to establish his practice here in the Swiss ranks. It's the only way we'll survive. He's almost back to the top. A teenage daughter with an illegitimate child would ruin him. Ruin us. We simply cannot risk that reputation."

"What are you saying, Mother?" Lara's tone was panicking. But Marlene was lost in thought, her mind going a million miles an hour trying to come up with a solution to avoid a catastrophic situation.

"Mother?"

Marlene snapped to focus, her hand coming to rest on her forehead. She stared at the terrified face of a girl, who at one time had so desperately wanted to be a woman but now looked no older than a child. Her heart crumbled for all that was about to be lost.

"Come here, darling." She pulled Lara into a tender hug. "It's going to be okay. We'll figure this out. Let me talk to your father. We'll come up with a plan. Until then, don't say anything to anyone—not even your siblings."

"Okay." Lara stifled a sob. "I'm so sorry, Mother."

Marlene brushed a piece of hair from Lara's face and ran her hand down the girl's tear-stained cheek.

With a voice on the edge of breaking, Lara was able to utter four more words: "Will God forgive me?"

"Of course He will." She gave Lara's hands a gentle squeeze. "Now, go get a bit more rest before everyone gets up." Lara crept softly back toward her room at the end of the hallway, her head hanging.

Marlene sat for a moment before walking heavy-footed to her bedroom and slipped through the door without a sound. She eased in bed beside Gerald who, she was relieved to see, hadn't budged since she'd left. Sliding under the crisp quilt, she swallowed the lump in her throat and closed her eyes.

Terrifying images danced behind her lids, one more dreadful than the next. She shivered at the thought of the public disgrace that would befall the family should this news get out. Without specifics of the night in question, she was left to her imagination to piece it all together.

How could Rubin have taken advantage of her? How could Lara have been so foolish?

The sick questions and painful possibilities rolled through her mind one by one like a runaway locomotive. Despite all efforts, Marlene never fell back asleep. Instead, she tossed and turned, imagining the various outcomes of Lara's circumstance.

* * *

The first hints of light trickled through the curtains. Marlene usually greeted the new day head on and with a jovial spirit. Each morning was an opportunity to be grateful, and she epitomized the mantra of "seize the day." But today felt different. Today was ominous.

She decided to keep Lara's situation to herself, letting it sink in and giving herself a chance to formulate options. It wasn't easy to pretend nothing was wrong—she and her husband shared everything, and he was the greatest source of support in her life, but she kept her tongue quiet, allowing her brain to think.

Marlene went through the day's motions, trying not to draw alarm. The house was warm, but she still felt numb.

The following morning, a soft set of lips on her forehead stirred her from her light sleep. She rolled to lie face to face with her husband. His dark hair sprinkled with faint streaks of gray gave him a distinguished look, even first thing in the morning, when he was tousled from a restful night.

At least one of them had slept well.

"Good morning, beautiful," Gerald kissed her head, followed by each cheek and finally trailed his lips to her mouth. She'd usually match his advances, bringing her body close to his and letting hands roam wherever they went. But not today.

"Gerald, we need to talk."

"Mmmm. We can talk later." He ran his fingers up her thigh.

She pushed him back gently, making room between them. Her serious expression startled him, and his smile faded.

"What is it?"

"It's Lara." She paused. "She's pregnant."

"What?" He jerked back, smirking at the absurdity of her statement.

"I'm serious."

The smirk disappeared. "How? I mean, when? With who?" He gestured wildly with his hands. Marlene grabbed his arm to stop him from banging his hand against the bedpost.

"Rubin," she said.

"Rubin? You're kidding me. No, it can't be!"

"It's true. She told me. And I've been noticing her symptoms for a while now."

"Before we left?"

"Yes, she said just before we left."

"My God."

Marlene took a deep breath as Gerald ran a hand through his wild, morning hair. It was a relief to tell him. Even though she'd only held Lara's secret for less than twenty-four hours, the burden had grown heavy. Letting Gerald in meant she had a partner to help her problem-solve.

"I can't believe this," he said.

"I know."

"What do we do? I mean, we certainly can't let it get out. Her reputation would be ruined. I could lose my position."

"Yes, I know. Well, I've been thinking."

"Thinking? How long have you known, Marlene?"

"I've suspected for a little while. But only just talked to her yesterday morning." Gerald stared off into the distance, shaking his head. "We have to prevent any rumors before they start," Marlene continued. "We need to hide her."

"Hide her?"

"Yes."

"You mean, let her have the baby?"

Marlene was aghast. "What's the alternative, Gerald?"

"Marlene, there's ways of stopping a pregnancy. Even I know that." He grabbed her hand.

"Absolutely not!" She pulled away, disgusted. "No. We could never. That's God's child. I could never live with myself."

Emotions rising, Marlene stood. "I can't believe you'd even suggest such a thing," she said before disappearing out of the bedroom. Gerald grumbled, embarrassed. The conversation was over—at least for now.

Two days later, after tucking the last of the children into bed, Marlene settled on the couch with her husband. It wasn't like them to disagree, and she didn't like the tension between them. She curled up next to him, letting her body sink into his.

"I'm sorry," he said. "I shouldn't have suggested what I did. It was my instinct to just make it all go away."

"I know. But honestly, Gerald, we need to figure this out. There's a baby coming whether we like it or not."

"Okay. So she has the baby. Where? How? And then what?"

"Well, it's summertime now, which is good because she won't be showing until the fall. She'll be able to hide it more with heavier clothing. Once fall and winter come, we'll have to keep her inside. No visitors. She can have the baby here, and no one needs to know."

Gerald stared at his wife, dumbfounded by the glaring omission of her plan.

"Say that goes without fault. There's still a baby. How are we going to explain that?"

Marlene deflated. She'd been thinking obsessively about the pregnancy, she hadn't given much thought to the aftermath. Before she could speak, her husband shot a finger in the air.

"I've got it! We pass the baby off as ours."

"Ours? How?"

"We're newlyweds, Marlene. The timing makes perfect sense."

"But I'm not pregnant. I won't look pregnant."

"We can fake it. A pillow under your shirt is all you need. As long as you keep people from getting too close, from a distance there would be no reason to question it."

Her mouth dried. It was all starting to sound too real—too wrong. Deceit wasn't a feeling she was used to. They were quiet for several minutes as they considered the plan. Could they pull it off? *Should* they pull it off?

"I'm overcome with guilt already," Marlene confessed, as her eyes filled with tears.

"Shhh... it's okay." He pulled her into an embrace and ran his hand over her hair and down the back of her neck.

"The Reverend Mother would be ashamed," she whispered.

"The Reverend Mother would want you to protect your family. That's what we're doing. It's for the best."

They left it at that. With little thought of any long-term implications, their decision was made. Now all they needed was to tell their daughter.

SIX

Lara did not take the news well.

Within a few days, she had been told she was not only pregnant, but that she would have to carry and deliver the child, only to have it secretly raised as her sibling. She was outraged.

The vigor with which Lara protested came as a surprise, given the girl's recent bout of exhaustion that had kept her mostly bed ridden for the past several weeks. With a guttural howl, Lara flung herself onto the chaise lounge in her parents' bedroom. She'd worked herself into a sweat and the hair at the base of her neck turned into a stringy, wet frizz.

"No! I won't do it! How could you ask me to do such a thing?"

"Lara," Gerald soothed, "trust us. We're looking out for your best interest. Do you know what happens to unwed teenage mothers? Not even our social position can save you from the persecution you'll encounter. This could ruin your chances for any sort of future."

"But it's a lie!"

"Not all lies are bad, Lara. Not when they're designed to protect someone."

"I can't and I won't." She fled the room, stomped down the hall and slammed her bedroom door.

Gerald looked to his wife. "Well, that didn't go well."

"Give her time. It's a lot to take in."

"I don't know, Marlene. What if she never forgives us for this."

She couldn't offer a way to ease his worry—mainly because she was thinking the same thing.

* * *

The revelation of her condition marked the start of Lara's despondency. She buried herself under the covers of her bed, hiding from reality.

Pregnant.

How did this happen? Well, she knew how it happened, of course. The question was more a self-imposed punishment. She'd let it happen. Even when her conscious flapped a glaring red flag (*"Warning! Warning! Maybe this isn't a good idea!"*). She'd shaken away her hesitation, putting all her trust in Rubin.

The memory was as vivid as a freshly-painted canvas—rich and theatrical, in an abstract sort of way. Recalling the details was easy.

She'd snuck out of her room that night, climbing down the drain pipe from the second-story window to where Rubin waited in the shadows below. The act felt all too familiar. Scaling houses in the dark was becoming a bit of a habit.

"Lara!" Rubin hissed from behind a towering maple tree. She caught sight of his blonde hair. He waved her over.

Lara dashed away from the house, her feet skimming over the ground, light and carefree. There was something exhilarating about breaking the rules—not that "sneaking out of the house at midnight to rendezvous with a boy" was a formal Weiss precedent, nonetheless she assumed it would be gravely frowned upon.

They joined hands and Lara giggled as they headed toward a clearing behind a dense group of trees.

"Did anyone see you leave?" he asked.

"No. Everyone's asleep. Frau Schuster sleeps like a rock. Besides, she'd never expect me to sneak out anyway." With her parents gone on honeymoon for a month, the old, frigid housekeeper was also promoted to babysitter.

"Devious girl." He leaned in and kissed her, releasing an urgent "Mmmmmm" as though her lips were nothing more than the sweetest, ripest strawberries he'd ever tasted.

A rush swept through her body—a mixture of adrenaline and lust. Rubin's hands moved from Lara's face down her neck and to her chest. They rested so the heel of his palms nestled into the curve right above her breasts.

She gasped at his forwardness. It felt dangerous—but in a good way.

"I want you so bad," he breathed against her lips.

"You have me. I'm here." *Silly*, she almost added at the end but then didn't, as it seemed childish in some way. *Don't be coy*, she told herself.

"No, I want you more than that. I want all of you."

She stared, fairly certain she understood.

"Come on," he said, taking her hand again and pulling her along. She'd let him pull her anywhere.

They ran a bit further until the trees cleared giving way to a small, open patch of grass. She skipped along behind him, practically buoyant. In the glade, Rubin spun her around so they faced each other. He pulled her tight against his body and kissed her eagerly.

Before she knew it, Lara was on her back. The grass felt damp and she wondered if it would leave marks on her dress. It was new—white with a yellow sash. She'd gotten it for her father's latest dinner party, feeling special and grown up. Tonight, she'd chosen it to bring back those same feelings.

Rubin pressed himself on top of Lara, using one elbow to prop himself up, and the other to explore her flesh.

She kissed him back, surprised by the pleasure stirred up by such a simple act. Kissing felt good and her body responded.

"I've been dreaming of this," Rubin said. He unbuttoned the top of her dress to the base of her sternum and slipped his hand in to cover her breast. Her eyes flashed open. Was his hand really under her bra?

That's when everything started tingling.

Rubin panted, moving faster and faster—seemingly unable to get enough of her. She was so consumed with the thrill of it all, so absorbed with the pleasure pulsing through her veins, it was as though she were floating on a cloud high above—that is, until her cotton underwear began to slip down her legs.

"Wait," she said, reaching to push his hands away.

"I want you, Lara. I need you." He kissed her with passion that made her feel she was the only girl in the world. Rubin made his move again.

"I don't know if we should."

"This is so right. Doesn't it feel good?"

"Yes, but—"

"Then what's wrong? Let it go, Lara. It will be perfect. I love you."

"I love you, too."

He loves me, she thought. *He loves me.* She repeated it as she gave in, letting him take her.

* * *

Marlene knocked on Lara's door.

"Are you coming down for breakfast?"

"I'm not hungry."

Three days had passed since Lara refused her parents' proposal to hide the pregnancy. She'd shed more tears in these days than at any time in her young life. It was impossible to wrap her head around the fact that she was pregnant, let alone the scheme her mother and father had suggested. That, along with the hormones flooding her body, meant that Lara was, quite simply, an emotional mess.

"You need to eat, Lara. Now more than ever, it's important to stay healthy."

"I said I'm not hungry." Her voice wavered, on the verge of tears.

Marlene closed the door, leaving her daughter to her solitude. *One more day*, she told herself. *Then we need to broach this again.*

Marlene was true to her word. The following day, she and Gerald brought Lara to their room for another deep conversation.

"Have you given it more thought?" Marlene asked.

Lara frowned. She looked terrible—weak and pale—having had many nights of fitful sleep and days filled with nothing but anxiety.

"I don't know what to do," she admitted. "But I know I want to keep my baby. It was created with love." She put a hand gingerly on her belly. Flat as a board, it was hard to imagine a poppyseed inside it, one with a flickering heartbeat that would grow into a human.

Gerald grimaced. The hatred he felt for Rubin bordered on madness. His daughter swooning over a double-crossing Judas was enough to make him lose his breakfast. Marlene, sensing her husband's fury, put a hand on his arm. Insulting Rubin in front of Lara would do nothing for their cause, and Marlene knew it.

"We never suggested otherwise," Marlene said.

"That's exactly what you're suggesting! The baby wouldn't be mine."

Lara breathed heavily, her face flushed with pain. Her palms were damp with sweat. Marlene sat beside Lara on the chaise and rubbed her back.

"Your father and I love you so much and don't want to see anything happen to you. This is the only way, Lara."

"It's hard to see it now," Gerald added, "but we're doing this *for* you."

"But it's my baby. How can I just pretend it's my brother or sister?"

"We'll always know the truth," Marlene said, "but no one else can. It has to remain between us."

Gerald joined them on the couch, placing another hand on Lara's back, as though he and Marlene were spiritual leaders blessing the unfortunate. "Yes," he said, "and you'll be able to watch the baby grow up here in this family, which is a blessing compared to lots of other young girls who have to give up their babies completely."

Lara bent in half and sobbed. Without much more to say, Gerald left the room solemnly, giving his wife the space to work her compassion and convincing. There was something about Marlene that made the world feel like everything would be alright in the end. It was one of her gifts.

Marlene ran her fingers through Lara's hair and wiped tears from her eyes. They didn't speak, just sat. They held each other. In that moment, Lara fully appreciated the love of her stepmother.

Each woman was a critical part the other one never knew she needed.

Marlene let Lara cry until her body could cry no more. Quiet whimpers and deep wails, that fell from her eyes like a faucet without an off switch. The sobs came and went, but the two stayed together in the room for another hour.

Lara wrestled with the decision in front of her. Go along with her parents' plan? It would be devastating. But what was the alternative? She was seventeen. She had no money of her own, had never had a job. Her world view was very narrow, to say the least.

When the silence of the room became too much to bear, she lifted her head and spoke.

"Okay."

From that moment in the bedroom, with her single word of concession, their plan was set into motion.

* * *

Lara stayed close to home even though there was nothing detectable about her appearance—so thin and slender, any hint of a bump wouldn't emerge for months. Still, there was an unspoken safety she felt from the comfort of her four walls. Outsiders were none the wiser. But she knew the truth. And the nausea that came along with that knowing, only added to the morning sickness, which struck her nearly every day.

It was a curse, a daily reminder of the choice she had made—both at first, that night in the field, and later, upon agreeing to the deception.

The three of them agreed not to say a word to the other children—Miriam's jabber-mouth would certainly blow their cover. When any question of Lara's despondency arose, Marlene quickly dismissed it with a clever excuse.

"Oh, she's just extra tired today."

"A little homesick, that's all."

But by the time October arrived, it became much harder to hide Lara's growing belly. She ventured out less and less, succumbing to the walls of the house. It was to be her final year of high school, but teenagers were, perhaps, the most observant living souls, and Lara would never have been able to get her secret past them. Instead, Gerald and Marlene settled that once the baby came, Lara could finish her schooling at home.

At the same time Lara's stomach threatened to pop the buttons on her blouse, it became obvious that Marlene would need to craft a false bump if they were to make their timelines believable.

So the facade grew. Another day, another lie.

Marlene had always been a thin woman, boyish really, with a straight appearance and few curves. Never bearing her own children, she didn't have the postpartum pooch at her midsection like other thirty-year-old mothers. Her figure was envious, youthful and slim. But that didn't help the appearance of being with child. They knew they must be strategic.

At the store, Marlene bought four new pillows of varying sizes: a small decorative cushion, all the way up to a full, round bolster. She'd kneaded and prodded the filling, testing it for shape and softness. *These should do*, she thought.

One evening, after the children had gone to bed, Marlene, Gerald and Lara gathered in the master bedroom: what had become their private convening spot. A chamber for executive decision-making.

"What about this one?" Marlene turned to the side, examining her profile in the full-length mirror. She jabbed at the padding under her shirt, positioning it just right.

"Too big," Lara said soberly.

Marlene pulled the pillow from her shirt. She grabbed a smaller option and replaced it where the larger one had been.

"That's better," Gerald said. "Looks about the same size as Lara."

Marlene regarded her new silhouette. The mid-sized bump jutted out from under her gabardine bodice. She'd have to give up her lace up tops, which was a shame, as they showed off her willowy waist. Now, admiring the bulge, she felt a mix of shame and longing.

From the moment she fell in love with Gerald she dreamed of adding a baby of their own to their family. She was young—only in her mid-twenties—so her maternal urge was strong and her body was primed for pregnancy. Never did she think *this* would be how a new life would come into their family. The thought produced a taste of bile in her mouth.

Lara watched her mother push at the pillow until it formed a realistic shape. The image of her mother pregnant, which she knew was a lie, delivered a sudden anguish like a slap across the face. Lara burst into tears, collapsing to the chair. Her body weight slid the chair backwards and it collided against the wall with a loud bang.

"I just can't believe we're really doing this," Lara cried. Marlene and Gerald looked to each other for reassurance.

Lara wiped her cheek. Marlene glanced to the mirror again but whipped around when the bedroom door flew open. There in the frame was Felix. He looked from Lara to his mother, then to his father and mother again. Horror spread across his face as he took in the sight of his mother cradling a burgeoning belly that wasn't there hours earlier.

"Felix!" Gerald seethed. "You're supposed to be asleep."

"Wha—, what's going on?" Felix stuttered.

"Come in. Quickly." His father pulled him into the room and shut the door.

"I heard a crash," the boy said, apologetically. "I was coming to make sure everyone was alright." Lara's face drained of color. Felix fixed his eyes on Marlene, who stood frozen. "Mother, why—."

Gerald dropped his head, then regained eye contact with his son. "This is probably very confusing," he said, palms out. "Let us explain." He gestured to an open spot next to Lara. "Come. Sit."

Felix sat, as instructed, next to Lara on the chaise lounge while his parents told him the truth. They had wanted to keep everyone in the dark, but their son's unexpected appearance changed that.

"You mustn't tell a soul," Gerald ordered. "I hope we can trust you, Felix." Felix nodded, stunned. At sixteen, they hoped he was old enough to keep the secret. Obedience—or at least the expectation of such—ran strong through the Weiss family, but this was big. This was a lot of pressure to put on a boy.

Felix looked to his sister, his face long as a fiddle.

"I'm so sorry, Lara," he said. And with tears dripping down both of their chins, the siblings held each other. It was an understanding of the worst kind.

From there, they lived out the façade, day by day lying a little more. A few weeks later, Marlene and Gerald decided it was time to tell the children about the pregnancy—Marlene's fake pregnancy, that is. They gathered the children into the den for a family meeting.

"We have some exciting news to share with you," Gerald announced. He wrapped an arm around Marlene's waist and they both put on smiles that only the youngest wouldn't see as insincere.

"Oooh, I bet I know," Lena said excitedly. What other news would a newlywed couple have?

"We're going to have a baby."

"I knew it!"

"Yay!" the little girls cried.

"Oh, Mother, how wonderful!" Bettina said.

The children shouted in elation at the idea of a new sibling. The youngest bounced up and down, giddy and slap-happy.

No one noticed Lara and Felix sitting quietly to the side.

"The baby will be here after the new year," Marlene announced. The children gathered around, talking over each other and sharing their opinions on the newcomer—where it should sleep, who would be its favorite sibling.

The joy on their faces broke Marlene's heart even further. She couldn't bring herself to meet Lara's eye.

As winter approached, Lara took to hiding her growing belly with oversized shirts that Marlene sewed—blouses with high collars and gathered yokes that flowed over her midsection. She declared her looks the latest style craze, and even though her siblings didn't see other seventeen-year-olds sporting such fashions, they didn't disagree. In their eyes, Lara could do no wrong.

Most of the changes to her body happened on the inside, unbeknownst to the naked eye. She gained little weight—still struggling with nausea and a suppressed appetite. So aside from her stomach, round as a basketball, Lara looked largely the same.

As often as possible, Lara made excuses to stay in her room, and the children, being young and impressionable, didn't think much of it. Instead, Marlene kept them busy with outings and activities to distract from Lara's absence. Neither did they probe Marlene for her continued stream of energy.

They were naive. *Mother is having a baby, and that's that. Why would she be any different?*

With each week that passed, Marlene stuffed larger pillows under her clothes. She'd never worn so many empire-waisted tops in her life. She was grateful when winter came, so she could wear bulkier items to help hide the scam. Loose tops and open cardigans drew less attention to the inconsistent shape of her bump, as every day's belly looked slightly different than the day before.

At times, she'd look in the mirror and imagine the bump of pillow filling was really the elbow of a baby.

Unlike Lara who could barricade in her room, however, Marlene's responsibilities meant she had to leave the house. It had only been a handful of months since their arrival in Zürich, and the family was still meeting new people in the neighborhood. Marlene was relieved they didn't need to make a grand announcement of her pregnancy to friends—there were really only a couple ladies she had gotten to know as acquaintances thus far.

Instead, she revealed her "news" with little fanfare. She told them they'd be welcoming a baby later in the winter, careful to never use the words "I'm pregnant." Somehow avoiding this phrase made her feel a *little* better about the lie. It's amazing what will ease a conscience.

"That's wonderful news!" her friends cheered with excited great hurrah. And of course it would have been wonderful news, if it hadn't all been built on deceit.

Still, Marlene had to be prepared each time she ventured from home, knowing it would only take one slip for their farce to come tumbling down.

On a cold January morning, Marlene and her two youngest daughters were at the store when an elderly woman with tight gray curls and a hunchback hobbled to where they stood at the meat counter. Marlene greeted her with a polite smile, stepping aside to let the woman view the cuts behind the glass.

"Such a blessing," the lady said, gesturing to the hump protruding from under Marlene's coat.

"Oh, yes, thank you," Marlene responded, placing a hand on her abdomen.

"How much longer? You look like you're about ready."

Marlene felt her cheeks flush. "Any day now!"

"Ah, so wonderful. I just love babies. May I?" The woman reached out to touch Marlene's stomach.

"No!" Marlene shouted. The old lady gasped, retracting her hand as if she'd just come close to the flame of a candle. Another shopper near the counter turned sharply at the sound of the commotion.

Embarrassed, Marlene quickly diffused the situation with nervous laughter. "Sorry," she said smoothly. "I'm just really particular about my space. I don't even let the children feel the baby."

"Oh," the woman responded, baffled. "I see. My apologies. I meant no harm."

"Of course not, it's just me. I'm sorry for startling you."

The elderly woman shuffled off, glancing once more over her shoulder and considering Marlene's peculiar reaction to such a common gesture. Marlene felt the tingling panic begin to subside, and her breath returned to normal. It was true, she never let the children touch her stomach—she'd never offered, and they'd never asked. She'd resorted to altering the way she hugged them, too—never straight on.

Marlene's life had become one big game of charades.

It was a trying several months. Honesty was a core pillar of her being, and she felt a piece of her integrity chip away each day that passed. When Lara made it to thirty-nine weeks, Marlene knew the time was near. Even staring down the never-ending road of deception ahead, she was greatly looking forward to putting at least this part of the lie far behind them.

SEVEN

The pains struck on a bitter cold night in the first week of February. Lara had been asleep for a few hours when an intense cramp tightened her midsection, wrapping around to her lower back. The spasm jolted her from her sleep and she cradled her belly, rubbing her hand over the skin that had been stretched taut for the past nine months. Sharp and deep, it was different from the small pangs of the last few weeks, which were uncomfortable but bearable. This was squeezing, like Lara had never felt before. She imagined an octopus strangling its prey.

The contraction eased and her muscles softened again. With a beat, her shoulders relaxed. *Whew, what was that?* she thought. Taking a deep breath, Lara ran her tongue across her parched lips. Her throat stung from the dry air in the room.

She lifted her head to see if her squirming had woken her sister. To her relief, Lena slept soundly in the matching twin bed a few feet away. Their white headboards featured a bubblegum pink bow painted at the center. The innocence of it fitting for Lena, but fraudulent for Lara.

Not three minutes later, her belly tightened again, slowly at first, then increasing in intensity. Lara drew a sharp inhale. The pain seized her, and she pushed herself up to sit on the edge of the bed, clenching her teeth and squeezing the sheet in her hands to keep from crying out.

When the pain receded and she was able to think clearly, she gathered the first contraction hadn't been a fluke. Yet another wave crested, then fell. She sat for a while longer, realizing the contractions were coming in regular intervals.

Lara knew she needed help.

She stood from her bed, using her arms to lift her heaviness. As she did, a warm stream of liquid trickled down her leg, soaking into the top of her shearling sock. The light was off. Nothing but darkness and fear surrounded her. Scared and shaken, she shuffled, wide legged, down the hall to her parents' room.

Marlene and Gerald were sound asleep, their bodies nestled together and his arms draped over her waist. They always slept with the curtains open, and now the moon's luminescence showed Lara's wet footprints on the hardwood. Lara lifted a leg and saw a discoloration at the ankle of her sock—clearly not urine.

Quietly, Lara shook her mother awake.

"Mother, I think it's time."

Marlene flew out of bed, waking her husband in the process who looked around with a mix of confusion and alarm.

"What? What is it?" he blathered, half asleep.

Lara, in the clutch of another contraction, leaned against the tall armoire, eyes closed. She rocked her head to the rhythm of her long, slow exhale.

"The baby's coming," Marlene hissed, trying to keep her voice low. "Call Elena."

Marlene and Gerald had divulged their secret to only one other person: a midwife. Elena had a glowing reputation in Zürich for her knowledge and skill—two things Gerald insisted on for the care of his daughter.

During her first visit to the Weiss home, Elena examined Lara with gentle hands and a confidence in her voice that made Lara feel safe. She was as wide as she was tall, with boyish hair that looked like she cut it herself. With her frumpy clothes and not a stitch of makeup, Elena was far from glamorous. But she was good at what she did, and that's all that mattered.

Upon their first meeting, Gerald offered Elena a generous sum of money for her discretion. "We appreciate your confidence in this delicate matter."

The woman adamantly declined.

"You may pay for my services like any other patient," she said bluntly, draping a stethoscope around her neck. "But I will not take anything else from you. I know how to keep secrets, sir, and I have no reason not to. My job is to get this baby here safely. I care of nothing else."

At that, she had given Lara instructions and then departed, leaving them no choice but to trust her.

Elena visited the house every month, her appointments increasing in frequency as Lara's belly grew. Along the way, she educated both Lara and Marlene on the course of gestation, including what to expect as labor drew near.

"You will call me when contractions are a minute apart, no sooner. That, or if your waters break."

"How will I know if they break?" Lara had asked.

"You'll know."

Elena answered their concerns with frankness that might have been interpreted as poor bedside manner. But Lara appreciated her straightforward approach. The two formed a connection. Each time Elena treated Lara compassionately, and without any hint of judgement. Her words were crisp, but her hands were gentle. She left every appointment by giving Lara a kiss on the cheek.

Still leaning against the armoire, Lara let out a quiet moan and cradled her stomach. She breathed through gritted teeth.

Gerald hurried to the kitchen and used the home's only phone to call Elena. He glanced at the clock above the stove: one o'clock in the morning. Would she answer at this hour? Relief came when she picked up on the second ring.

"Elena," he gasped. "she's in labor. We need you."

"I'll be right there." The line clicked on the other end.

When he returned to the bedroom, the scene had changed. Marlene propped several pillows against the headboard behind where Lara sat in the middle of the bed. The girl reclined against the softness. Her face was ghostly with fear and discomfort. Her bent legs formed a tent with her nightgown, and the intimacy in the room made Gerald blush and turn away. This was his daughter, his little girl, not some grown woman about to birth a child. The scene conjured images that felt too private, too wrong for him to be witnessing.

"What can I do?" he whispered to his wife.

Marlene, in her own floor-length nightgown, gathered towels into a pile near the foot of the bed. "Nothing, I suppose. I'm just trying to keep her comfortable—and quiet—until Elena gets here."

Gerald took a seat in the corner, balancing his elbows on his knees. His legs bounced nervously. With each contraction, his body tensed along with Lara's. It was as though he could feel the pain through her. Gerald bit his lip so hard he tasted blood.

When the midwife finally arrived after twenty minutes that felt like an eternity, she was fresh-eyed and ready. She swooped in with authority and confidence. Gerald, relieved, gratefully excused himself from the room.

"I'll, uh, just be downstairs if you need me." His clumsy announcement met no response, as the women's full attention was on Lara whose hairline had become wet with perspiration. When Elena whipped up the hem of Lara's white nightgown, Gerald turned so fast he nearly hit his nose on the doorframe.

The plan they'd agreed on in advance was simple: Keep the door locked until the baby arrived. No one in and no one out. And for the children? They would be told that their mother was in labor and that Lara was assisting the midwife.

It was true—almost.

As the dark hours of the night passed one by one, Gerald's bare feet paced the floor. He traced a path through the kitchen, dining room and sitting area, hoping each lap would be the last before the baby came. A finger pour of whisky helped ease his nerves. The amber liquid burned his throat, but he took the punishment willingly.

The grandfather clock struck four, then five. How long would it take? He hadn't been present for the births of his own children—a lifetime ago, it seemed, before his first wife died in childbirth with Gloria. That wasn't something in which men of his position participated. All he remembered of those times was being told his baby had arrived. *Congratulations, you have a daughter! Cheers, sir, you have a son!* How many hours had it taken? He couldn't even begin to guess.

Gerald prayed—for the first time in a long time—for the safety of his daughter and her unborn child. Not one to label himself religious, he'd opened up to the idea of a higher power thanks to Marlene. She was, after all, a highly spiritual person, given her time volunteering at the abbey and teaching nursery school alongside nuns.

He willed Elena to do her magic, to deliver the baby without complication. The room above was quiet—the dull pattern of footsteps on the ceiling the only sound in the hushed house.

A few times, when curiosity got the better of him, he climbed the staircase and leaned his ear against the smooth wood door, and only then did he hear a rhythmic panting that sent him running back downstairs.

At the strike of seven, a bright orange sun inched up over the horizon. The day dawned new and clean despite the messy situation upstairs. It wasn't long before soft, morning pitter patter filled his ears. Gerald stirred, having surrendered his pacing for the comfort of an armchair where, after strumming his fingers anxiously for another hour, he'd eventually rested his head in his hand and gave in to the allure of sleep.

Gloria and Miriam were always the first ones up, well-rested and cheerful after a full night of sweet dreams. They bounded into the kitchen—all rosy cheeks and flyaway hair—expecting to see the familiar sight of their mother. Instead they met a father with dark circles under his eyes. He was in plaid pajamas—an altogether unfamiliar sight.

"Father, you're home? Where's Mother?" Gloria asked.

"Your mother is having the baby!" He put on an enthusiastic smile he hoped they wouldn't see through. The last thing he wanted was his unease to rub off on the children.

"She is?!"

"Shhhhh!" he playfully scolded. "Yes, but keep your voices down. We need to stay quiet so they can focus."

But their gasp was enough to wake the other children, and within minutes they had all made their way from their bedrooms to the kitchen.

"What's the commotion?" Bettina asked.

"Mother's having her baby!" the girls exclaimed in unison.

A sense of excitement filled the space, as the children spewed questions—"When?" "Is it a girl?" How much longer?"—at their father and he tried to answer strategically. Only Felix met his father's gaze with misgiving.

"Where's Lara?" Karl finally asked, noticing she was the only one missing.

"She's with your mother. She's helping the midwife, so she'll probably stay in the bedroom until the baby comes."

"Oh I hope it's a girl," Gloria said again, crossing her fingers.

"No way, we need another boy in this family," Karl inserted. "We're already outnumbered."

The group looked to each other awkwardly, unsure what to do on the cusp of such excitement. "We'll just carry on with the day while we wait," Gerald answered the question no one had asked but all were wondering. "But you must stay down here. They need privacy upstairs." The children complied.

Lena made breakfast for the group—poached eggs on toast and fresh fruit. She spooned a serving to each of her siblings, feeling a sense of pride at being promoted to the eldest female in attendance. They ate, every few bites interrupted by giddy giggles.

Karl requested seconds—per usual—which was turned down by his father. The fever in the room climbed with anticipation.

As the children finished and began to clear the dishes—Gerald's nerves squashed his appetite—a deep moan echoed from upstairs. It was primal, unlike anything they'd heard before. Lena gasped. Everyone froze in place, then looked toward Gerald.

"Is Mother okay?" Miriam asked, nervously.

"Yes, darling. She'll be just fine," he soothed her with a pat on the head.

Another loud wail reverberated through the house. The children again looked to each other for reassurance. Gloria reached for Lena's hand as a growing sense of worry filled the kitchen. They were helpless. Helpless and a little afraid.

"Why don't we sing," Bettina suggested. "Remember how Mother taught us that song when we were scared of the dark?"

"Yes," her siblings replied.

"Maybe it will make us feel better."

Bettina began the first verse, a bubbly tune about kitten's whiskers and woolen mittens. The children linked hands as they joined in.

They finished with lighter faces, until a cry erupted from above. But this time it wasn't the guttural howl of a woman in labor. It was the shrill shriek of a newborn baby.

Gerald jumped from his chair, heart in his throat, and ran up the stairs two at a time. Bursting through the bedroom door, he saw Lara, red-faced with sweat beaded on her neck. A folded washcloth laid across her forehead.

Lara looked up when he entered and managed a weak smile before returning her gaze downward. In her arms, a tiny pink face poked out from a swath of receiving blankets. The baby's eyes were open, blinking away the residue of birth. Lara stared in awe, intoxicated with love for a creature she'd known only minutes.

Gerald looked to Marlene, who sat on the edge of the bed leaning into Lara and holding her hand. Marlene's fingers were stained crimson, and he noticed splotches of blood on her apron. At the foot of the bed was a pile of drenched linens, the after effects of the messiness of birth.

"It's a boy, Gerald," Marlene said. The sting of grateful tears pricked her eyes.

Gerald rounded the other side of the bed and bent down to kiss his daughter on the head. He glanced at the tiny baby, whose cry he'd heard only seconds ago, but who now was comfortably resting in his mother's arms.

"A boy," he said. Then looking to Lara, "Well done, my dear."

The midwife interrupted the moment, scooching past Gerald and gently lifting the bundle from Lara's arms. "Need to get his vitals," she said.

They watched as Elena unwrapped the baby and placed him in a cotton sling attached to a scale. The baby's arms shot up in reflex and his bleating cries protested the cool air of the room. Elena lifted the sling in front of her and squinted at the number.

"How is he?" Lara asked.

"He's perfect. Just over three kilograms. A very healthy weight."

"You did so wonderful, darling," Marlene said, wiping Lara's forehead with the washcloth. "You were so brave."

Elena handed the swaddled baby back to his mother. The boy flinched and made a cooing sound as he relaxed into the cradle of her arms.

"Have you chosen a name?" Elena asked.

The three Weisses looked back and forth at one another before Marlene finally said, "It's your choice, Lara."

She thought.

"Erich. His name is Erich."

Marlene and Gerald gazed lovingly at the baby. "Erich," Gerald whispered.

He walked around to Marlene and she rose to embrace him. They stood, side by side, their arms around each other's waists, looking down at their daughter and grandson. Lara stroked the newborn's check with the pad of her finger.

"Hello, sweet boy," she said. She'd never experienced such bliss. This was heaven.

"I'm so glad it's over," Gerald said to Marlene.

"Darling," she replied, with a gentle touch to his forearm, "this has only just begun."

EIGHT

Present

In the year since his birth, Lara had watched her son grow into a smart little lamb. He crawled early, and easily followed instructions, even shaking his head "no" when he knew he wasn't supposed to do something, like touch the log pokers that hung near the fireplace.

With each milestone Erich reached, her heart overflowed with quiet maternal pride. She'd been present for all the big things: when he first sat up unassisted, his first taste of baby food, when he learned to crawl, and most recently, as he practiced taking his first steps.

He knew her—loved her—even if it was as a sister.

Erich's arrival brought fresh elation to the house, which was greatly welcomed after the stress of the family's immigration to Switzerland. He was a true joy; always cheery and quick to placate on the rare occasion he was sour. Entering such a large family, it was as though he knew he'd have to be easy-going, always along for the ride to wherever his mother or siblings were headed.

The tagalong, they called him. As if he had any other choice.

Erich melded right into the fold of his siblings' close bond. Each morning before the children set off for school, they'd plaster Erich with kisses, and he'd chortle as they nuzzled their faces into the rolls on his chubby neck.

Lara wasn't shy with her affection either, showering the baby with love, yet never uttering the words she longed to say. Every time her lips touched her son's smooth skin, her heart broke a little more. Naturally, her feelings for Erich were different from the rest of her siblings'. They all doted on him, but Lara understood love on a deeper level. She'd jump in front of a train if it meant sacrificing her life for his.

The love she felt for him was ingrained to her core. Boundless and eternal.

Erich was her child, her flesh and blood—even though no one outside her parents and Felix knew the truth—and with the passage of time, the lie became more painful. She wondered if she could bear it much longer.

Lara rolled a small ball across the braided rug that covered the center of the living room floor. On the opposite side, Erich waited for the toy to get close, then lunged for it and missed. The rubber ball hit his shin and bounced off. The boy grabbed it before it was out of reach. He looked to Lara.

"Throw it back," she instructed. Erich tossed the ball one handed and it landed only inches from where he sat. Lara laughed. "Good try," she said. He crawled forward and picked up the ball again, determined to throw it farther. Their game of catch went on a bit longer, until Erich's attention dwindled and he became distracted with another toy.

Erich crawled across the rug to where Lara sat cross-legged, her shoulders slumped forward. He climbed into her lap and she gave his bum a pat.

"Want to do Patty Cake?" she said, grabbing his hands and clapping them to the tune. Erich grinned, wide mouthed, and as he giggled a trail of drool trickled from the corner of his mouth.

Marlene entered the room with a basket of dirty laundry on her hip. She stopped and smiled at Lara and the baby.

"There you are," she said, dropping the basket to the floor. She arched her back for a good stretch.

"Mama!" Erich pointed a stubby finger at Marlene. Lara's stomach clenched. She cringed every time she heard this address. It had been a year, but she still hadn't gotten used to her parents being referred to as Erich's mother and father.

It's just a title, she tried to convince herself early on. But it was no use. The name held power.

"Hello, sweet boy," Marlene said. Then to Lara, "I have to go to the store. We need more formula for Erich, and I'm going to pick up some fresh strawberries. Do you need anything?"

"No, thank you."

"Want to come along?"

"That's alright. I'll stay here with Erich if you don't mind."

"Sure." Marlene watched adoringly at the pair playing on the floor. With Erich's dark hair and blue eyes, he looked so much like Lara, who in turn got her looks from Gerald. The physical similarities made their ruse even more believable. To strangers, Erich and Lara had a striking sibling resemblance—nothing more.

But when Lara looked at her son, she saw the truth: the crinkle in the corner of his eyes was all Rubin. Certain expressions—the look of resolve when he was absorbed in play, or when his nose wrinkled at an offensive smell—reminded her of the man who'd once charmed her.

Marlene buttoned the toggle clasp at the neck of her cloak. The Peter Pan collar only accentuated her well-preserved youthfulness. She hurried out the front door, tote over her shoulder. At the base of the front steps, Karl was teaching Miriam and Gloria how to play hopscotch, while Bettina sat on the stoop with a thick book in her hands.

"I'm headed to the store. Lara is inside if you need anything," Marlene said, to which the children agreed and sent their mother off with a wave.

Back in the house, Lara cuddled Erich in her arms. Swaying back and forth, she hummed a lullaby. Erich sat still, perfectly content in the moment. When they were alone, she imagined what it would be like to live outwardly as his mother. She envisioned a small cottage in the country, modest yet cozy. Chickens roamed the yard and they'd play barefoot in the grass until the sun went down. But in her fantasies, it wasn't just the two of them—Rubin was there, completing their perfect family. She pictured their life together. Rubin would prop his boots by the fire in the wintertime, and she'd hang laundry on the clothesline in the summer. It was a simple existence, far from grand, but to Lara it was ideal. It was utopia.

Such daydreams plagued her regularly—in the shower, during her lessons with Frau Zimmermann, as she set the table for dinner. She relished in them, letting the fantasies evolve and grow from something bitter to something beautiful. Like caterpillars, Lara's dreams always blossomed into butterflies.

But then she came back to reality with a smack. And the truth was even harder to swallow.

"Ba-ba," Erich said, touching his mouth with his palm. Lara stopped humming and looked down to his little face.

"You thirsty? Want some milk?"

Lara stood and carried him to the kitchen where she warmed a cup of water and mixed in a scoop of white powder to make formula. She handed the lidded cup to the boy, who took a long sip.

When Erich was born, Elena had suggested he stay with Lara for only the first day.

"Once your milk comes in, he'll be able to smell it," she told Lara. "And he'll fuss if you don't give him your breast." Marlene looked to her daughter with concern, waiting for Lara to protest.

"Oh, I didn't think of that," Lara said.

"I'm not sure breastfeeding every other hour fits into your cover story. You'll need to get some infant formula. But don't worry, he'll take it fine."

"What will happen to me?"

"If you don't nurse the baby or express your milk in any way, it will eventually dry up," Elena explained. "It'll take several days, and might be a bit painful, I'm afraid." Then to Marlene, "Make sure you have cold compresses to help with her discomfort."

Marlene nodded, listening intently to Elena's postpartum instructions. She felt inept, having never bore a child of her own. Elena sensed Marlene's concern and left the house with some final reassuring words.

"Feed the baby and make sure Lara rests. That's it. I'll be back to check on everyone in a few days."

After that, they were on their own.

Lara spent a week in her room recovering. Her body was sore and swollen, and she struggled to find a comfortable position. Once, she'd made the mistake of using a hand mirror to look between her legs, only to be shocked and horrified by what she saw. She was mangled. Prickly black stitches poked out from her tender flesh.

Shocked by the effects of childbirth on her body, she crawled back into bed, wondering if she'd ever look normal again.

To explain her absence, Gerald told the children Lara had been struck with the flu, and they were happy to keep their distance. Lena bunked up with the younger girls for two weeks, not wanting to risk getting sick. By that point, Lara could at least walk without waddling, and her tummy had already shrunk by at least half.

It was almost as if nothing had even happened.

During the first few days following Erich's birth, Marlene checked on Lara regularly, helping her to the bathroom and massaging her belly—as instructed by Elena—to contract her uterus back to size. On the fourth morning, she opened the door to find Lara weeping.

"What is it, darling?"

"I just can't stop crying. It's like I have a never-ending supply of tears." Lara pressed up in bed to sit and Marlene noticed two wet circles on the front of the girl's night shirt.

"Oh, sweetheart. Here, let's put these under your top." She grabbed two cloths and helped Lara place them into her soft, cotton bra to soak up the leaking milk.

Lara blushed. "This won't stop either," she cried, pointing to her breasts. "Every time I think of him, I get the strangest feeling and before I know it, my shirt's all wet."

71

"Remember what Elena said. It could take several days for your body to adjust. It's normal."

"I know, but it's all just so hard to grasp."

Marlene didn't know what to say. She'd been the one to form this entire scheme from the beginning, and rarely did a day go by when she didn't wonder if they'd made the right decision.

Despite Elena's suggestion to separate the baby from Lara at the beginning, Marlene couldn't do it. The thought of Lara alone in her room, recovering from the trauma of childbirth crippled her. She couldn't keep Erich away—what kind of heartless person could? So she often took to sneaking Erich into Lara's room that first week for short visits.

Lara would prop him up on her bent legs and pore over his delicate features: long, silky lashes, pudgy toes, and skin covered in peach fuzz. She was, quite simply, amazed. *I created this. He came from me.* She breathed in his newborn sweetness, rocked and swaddled him, but never took him to her breast.

The lies continued, and Lara remained hidden, but no one thought twice—not when there was a newborn in the house on whom everyone's attention was focused. Babies, much like clumsy puppies or furry kittens, have the mysterious ability to hush all other worldly noise.

Once Lara's body healed, she emerged from her room a ghost of the person she had been. She was somber and quiet, trying to adjust to her new unwanted role. What was her place? How much—or little—should she contribute? When Erich cried, intuition told her to soothe him. Maternal instincts haunted her brain, but she resisted, instead allowing Marlene to step in.

It was agonizing.

Nonetheless, Erich thrived under the constant care and love of his family members. And for that Lara was grateful.

Weeks turned into months, and Erich quickly changed from a fragile newborn to an adorable, bouncing infant. His body filled out with so much soft baby fat, Marlene once joked that Erich had more rolls than the local baker.

"Mmmm...and you're even more delicious!" she'd poke at his chubby legs.

He was happy, well-adjusted. The family settled into a comfortable routine with a little one, and the children were thrilled to have a new sibling. They were all content—except, of course, for one.

With each passing day, Lara thought her spirits would lift. They never did. *What's wrong with me?* she thought. *I should just be thankful.* She'd gone along with her parents' plan with blind trust. Yet, as time moved forward, the resentment she carried grew.

* * *

As Erich's first birthday approached, the family planned a celebration to mark the special occasion.

"You only turn one once!" Marlene chirped as she strung a banner across the bay window. Gloria and Miriam helped Marlene bake a chocolate cake and piped the boy's name on top in shaky white letters—the E and R taking up most of the space, so that the remaining letters had to be squeezed in.

Later, they laughed when Erich dove headfirst into the slice on the tray of his highchair, grabbing handfuls of deep brown crumbs and bringing them to his lips. By the end, more frosting landed on his face than in his mouth.

"What a mess! I hope that was good, silly." Marlene lifted him from the chair to give his naked body a wipe down.

"Time for presents!" Gloria squealed as she dashed from the room. Miriam and Bettina followed, more excited for Erich's gifts than the unaware one-year-old.

Fresh and clean in a t-shirt and diaper, Erich crawled into the den. Marlene placed a small box in front of him, and he tore through the paper, sending shreds into the air. Gerald watched from his recliner, lovingly amused. Inside the box was a pale blue bonnet embroidered with little yellow ducks. Marlene placed the bonnet on Erich's head.

"You look positively handsome," she said, giving the bonnet a pat, before the boy ripped it off and threw across the room. He picked up a piece of the wrapping paper from the ground and crunched it in his fist. Paper: much more interesting than a bonnet.

Lara handed Erich another box. She helped him hold onto the tail of the ribbon and showed him how to pull to untie the bow. He opened the lid to find a creamy, white sweater with small, ivory buttons.

"How beautiful!" Marlene exclaimed.

"I made it myself," Lara said, her chest puffed with pride.

"Wow, what a talented sister you have," Lena said to Erich, as she poked his soft belly with her finger. "You'll be the most dashing one-year-old on the block." Lara blushed.

"One more!" Miriam said, placing a final box on the floor in front of Erich. Inside was a wooden train set. Each car featured a letter so that when hooked together, it spelled his name.

"Gloria and I picked it out at the store with Mother," Miriam boasted. Much more interested in the train than the bonnet and sweater, Erich rolled it back and forth while the girls provided sound effects. *Choo-choo!*

With the presents concluded and the children's bellies full, Marlene tidied up the kitchen before taking the little ones to bed. Erich fell asleep in Gerald's lap, and Lara watched as her father gently shifted the boy in his arms as he stood to take him to his crib.

Gerald was so warm with her son. Such a natural. Lara wondered if he'd been like that when she was first born.

Observing the interactions between Gerald and Erich made her thoughts drift to Rubin. She often wondered what he was doing and where life had taken him over the past year. Was he still caught in the twisted grip of the Nazi regime? Her parents insisted Rubin was a traitor to his country, a dangerous man who shouldn't be trusted. They'd done everything possible to erase his existence from her mind.

But love is a powerful drug.

Despite what her parents said, Lara held a soft spot for Rubin. She was horrified by his actions—he'd almost single-handedly thwarted their getaway—but she convinced herself there was a good person underneath. She'd seen it. She'd felt it. Somehow, in her mind, the moments of tenderness they shared meant more to her than his casual cruelty.

I love you, Lara. You're it for me.

She got butterflies in her stomach whenever she thought of their rendezvous near the boat house, the night he'd first kissed her. He was so charming. She'd fallen hard—and fast. That was the first, but not the last. They'd used every chance possible to touch—sometimes just a brush of hands, other times, when they checked for onlookers, a caress. The lust had culminated in that small patch of grass in the clearing, where he'd taken her virginity and given her a child.

Now, she couldn't help but picture him as a father to their son. Erich deserved his real father. She was sure Rubin would be just as attentive to Erich as he was to her. If only she could tell him the truth.

When Erich had been about six months old, a new family moved to the neighborhood. Friends along the street buzzed with the revelation that the family had come from Austria—just like the Weisses.

"Oh, we must meet them!" Marlene said. "I hear they lived in Salzburg!"

Always the consummate diplomat, Marlene was among the first to drop off a fresh loaf of bread and a welcome letter on the new neighbor's doorstep the following morning.

"They were so appreciative," she told Gerald after her visit.

"Must be that good Austrian breeding and manners." He winked. "Let's invite them for dinner."

"That's a wonderful idea, Gerald."

And so the couple, along with their baby girl, squeezed around the Weiss dinner table on Friday evening. Gerald was right—they were cordial and polite. Amid bites of Käsespätzle, the adults spoke of Salzburg, discovering many connections between themselves.

Lara listened intently, her heart aching for news of people she'd left behind. Desperate for updates, her zeal got the better of her.

"Did you know a boy named Rubin?" she blurted only a few minutes into the main course. Hope twinkled in her eyes—she couldn't help it.

The man and woman, forks full of cheesy noodles to their mouths, stared at her blankly, and Lara quickly realized the absurdity of the question. There were hundreds of men in

Salzburg named Rubin. How daft to think anyone would know a particular young man with blonde hair and broad shoulders.

"Nevermind," she mumbled.

Gerald made meaningful eye contact with Marlene, then quickly changed the subject. Lara finished her meal in silence, picking around the crispy onions on top to the gooey gruyere below. As the dinner concluded, a sense of doom settled in her stomach for the lecture she anticipated.

She was right.

After the neighbors left, Gerald addressed Lara in private. The frustrated look on her father's face said it all.

"Lara..."

"I'm sorry, Father, it just came out."

"We have to be careful."

"I know. I was just curious."

"You must forget about him, Lara." He shook his head, exasperated.

Her face dropped and her eyes became misty. "But I love him, father."

"Love? How can you say that? Remember what he did to us? He doesn't care about you; *that* he made perfectly clear."

"He's Erich's father! Doesn't that count for something?"

"Shhhh, quiet," he hissed, pressing a finger to his lips. "You know you can't say that when the children are around."

Marlene entered the room and immediately consoled Lara who was now blubbering openly. The girl's arms folded firmly across her chest, but Marlene hugged her anyway, stroking the hair that fell down the back of her neck.

"My darling, your father is right. You have to move on. You have a bright future ahead of you and I know you're going to find a wonderful man to love." Albeit soft, she was also persuasive.

"But I don't want another man. I want Rubin. He said he loved me. We should be together—the three of us. I know he'd leave the Schutzstaffel if he knew about Erich. I know it. We could be a family." The last words were no more than a whisper.

Marlene sighed and looked to her husband.

"It's not possible." Gerald's response was terse. His voice deepened with anger. "You made choices, Lara, and now you must live with the consequences." Marlene, shocked by his sternness, blinked as if she had misheard.

Lara looked aghast, her eyes wide and mouth open. Before Marlene could mollify her husband's brashness, Lara stormed from the room in tears. At the end of the hall, they heard a door slam shut—a familiar sound. Marlene turned, disappointed.

"Oh, Gerald. A little compassion goes a long way."

NINE

Erich's first birthday marked a critical turning point for Lara. She'd spent the past year depressed—weaving in and out of a heavy fog, one so confining it felt like a cage without a key. The loneliness was crippling. Each day was a haze of emotion so confusing she often found herself falling into bed at night unable to pinpoint her true feelings. Was she bitter? Or was it regret she felt—topped off with a splash of hopelessness?

At times she'd go days with a surprising turn of optimism, greeting the morning with a smile and maintaining a positive mood all day. These stretches teased her parent's hopes that the girl had come to accept the reality of their situation. But they never lasted. A new day would dawn and Lara would fall yet again into a deep despair that bound her to her room.

The children were perplexed by Lara's behavior—the bright young woman they all looked up to ceased to exist. She was a shell of her former self.

"What's wrong with Lara?" they'd each ask, in one way or another, to which Marlene would respond, "Everyone has difficult phases in life. Just give her time." Puzzled yet appeased, the children went on with their lives, hoping their sister would one day come back.

Lara knew she was off. She felt it deep in her bones. But how could she possibly remain the same girl that lived so free and easy in Austria? New Lara had made dangerous decisions with heavy repercussions—ones her siblings could never understand. The life she knew was a lie, and the lie was slowly eating her from the inside out.

As she lay in bed, she'd pull the quilt over her head and bury her face in the pillow to stifle the sounds she'd lost control of. She cried for the unfairness of her plight and the lifetime of secrets to which she was sworn. When there were no more tears to be had, she'd fall asleep with her cheek against the dampness of her pillow only to wake the next morning to the same harsh light.

But as her little boy's first birthday came and went, something inside Lara shifted. The occasion seemed like such a significant point in not only Erich's life, but hers, as well. She'd survived a full year of living in deception. A whole year!

In some ways she felt the months had flown by in the blink of an eye. Hadn't it just been yesterday when she'd given birth? So vivid was the sensation of his head crowning that a shiver tickled her spine when she thought of it. It was the most physically painful moment of her life; her body being ripped in half by the force of Erich barreling into the world.

He wasn't planned. But that didn't mean he wasn't wanted.

She'd do it again in a heartbeat.

The memories were fresh, the year not long enough to soften their edges. Yet, in the same breath, Erich's birth felt like a lifetime ago. Hours ticked by, slow and forced, as if being pushed back by a powerful wind.

One year felt like ten. And the future looked daunting. Lara questioned her ability to keep up the façade for decades to come. If a single year had been this difficult, how would she ever make it sixty more?

Something needed to change. As the days following Erich's birthday went on no differently than before, Lara knew she had to choose. With a renewed certainty, she made a silent vow to resolve her situation, regardless of the cost. She pledged to choose happiness.

Even if her happiness brought heartache to others.

* * *

The next morning, Marlene popped her head into Lara's room just as the girl was buttoning her dress. Lara's figure had snapped back quickly following Erich's birth. The few pounds she'd gained melted off with ease, leaving her with the wispy waist and defined silhouette from before.

"I'm leaving in a few minutes to take the children to school," Marlene said. "Do you want to walk with us?" She predicted the answer, but always asked anyway.

"I think I'll stay here today."

There it is.

Lara waited for her mother to ask if she'd keep an eye on Erich while she was gone, as Marlene often did.

"Ok. Oh, I'm taking Erich, too. He could use some fresh air."

"Alright."

Lara was relieved, actually. Time with her son was typically savored, especially when she could strengthen their bond one on one. But on this day, Lara didn't want any distractions. She needed to be alone, to concentrate. She had a mission, and it needed to be finished before her mother returned.

Marlene and the children left through the front door, their voices fighting over one another in a slew of separate conversations. With Felix and Lena at friends' homes, Lara found herself alone in the house, which was just as she'd planned.

Once her family rounded the corner and was out of sight, Lara hurried to Gerald's study and slid open the solid, pocket door. A generous mahogany desk sat in the center of the room, framed by built-in bookshelves stretching from floor to ceiling. The desk lamp with a rounded, green shade and delicate pull chain signaled the formality of the space.

This was a private room. Lara felt like a trespasser, but her will drove her forward.

She pulled open the first drawer of the desk to reveal a stack of crisp ivory stationery. She'd seen her father write correspondences on them, the black words soaking into the porous linen. Without room for a desk in her own room, much of the office supplies were housed in Gerald's desk. He would have gladly shared with her had she asked. But that would mean revealing her reason—that, or lying once again.

She couldn't handle another lie.

Taking a piece from the top, Lara took her father's fountain pen and began to write. Her hand shook as the ink took shape.

My dearest Rubin,

I hope this letter finds you well and safe. I can hardly believe it's been two years, as it seems like yesterday when we parted. So much has changed, and I want you to know that despite what happened, I forgive you. I believe you're a good man, a man who made a mistake. But haven't we all?

I've missed you so, and often find myself dreaming of the time we spent together. I still feel the depth of love for you that I expressed all that time ago. What we had was real. And I know this because I have proof of it.

Rubin, we have a son. His name is Erich and he was born eight months after my family left Austria. He has your smile and my dark hair. When I look at him, I see the love we once shared, and I desire nothing more than to be together as a family.

If this letter finds you, I pray you will reply. Until then, I remain yours, faithfully.

All my love,

Lara

She read through her words three times before feeling satisfied. Folding the sheet in half, she slipped the crisp paper into an envelope from the desk drawer. But where to send it? Where did he live?

He'd been to her home in Salzburg many times, first as a grocery delivery boy and later as her secret suitor. It occurred to Lara in that moment that she'd never seen his house. Was it big and white? Modest and blue? Did he share a room with a sibling? Did he even *have* a sibling? It struck her how little she actually knew about the man she claimed to love.

Small details, she assured herself.

On the front of the envelope, Lara wrote the only address she knew that might land her letter into Rubin's hands: an outpost where he'd once been stationed. She didn't dare include a return address, but that didn't matter—if it didn't get to him this time, she knew no other address to try. This was her only shot. Instead, she added a postscript at the end of her letter, telling Rubin where he could reach her.

Here is my address. I'll wait with bated breath for your reply.

Grabbing her coat and hat, Lara dashed out the door and down the sidewalk toward the post office—thankfully in the opposite direction of the school—where she could send the letter. She needed to be quick before her mother returned—or before her courage evaporated.

The small brick building came into view, large block letters spelling "POST" across the archway. Lara was out of breath when she reached the mailbox. Her hand shook as she pulled the letter from her pocket. She stared at the white square grasped firmly between her fingers. If she did this, there would be no going back.

With a deep sigh of resolve, she pushed the letter through the slot. As the envelope slipped from her fingertips into the collection bin, she watched it tumble in slow motion onto the pile of other outgoing mail, taking with it all her hopes and dreams.

* * *

The weeks that followed were fresh torture. Each day Lara waited for the mail to be delivered, then eagerly sifted through each piece, searching for her name.

Nothing came.

Her faith lingered dangerously close to defeat. But just when it threatened to surrender completely, her heart found excuses for the lack of response.

The letter was lost in transit.

The letter was intercepted and never made it to Rubin.

Rubin was no longer in the same position within the German military.

What she refused to accept was the alternative: That Rubin *had* received her letter and chose not to reply.

TEN

A bright morning in April brought with it an upbeat mood to the Weiss home. Lara awoke to birds chirping outside her window—a sound she'd recently found so irritating. How dare the birds carry on so happily when she was so terribly miserable? Today, though, she welcomed the conversation between the little sparrows as a hopeful sign of spring and new beginnings.

Maybe today's the day.

She peered out over the windowsill near her bed. Tulip sprouts pushed through the earth in the small courtyard below, begging to greet the spring air. Closing her eyes, Lara listened to Mother Nature's orchestra: wind rustling through leaves, the rhythmic tap of a woodpecker against the trunk of a soaring oak.

Everywhere she looked, things were living—if only she could join them.

A squeal from somewhere in the house brought her back. Erich's joyful laughter echoed through the hallway, making

Lara's heart lurch. He was her greatest accomplishment, causing her equal parts unbridled love and deep sorrow. In truth, it was Erich who kept her going—without him, she felt little reason to live.

Standing from her bed, Lara reached her arms toward the ceiling and rolled her head around to stretch the muscles in her neck. She slipped into her plush robe and fastened the pastel pink tie into a knot at her waist.

"Good morning!" Marlene said brightly as Lara entered the dining room. "Such a gorgeous day, the sun woke me up even earlier than usual." Her mother was always so peppy and full of life, Lara wondered if the woman ever had a down day. (Marlene did, of course—she just chose not to show it).

"Morning, Mother."

Bettina, Miriam and Gloria sat at the table, a bowl of steaming porridge in front of each of them. Gloria spooned a heap of brown sugar on top, licking her lips as it melted into a dark river among the oats. ("Would you like some oatmeal with your sugar?" her father would have joked had he seen it).

Across from Gloria and her dessert breakfast, Lena bounced Erich on her knee, giving him bites from a small dish. A deep bowl of fresh fruit sat in the middle of the table, and Lara reached for a banana, peeling it while she spoke.

"Where's Felix?"

"Still asleep," Lena replied.

"Karl?"

"On his paper route."

"Oh, I forgot he was doing that now."

"Beautiful day for a long walk," Marlene inserted, coming to join the children in the dining room.

Bettina snickered under her breath. "A little exercise will do him good."

"Be kind, Bettina," Marlene scolded. "No one likes a nasty tongue."

The children stifled a laugh. Poor Karl always got the brunt of their jokes.

"What shall we do today?" Marlene changed the subject. She rounded the table until she stood behind Gloria. The girl's long, golden hair flowed over her nightgown in perfect tendrils past the middle rung of the chair. Marlene fingered the soft locks, then began to braid them into a thick plait down Gloria's back, tying it with a ribbon.

"Let's hike in the hills!" Miriam exclaimed.

"Or ride our bikes through town," Bettina added.

Gloria nodded enthusiastically. "Yes! Can we, Mother? I miss our old adventures."

It was true, the family routines transformed when Marlene came into their lives. She loved taking the children out of the house to discover the city and find joy in the smallest things. The world was her playground, and Marlene intended to explore every inch.

Since establishing themselves in Switzerland though, and especially with Erich still being so young, they'd had fewer opportunities to go roaming. Marlene could sense the children's restlessness.

"Those all sound like wonderful ideas," she said. "But—"

The close of a door interrupted the conversation, as Karl slunk into the room and collapsed into a chair at the head of the table. His shirt had come untucked from his knee-length shorts. One suspender hung on the edge of his shoulder. His cheeks were flushed from obvious exertion.

Marlene chuckled. "Tired?"

"Exhausted," he said, extending his legs out and sinking down into the chair like a wet noodle. "Feels like my route gets longer every day."

Bettina rolled her eyes.

"Oh, I almost forgot," he said, straightening up again. "Before I left the post office I grabbed our mail." He pulled a stack of envelopes from his bag, tied together by a rough piece of twine. "There's something for you, Lara." He extended a small, white envelope to her.

Who could possibly be writing to her? Marlene wondered.

* * *

Lara's stomach dropped. Her fingers tingled as she took the letter from her brother. *Act normal*, she told herself. Feigning indifference, she discreetly slipped it into the hip pocket of her robe before excusing herself from the table.

The letter—no heavier than a feather—held enormous weight. In the safety of her room, she tore open the envelope and removed a thin piece of paper. Unfolding it, she was struck by the severity of his angular penmanship—so opposite from her smooth strokes. Her eyes devoured the page.

Dear Lara,

I must admit I was stunned to receive your letter, assuming I would never see you again after you left Austria. Your words brought me to my knees. A son! What a blessing that could only have come from God. It's true, Lara, that I made many mistakes in recent years, choices I'm not proud of. But since you've been away, I've changed. I'm no longer conspiring in favor of Hitler's agenda. Austria is my home, and I've decided to be faithful to serving and protecting my birthplace.

Oh Lara, how I miss your beautiful face and sweet innocence. You are right: What we had was real, and our dear Erich is proof. If only we could be together again. I would vow to love and protect you and our son for as long as I live. Regret fills my heart and I wish I could go back and change what happened.

What the future holds, I cannot say. But I hope you receive this letter so you at least can go on with the peace of knowing the magnitude to which you capture my heart.

Yours,
Rubin

Lara dropped the paper to her lap, as her chest constricted with sharp, tight breaths. Her instinct was right—he *did* love her. And he wanted to be together. Tears sprang to her eyes at the possibility.

Her first impulse told her to march down to her father's office and pour her heart out onto another piece of stationery, but her second knew that this was impossible, considering the busy constraints of her family home. She'd have to wait until tomorrow when her parents were out. Instead, with shaky hands, she folded the letter and placed it within the creamy pages of a book on her nightstand where she was sure no one would find it.

She smiled, dizzy.

Not wanting to cause suspicion, Lara made her way back downstairs where her family sat finishing breakfast. She felt flushed. She hoped her neck wasn't blotchy.

Marlene eyed Lara curiously, and the girl put on her best blank face.

Please don't ask about the letter. Please don't ask, she thought. She didn't want to lie again—although she'd become quite good at it.

The children were still formulating their plan for the day when Felix meandered in, his nightshirt wrinkled from the deep sleep of a teenage boy and his rumpled hair sticking out to the side.

"Well good morning, sleepy head," Marlene said. "I thought you'd never wake up. It's nearly ten!"

Felix grinned and sat beside his mother, putting his head on her shoulder. Even as a boy on the cusp of manhood, he'd formed a soft spot for Marlene. She wrapped her arm under his chin and patted her hand on his cheek.

"Let's do Rieter Park today," Marlene said. "Sound good?" The children whooped in agreement.

"Mother, would you like me to fetch the groceries today while you're all out?" Lara asked with unusual enthusiasm.

"You don't want to come with us?" Marlene replied, disappointed.

"No, I'm afraid I have to catch up on my schoolwork. But I'd be happy to run to the store to save you a trip later."

"That's thoughtful, Lara. Thank you."

The children cheered at the prospect of a full day of adventure with their mother. Her spontaneity had always been one of the traits that drew the children into her sunny orbit. Marlene smiled at them, all the while keeping a skeptical eye on Lara.

Something changed, she thought.

Grabbing her purse from the kitchen counter, Marlene pulled twenty francs from her wallet and handed them to Lara.

91

The gold coins were cool to the touch and they jingled as Lara put them in her pocket.

"Just get all the usual things."

"I will."

Lara smiled, revealing a deep dimple in her right cheek. Was she coming across as natural? She hadn't offered to do much over the past year. Would Marlene see through her? Quickly breaking eye contact with her mother, she went upstairs to dress, while the rest of the family dispersed for their various outdoor activities.

Alone in the house once more, Lara took the opportunity to draft another letter to Rubin. She signed it "affectionately," and dropped it in the mail slot on her way to the market.

Plop! As simple as that, their correspondence began. Why hadn't she thought of it sooner? Could she have saved herself a whole year of heartache?

Lara walked the rest of the way to the grocers with a spring in her step. Her mind was busy, her world re-opened, and she felt a purpose had returned to her life. The fresh air brushed away all of the cobwebs that had formed in her mind over the past twelve months.

Things were finally falling into place.

At the market, Lara filled a basket with the essentials to feed a family of ten. In addition to the staple items, she grabbed an extra bag of flour, chocolate morsels and confectioner's sugar. Her mood called for celebration. Placing the items on the counter, the woman behind the register smiled knowingly.

"Let me guess," she said. "A cake?"

"Yes, actually," Lara replied sheepishly. "My birthday is this week."

"Oh, lovely. How old?"

"I'll be eighteen." She stood a bit taller at the sound of her words. Eighteen—such a milestone—once seemed so far away, and yet here it was. What should have been a time to celebrate impending womanhood, now felt silly given all she'd been through. Surely conducting a secret pregnancy, bringing a child into the world, and then living a devastating lie matured her more than any birthday could.

Eighteen was once something she wished for, but she never thought it would look quite like this.

"A big one!" the woman replied. "Officially an adult. How exciting. Well, I hope you have a lovely birthday, dear."

"Thank you."

Lara paid for the groceries. At home in her room, she emptied the change into the glass mason jar under her bed. It was half full now. A jumble of bronze and silver of varying sizes layered two inches from the bottom. Lara hadn't counted it for a while, but she knew she was getting close. With a twist of the lid, she pushed the jar back beneath the shelter of her mattress.

From there, twice weekly grocery shopping became a new chore, one she willingly agreed to, for reasons only she knew.

ELEVEN

"Happy birthday to you
   Happy birthday to you
Happy birthday, dear Lara
Happy birthday to you!"

Their voices rose in harmony, led by Marlene and her natural
gift for song. Lara smiled, perhaps more genuinely than she had
in years. The family gathered around the dining room table.
From the kitchen, Gerald emerged, gingerly carrying a cake
topped with candles with wobbling flames.

Lara sat at the head of the table—a birthday tradition—and
grinned as her father placed the cake in front of her. Buttercream
frosting smothered the double-layer confection, dripping with
yumminess over the edges down to the silver platter.

"Make a wish!" Miriam yelled.

Lara closed her eyes and paused, thinking. Then, with a deep
inhale, she leaned forward and blew out each candle in a single

breath. Everyone clapped and the children cheered, much to the delight of Erich, who banged on the table excitedly.

"What did you wish for?" Miriam asked.

"I can't tell! Or else it won't come true." Lara pinched her sister's cheek.

She's in an awfully pleasant mood today, Marlene thought. Then again, she never got her hopes too high, as Lara's good humor was typically short-lived.

The family savored the rich, vanilla dessert. Marlene was proud of the result, and the family's approval pleased her. She'd become quite a skilled baker, always scouring cookbooks for new recipes. When the pantry didn't have exactly what she needed, she experimented with ingredients, often coming up with something unexpectedly delicious.

"Seconds?" Karl asked, hopeful.

Marlene gave the boy a sideways glance and shook her head.

"Heavenly, Marlene," Gerald said, using his fork to get every last crumb.

"Yes, thank you, Mother," Lara echoed.

Marlene nodded, delighted with their satisfaction. She carried the leftover cake to the kitchen where she placed it under a glass cover. Plenty left for tomorrow. She returned to the table with a wet washcloth for Erich whose face was covered in a thick layer of icing.

"You sure got Father's sweet tooth," Bettina said. Erich grunted and swatted at Marlene's hand as she gave him a thorough wiping. His fair skin turned rosy from the rag's roughness.

Gerald, who had disappeared briefly after the cake, reappeared a moment later. His right hand was behind his back, hiding something, and the children studied him, waiting for the reveal. Gerald turned to Lara and unveiled a deep green bottle of champagne. It was embossed with a fancy label and had gold foil covering the top.

"I was saving this for your mother's and my anniversary next month," he said, holding up the bottle, "but I think my oldest daughter's eighteenth birthday calls for a special celebration."

Lara's eyes lit up. Her father had never let her taste champagne before. He extended the bottle and used his thumbs to pop the cork. The little girls jumped, then giggled when an ivory foam flowed from its mouth. Gerald filled a small, crystal glass and held it out to his daughter. Lara felt very poised with it in her hand.

"May I have some, too?" Lena asked.

"I don't think so," he replied, giving her a wink. Then to the group, "Cheers to Lara. Your mother and I are proud to call you our daughter."

Lara brought the flute to her lips. The clear liquid sparkled on the surface and she felt little bubbles tickle her nose. Tasting her first champagne, she was surprised by its sweetness.

"You like?" Gerald asked.

"Yes, very much." Her cheeks flushed. By the time her glass emptied, she felt an all-over lightness—she couldn't remember a time she felt more uninhibited. The effects of the alcohol not only relaxed her mind but eased the pain she'd felt since Erich's birth.

So this is why people drink, she thought.

Lara went to bed that night a day older yet no different. Aside from a glass of champagne, her birthday had been an average day filled with average events. Still, she knew this milestone was a significant one.

Things were changing—or at least they were going to soon if she had her way.

Lena slept soundly nearby, only a lamp atop a small nightstand separating their beds. Reaching for her book, Lara rolled over to make sure Lena was still asleep. The girl breathed deeply. Facing the wall, Lara cracked open her book. Three sheets of folded paper tumbled out onto her quilt: the first correspondence from Rubin along with the two additional letters she'd received over the past three weeks.

She reread each one, word for word, savoring his sweet prose. Each letter concluded with a declaration of love. *Yours forever. Devotedly. More than words.* He signed his name in the same slanted font.

Rubin—the man she loved, and the man her father hated.

How could her father despise someone who had given them such a beloved child? Surely, she thought, he'd come to accept Rubin. Deep in fantasy, she imagined running into Rubin's arms and being swept away to a place where they could live happily together. She'd be mama hen to a handful of little chicks—she wanted at least five—who'd follow her around their sprawling home. She and Rubin would throw glorious parties and spend their evenings strolling their grounds, hand in hand.

Lena stirred. Lara quickly shoved the letters back into the center of the book and replaced it in the nightstand drawer. She could not risk the letters being found.

Laying her head back on her pillow, she pulled the covers to her chin and closed her eyes, summoning the daydream back into focus.

Soon, she thought. *Very soon.*

TWELVE

"We'll be at the little tavern on the corner." Marlene dusted her cheeks with a coral-colored rouge as she spoke. A cloud of dust puffed into the air each time the wand bristles met her skin.

"Be sure to get the little ones to bed on time. And don't let them talk you into more than three stories—you know how they get."

Marlene gave Lara a wink. She smiled and shut the powder compact, placing it back on the porcelain dish atop her vanity with the rest of her cosmetics. Marlene didn't wear much makeup—she preferred a natural look—but liked to toss on a bit of mascara and lipstick on special occasions such as this. A little color only enhanced her already stunning complexion.

"You know," Marlene said, "it's nice to be together like this— here in this room—under good terms. I miss our long talks. Hopefully we can get back to that place—someday."

Lara nodded with a slight smile, but secretly wondered if their choices had already set them on a trajectory of distance.

She watched Marlene brush her chin-length hair. The golden blonde locks were longer than she'd always kept them, having grown from the cropped pageboy cut of her adolescence. Marlene, whose carefree spirit and youthfulness once considered appearances the least of her concerns, now made an effort to look nice. She knew she'd never fit the mold of the glamorous women with whom her husband used to associate, but that didn't bother her. Gerald fell in love with a clumsy tomboy. With him, she'd come into her own as a woman, growing in grace and femininity. Their connection was strong, whether or not she was dolled up—she knew she could always be herself and he'd love her just the same.

Marlene turned. "How do I look?"

The hem of her emerald chiffon dress skimmed the floor. Covered buttons formed a perfect line up the center of the bodice, stopping at the hollow of her neck. Modest with a quiet air of sophistication, sheer sleeves gave the piece just the right amount of allure. Functional refinement, she liked to refer to her style.

"Beautiful," Lara replied honestly.

A gift from Gerald to mark their first year as husband and wife, the dress was the fanciest Marlene owned. When she'd opened it and parted the layers of tissue paper, she'd gasped at its beauty—the elegant silhouette, the soft-as-silk fabric. *Can I even pull off such a look?* she'd thought. For the longest time, the gown remained in her closet—not quite a practical choice for a busy mother of seven—but she had made a plan to pull it out each year on their anniversary, much to Gerald's pleasure.

"What about this belt on top?" Marlene held up a shiny, woven sash with a wide buckle.

Lara nodded. "The perfect finishing touch."

Marlene wrapped the brocade belt around her waist, fastening it at the center. She'd seen it on display in the window of a shop in town. The metallic glint caught her eye, and she'd almost walked right past before doing a double take. Curious, she'd tried to picture herself in such a flashy accessory. What would it feel like to have such fine fabrics against her skin?

The shop girl's compliments boosted Marlene's confidence, even if the oohs and aahs were a little overdone. In the end, she bought the belt. But like the green dress, it remained largely untouched, a symbol of a life she couldn't quite decide whether she wanted. Was one's outward style a true representation of their inner self? Could she still be the same uncomplicated person if she also indulged in frills from time to time?

Above all else, Marlene insisted on staying true to herself, even despite all the rather dramatic turns her life had taken. Such as marrying one of Austria's most esteemed physicians.

Some of the handmade clothes she'd brought from her past life still hung in her closet—what few things they could grab and take with them. But occasionally Marlene would reach for the belt and wrap it around her slender waist. A reminder of the joy that could be found in life's little luxuries.

"Almost ready?" Gerald hollered up the stairs. "I don't want to be late for our reservation."

"I'll be right down!"

Marlene grabbed the beaded evening bag from the corner of the vanity and slid her feet into strappy, satin shoes. She turned to Lara, poised as ever.

"Alright, darling. You know where we'll be if you need anything. I'm sure you'll be fine. The children will be well behaved," Marlene hurried toward the bedroom door, but before she could turn the knob, Lara intercepted her path with outstretched arms. Startled at first, Marlene's body softened as Lara wrapped her in a tight embrace, lingering longer than usual.

"Everything okay?" Marlene could count on one hand the number of times Lara had hugged her over the past year.

"Yes," Lara managed, her voice on the cusp of breaking. "I just wanted to say I love you. That's all."

"Oh. Okay," Marlene smiled to hide her confusion. "I love you too, my darling." She ran her hands down her daughter's arms until their hands met. She clasped them both and gave a little squeeze.

What is this all about?

"Marlene!" Gerald's voice boomed from below once more, his impatience rising.

"Coming, Gerald!" She swept past Lara and hurried down the stairs.

In the living room, Felix and Lena kneeled on opposite ends of a small coffee table. Each had one of the little girls to their sides, buddying up into teams for a game of cards. The youngest, forever begging to be included, did little to prove they could keep up. Their short attention spans were hard for Felix to handle.

"Gloria, for the love of God will you pay attention? It's your turn!" he griped. Gloria scoffed, then took the top card off the worn stack in the center.

On the floor nearby, Bettina helped Erich build a tower of wooden blocks. The little boy grinned when Marlene entered.

"Wow, you look beautiful, Mother," Miriam said, folding her cards face down on the table.

101

"Thank you, darling." Marlene brought her hands to her waist and looked down as she smoothed her skirt. The featherweight material flowed behind her with each step. "Now, we must be going. Lara is in charge. Be sure to mind her, okay?"

"We will, mother."

"No funny business," Gerald added.

"Yes, Father."

He stuck his tongue out and gave a silly face, which made the children howl with laughter. They couldn't get enough of his new playful side.

"Miriam, it's your turn," Felix lamented, regretting his willingness to play the game in the first place.

At the front door, Marlene stepped out into the cool evening air. Gerald followed, turning at the last minute to give a final word to his eldest.

"We'll be home by midnight," he said. "Don't wait up."

"Okay."

"Bye!"

"Goodbye, father."

She watched her parents walk to the family's car parked at the side of the house. Gerald opened the door for Marlene and she slid in gracefully, pulling the sweep of her dress in to gather at her feet. As the car backed out of the driveway, Marlene waved to Lara, still standing in the doorway. Lara raised a hand, leaving it up until the car was out of sight.

Goodbye.

Back in the den, Lara eased into her father's favorite chair to take in the scene, sinking into the impression from Gerald's weight. She found comfort sitting in the familiar leather grooves.

She let the children stay up later than Marlene would have liked, but only because she was savoring every minute. Miriam and Karl finally caught on to the card game and proved to be tough competition for their veteran older siblings. Gloria, having lost interest or maybe due to Felix's impatience, sat cross-legged with a rag doll in each hand. Their soft limbs flew wildly at the girl's imaginative play.

Erich toddled the length of the room, holding onto furniture, and moving from sibling to sibling, investigating each activity. *Hey, what are you doing? Oh, neat! Okay, what's going on over here? Looks like something fun is happening over there, I better go check it out!* As he made it around the perimeter and back to Lara, he let out a yawn and rubbed his tired eyes.

"Alright," Lara said. "Let's get you to bed, little boy. It's past your bedtime." She picked him up and he instinctively laid his head on her shoulder. "Say goodnight to everyone." She took his hand and flapped it up and down in a wave.

"Goodnight, buddy," the children said. "See you in the morning."

Lara climbed the stairs and made her way to the master bedroom where Erich's crib waited. She changed him into pajamas, digging to the bottom of his drawer to choose the warm ones with feet. The heat was on, but she knew how chilly it was outside.

Sitting in the wooden chair next to the crib, Lara rocked to the melody that she hummed in his ear. Erich's body became heavy, his arms lax. She looked down to see his eyes closed. A bead of sweat formed in the crease of her elbow from the heat produced between them. It trickled to the tip and fell onto her lap.

The moment felt perfect, and she didn't want it to end. But there were still things to do. Ever so gently, she stood and laid Erich onto the mattress.

Wonderment held her to the spot, as she watched his rhythmic breathing. How had she created such a perfect, innocent being? Staring at her sleeping son, her mind drifted. Should she dare risk his safety? His happiness? She shook her head—there was no time for doubt. Before her thoughts got away from her, she whisked from the room, closing the door softly.

"Okay, now it's time for the rest of you," Lara said as she rejoined her siblings downstairs.

"Aw, do we have to?" Karl whined.

"I'm afraid so. I've already let you stay up later than Mother instructed, and I don't want to get in trouble when they return. Come on."

Karl groaned but ultimately obeyed. The other children followed Lara up the stairs to their rooms. She took turns tucking each of the younger ones into bed, giving Gloria and Miriam a kiss on their foreheads.

"Sleep well, girls," she said.

"I love you, Lara. See you in the morning," Gloria replied through a yawn.

"I love you, too." Lara swallowed the lump in her throat. She took one last look at her sleeping sisters and shut the door.

In their room, Lena changed into her nightgown.

"Aren't you coming to bed?" she asked when Lara didn't follow suit.

"Yes, I just need to tidy up downstairs a bit. And then I might read for a while. You go ahead. I'll be up shortly."

"Okay, goodnight."

"Goodnight."

As an unsuspecting Lena climbed into bed, Lara retraced her steps back downstairs and tiptoed into the kitchen. She paused to listen. The house was quiet. The clock on the wall read nine o'clock. She had time—but exactly how *much* time, she wasn't sure.

Let's get started.

Grabbing the canvas bag her mother used for groceries, Lara opened the pantry and scoured its contents. *Quick, easy and light*, she thought. She wrapped a block of orange cheese in muslin and placed it in the sack alongside a half loaf of bread. From the counter, she took two apples and a banana.

Scanning the kitchen, she noticed her father's silver flask on one of the top shelves. Lara strained her arm until she thought her shoulder might pop from the socket, and just then was able to tip the edge of the flask off the shelf and send it tumbling down into her hands. It was empty. As much as she felt she needed a bit of liquid courage, Lara determined alcohol would do nothing more than cloud her focus. She filled the flask with cold water from the tap instead.

Now to wait.

Knowing she had to kill time before Lena fell asleep, Lara sat at the dining room table and stared blankly at the bag next to her. Her stomach clenched and she thought for sure she'd vomit from nerves.

Can I really do this? Yes, of course I can. It's only right and fair. But what about my parents? I could never hurt them like this. I can't. This is asinine. But don't I deserve to be happy? Yes, I'll do it.

Devils and angels played tricks with Lara's mind, forcing second thoughts—ones as powerful as her assured determination. With clammy hands, she wiped dampness off her brow.

Another glance at the clock. Nine-twenty.

The minutes crept by at an unbearable pace and her anxiety spiked higher with each second. If she didn't act soon, she very well might chicken out altogether. How much longer would her parents be gone? What if they cut their evening short? They could walk through the door at any moment.

And then what? How would she explain?

The thought of her plan being ruined was enough to force Lara from her chair. She crept up the stairs toward her room at the end of the hall. Not a peep from her siblings' rooms as she passed their closed doors. Lara said a silent prayer of thankfulness for her family being heavy sleepers.

She cracked open her bedroom door and peered in at Lena's side of the room. A mound under the covers, perfectly still. Lara opened the door further. The hinge, old and rusty, made a loud creak. She froze. But Lena didn't move.

Lara slithered over the knotted floorboards and knelt quietly at the side of her bed. She reached under the frame to pull out a knapsack from the far corner closest to the wall. The sound of fabric sliding across the hardwood echoed through the dark room, making her wince. Finally, with the bag in hand, she slinked out of the room without a sound.

In the hallway, Lara released a breath she didn't realize she'd been holding. The upholstered bag—rectangular with a full zipper on top—felt heavy on her shoulder. She reached inside and pushed past the folds of clothes to the bottom where her fingers met the cool metal of several Swiss francs. Guilt-fueled bile rose in her throat. It was stolen money; leftover change she pocketed on all her trips to the grocers. She'd hid the coins in a jar under her bed until she knew she'd accumulated enough—at least for now.

With food in one small bag and her clothes and money in another, she was ready. There was just one thing left to do.

Lara opened the door to her parent's bedroom. The deep breathing of a sleeping child met her ears before she even entered. On light feet, she crept to the crib. A long, thin blanket was slung over the rail. Its whimsical circus motif in blue and yellow represented everything lively and cheerful about childhood. Staring at it, Lara recognized the irony.

No time to overanalyze. *Focus.* She'd strategically put the cover there when she'd taken Erich to bed so that she wouldn't need to rustle through drawers and risk waking him—or anyone else.

The blanket was smooth in her hand. She stretched it to wrap around her torso and criss-cross around her back. The ends met in the front and she tied them into a snug knot, pulling with all her strength to ensure its security. Across her chest, the fabric formed a pocket—the perfect size for a baby.

With a deep breath, she reached down and slid her hands under Erich's tiny body. She lifted him from the mattress and his arms fell limp to the sides. The few drops of brandy she'd placed on his tongue earlier had worked—the boy was deep in dreamland.

Lara guided him into the fabric pouch with ease, tucking his little hands in, and positioning his head against her chest. She felt the warmth of his palm against the skin near her breast.

I'm doing this for him, she told herself.

Without another thought, she flung the knapsack onto her back and draped her food bag across her body, tucking the strap under the blanket carrier. She looked far from conspicuous. The weight of it all bore down on her petite frame, but Lara was fueled by the adrenaline of a hundred men twice her size.

Stepping into the hallway once more, Lara peeked in both directions to closed doors lining the corridor. Again, she heard nothing but silence. She breathed a sigh of relief.

One step closer.

Common sense told her not to get ahead of herself. She quickly hurried down the stairs to the front door, and brisk air hit her face as she opened it. She looked down at Erich, still asleep, and was glad she'd thought to put him in warm pajamas.

Tree crickets chirped a nighttime melody.

This is it. No turning back now.

She closed her eyes and willed her body to summon every ounce of strength.

Just as she reached back to pull the door shut behind her, a hand emerged from the darkness of the house and grabbed her forearm. She yelped. A body moved into the light—a familiar face, still a surprise.

"Felix!" she hissed.

"Lara," he spoke calmly, "don't do this."

Her voice broke. "I have to. You don't understand." She looked at Erich as a tear slipped down her cheek. "He's *my* son."

"Please, Lara. There has to be another way." His eyes pleaded with her.

"No. We have to go."

"But where?"

"Home. To Austria."

He looked at her in shock.

"Rubin is waiting for us," she said. "He loves me, and we're going to be a family."

"No, Lara. Please. Don't leave. You're making a mistake." He hadn't let go of her. She yanked her arm away.

"I'm going, Felix. I can't stay here any longer."

A look of helpless sadness crossed her brother's face. Lara felt sick with guilt.

"At least give me a head start," she said. Then, reaching out to touch his face, she softened. "I hope you all can forgive me someday."

And with that, she turned and disappeared into the night.

THIRTEEN

The train coasted into the station at Altsätten right on time. It was the early hours of the morning and the sun had yet to grant the day with even a drop of light. Mosquitos swarmed the lamp posts' blazing bulbs.

Lara shifted in her seat. Her back began to feel the throb of the extra weight she'd been carrying. Erich slept through the hour-long train ride, so instead of taking off the makeshift carrier, she'd left him alone, wrapped against her body. It was comfortable for him, not so much for her. But that's what mothers do, right?

She was relieved he hadn't been fussy. In the nights before she fled, Lara wrestled nightmares of Erich crying the whole journey. In her dreams, his wails drew the attention of authorities who questioned why a young woman and child were traveling alone in the middle of the night. She'd woken from each time drenched in sweat.

Now, looking down at Erich's long eyelashes and smooth skin, she was thankful for her son's calm disposition. Sweet boy, he'd granted her mercy, at least in this.

Lara lifted the sleeve of her coat to check her watch: two in the morning. She imagined the scene back at home. The image came freely: her mother frantic, her father furious.

* * *

After she'd run from the house into the darkness, it took every fiber of her being not to turn back to where she knew her brother stood watching them go. She couldn't bear to see his face, even though it was still clear in her mind: tortured with objection and understanding. Instead, she pulled the coat's hood over her head and hurried through the streets on foot, praying the farther she got, the less shattered she'd feel.

The train station was three miles to the east. She had an hour to get there.

Street lanterns cast umbrellas of light in regular intervals along the main roads. Lara dodged the glow, sticking close to the walls of the buildings she passed and weaving in and out of shadows for cover. Erich, roused from sleep, whimpered occasionally—her brisk pace made his head bob up and down against her chest.

"It's alright, little one," she whispered, putting a hand on his head for support. To soothe him back to sleep, she sang a familiar lullaby. An ode to the national flower of her homeland.

Edelweiss...

It was her father's favorite song. They'd sung it together many times. Now, she choked on the last words.

Erich relaxed, sucking his thumb for comfort. His eyelids drooped but he fought sleep the rest of the way. As planned, they

111

reached the train station in less than an hour, which meant they didn't need to wait long for their line to depart.

Another step closer.

Lara looked around. The station was nearly empty, unsurprising for the time of night, yet the openness of it surprised her.

Along a wide brick pillar, a woman with matted hair curled up on the ground. A ratty blanket covered her lower half, while layers of mismatched knits wrapped around her torso. From a distance, she looked like nothing more than a mass of drab, dirty textiles—until closer inspection revealed the woman's round face peeking from a chunky scarf. She used a stack of newspaper as a pillow.

Lara tried not to gawk as she walked past the pile of sleeping filth toward the ticket booth, but the existence of homelessness shocked her. Didn't everyone have a house with a four-poster bed and a closet full of clothes?

How raw was the world outside of the Weiss social circle?

At the ticket counter, a tired-looking man leaned his head on his hand, distractedly flipping the pages of a magazine. He addressed Lara robotically without looking up.

"Where to?"

"Altsätten, please." Lara's voice was soft, with a false sense of confidence. Could the clerk detect fear? She handed over two francs and the man slid a paper ticket across the counter.

"Thank you."

"Yup."

She took the ticket and headed to platform seven. They were headed a short way to a small town on the border of Switzerland and Austria. Once there, the second leg of their journey would begin.

The train waited with open doors. Lara boarded at one of the middle cars. It was vacant, save for one woman who sat alone in a window seat. As Lara passed along the aisle—the bags over her shoulders bumping against every bench—the woman glanced her way. A black shawl draped over her head, hanging low on her eyes. She looked young—Lara guessed a few years older than herself. The woman acknowledged Lara with a friendly nod. Lara slid into the seat across the row. *If we're the only two traveling, we might as well sit nearby.*

"Your son is cute," the blond woman said quietly.

"I'm sorry?"

"I said your son. He's cute."

Lara was taken aback. She'd never heard Erich referred to as her son before.

"Oh. Thank you," she said, cradling his head. He'd fallen back to sleep.

The woman leaned to get a better look at Erich, and when she did, her shawl fell back from her face. A deep purple bruise surrounded her right eye. It was swollen, her eyelid so puffy that it was nearly forced shut completely. The discoloration traveled to her cheekbone and the bridge of her nose. Around the edges, the purple faded to a grotesque blue-green.

Lara sucked in a gasp. The woman, realizing she'd let her guard down, pulled the shawl forward to cover her face.

Embarrassed and unsure what to say, Lara resorted to the obvious: two young women alone on a train in the middle of the night.

"Where are you headed?"

"Altsätten."

"Us too. Then to Salzburg." Should she be telling a total stranger?

"Austria?"

"Yes. We have family there." She couldn't stop oversharing.

"That's nice."

"Are you visiting anyone?"

The woman paused.

"No. I'm...I'm traveling alone."

"Oh. That's nice." *Stop being so nosy,* Lara thought.

Lara shifted toward the window and faced forward, giving the woman across the aisle privacy. As the train shifted into gear, a tangible tension in the cabin lifted. They rode in silence—two women escaping their own traumatic pasts and running toward a new life.

* * *

The ride was quick. Yet with every minute that passed, Lara felt further and further from her home and family, as if her choice had put an ocean between them rather than of a handful of miles.

As the train came to a full stop in Altsätten, Lara peered through the scratched glass of the window onto the platform. Bright, overhead lights along the terminal stood in stark contrast to the pitch black of the outside air. A man in a suit and overcoat followed the signs marked "exit." His briefcase swung in tandem with his stride.

Under the overhang, rows of benches sat empty. The station felt thick with loneliness at this early hour compared to the activity of daytime.

Her insides—twisted with anticipation—felt backwards and upside down. She searched the platform for the blonde hair and sun-kissed skin she remembered so well. She expected him to be

114

waiting anxiously (bouquet in hand?). Now, scanning the platform, she came up empty.

Could he have backed out? The possibility sent a chill down her spine.

A whistle pierced the air and, as the doors flung open, Lara grabbed her bags and shifted out of her seat, trying not to wake Erich. The weight of him in the carrier reminded her of the last few weeks of pregnancy when getting up from a chair was a chore in itself.

Across the aisle, her lone travel companion moved to stand.

"Good luck to you," the woman said.

"You, as well."

The women dipped their heads knowingly. Stepping off the train, Lara looked around, unsure of where to go. She hadn't considered what she would do, should she not be met on arrival.

Where was he?

The platform emptied quickly as the few passengers on the train dispersed. Soon, Lara was alone—a young mother, in a strange town, with a bag of belongings to her name, and a baby on her chest.

Her lip began to quiver, and she suddenly wondered if she had made a huge mistake. Should she have left the comfort and safety of her home? Was it really so bad there? Doubt devastated her mind until a familiar voice broke her thoughts.

"Lara!"

She turned to see Rubin jogging toward her. His jacket flapped open with each step. Dressed casually in khaki trousers and a blue collared shirt, Lara realized she'd rarely seen him out of uniform. He looked so different. So...average. But handsomely average.

Lara stepped forward, and then he was there. Rubin extended his arms and she ran into them, sandwiching Erich between their bodies. She breathed in his smell, spicy and clean, and buried her nose into the hollow of his chest. He seemed taller. Two short years had transformed him into a man.

"Oh, Rubin," she gushed.

"Lara, I've missed you." He leaned his cheek on the top of her head.

"I've missed you, too."

"I can't believe you're here."

She stepped back and looked down at Erich, who had been stirred awake from the commotion.

"This is our son, Erich," she said proudly. Rubin beamed.

"Hi little one," he said, reaching for Erich's hand. The boy wrapped his tiny fingers around one of Rubin's. "He's so beautiful, Lara. Just like his mama." Lara blushed, elated.

"Would you like to hold him?"

"Yes. That is, if he'll let me."

"He'll be fine, won't you, Erich?" She unwrapped the blanket from her body, releasing the baby from tight against her skin. His legs stretched long from being cramped in the carrier for hours.

Lara handed Erich to Rubin. "This is your daddy, my love." The boy's eyes widened and he looked to Lara for reassurance.

"It's okay, darling. I'm right here." Then repeated, as if she didn't believe it herself, "This is your daddy. Can you say 'Dada?'"

Erich looked back and forth between them, unsure what to think of the situation and the strange person who held him. Rubin laughed. "I think he's a little confused."

Leaning into his body again, Lara tipped her chin up to meet Rubin's face. Their lips met and she felt all her uncertainty melt

116

away. He held her face as they kissed, his hand soft and gentle. When they released, she stared at him dreamily, hardly able to fathom the scene. He was really there. They were finally together.

"Come on," Rubin said. "We better get going. My car is parked just over there."

He carried Erich in one arm and placed his other hand on the small of Lara's back, guiding them off the platform and down the stairs to the parking area. The train—the link between her past and her future—grew smaller as they drove away.

In the car, Lara held Erich on her lap. She gave him a sip of water from the flask in her bag. Replacing the bottle, she noticed the uneaten cheese, and her stomach rumbled. It had been over twelve hours since she'd eaten.

"I can't believe we're together," Lara said, still too excited to eat. She reached a hand across the car and gave Rubin's arm a squeeze. "I've been dreaming of this moment. Where will we go?"

"Back to Austria. I have a small apartment now, right in the center of Salzburg." He said it haughtily, as though he hoped his maturity might impress her.

"That sounds perfect!" she exclaimed. "Just the three of us."

"Just the three of us."

They didn't have far to drive before signs indicated the approaching border. A faint glow penetrated the darkness, as daylight made its entrance to greet the morning. Up ahead, Lara saw a small booth on the road, flanked by red stop signs.

Rubin slowed the car and got in line behind two other vehicles. They inched forward and Lara strained to see two patrolmen speaking to the driver of the first car. After a minute, the men let the car pass. Moving closer, Lara recognized the olive-green uniforms the guards wore. Multicolored badges and ribbons plastered their lapels. Pistols hung from their belts.

Lara's stomach clenched as she looked closer. On each of their left arms was a familiar red band featuring a twisted black symbol. The image made her shudder.

"Is that the SS?" she asked, panic rising in her voice.

"Yes, but don't worry. We'll be fine."

"But what if they ask for my papers? They'll see my last name."

"It's okay, Lara. Just trust me."

Rubin pulled a flash of red fabric from his pocket. Lara gasped when she saw the same black swastika at the center.

"Why do you have that?" she whispered. "I thought you said you left the regime?"

"Oh I did, darling, I did. But this is what will get us safely across the border. No one will question us when I show this. Don't worry, it's just for show."

She sat back, considering what he said. Just for show? Why would he still be in possession of Nazi propaganda if he no longer participated in their cause?

The car rolled forward and to a stop. The officer leaned down, peering through the driver's side window, his eyes cold and his mouth pinched into a thin line. Lara's heart skipped a beat. She tightened her hold of Erich.

Rubin rolled down the thin sheet of glass separating them from the SS patrolman.

"Purpose for crossing?" the officer gruffed.

Rubin held up his arm band. "Just out for a drive. Trying to get the little one to sleep." He pointed his thumb in Erich's direction. Lara gave a nervous smile.

The officer nodded and took a step back, extending his arm out in front of him.

"Heil Hitler!"

Rubin followed suit. Lara's stomach dropped when she heard the words leave his mouth.

The guard receded into the booth. Passing through the checkpoint, Rubin chuckled and shoved the band back in his pocket.

"See? Home free," he said. He turned to Lara who looked much more concerned than amused. "Don't worry, my love. It was just for show. I promise." He smiled as they continued down the darkened street.

"Okay." It was all she could manage as a tiny voice in her head screamed in warning.

Wasn't she supposed to feel content in this moment? They were together, on their way to a fresh start. So why, then, as they barreled toward the same place that had threatened her family's safety, did only one question run through her mind: *Can I trust a man who tried to capture my own father?*

FOURTEEN

When Marlene and Gerald returned home shortly before midnight, the train carrying Lara and Erich out of the city was already on its way.

"Dinner was lovely, Gerald. Thank you, I needed that." Marlene leaned across the car to kiss him on the lips.

"The pleasure was mine." He looked at his watch. "Only six hours until someone's going to wake us up. We better get to bed." They giggled, leaning together and feeling the wine making them lighter, easier.

"Can't we just sleep here?" Marlene asked playfully.

"I'm afraid not, my dear."

"Why not?"

"Because I have plans that require a bed, not a cramped car." He raised his eyebrows and Marlene smiled coquettishly.

She grabbed her envelope clutch and met her husband at the front of the car, taking his arm as they walked to the front door. They entered the dark house quietly, not wanting to wake their sleeping children. Marlene slipped off her heels by the door and rolled her toes on the tile. She wasn't used to wearing heels with such a point. Her pinky toe was sore.

"Coming?" Gerald whispered. She nodded.

Together they went upstairs and Marlene checked on the little girls before going to her own bedroom. She left the light off so Erich wouldn't stir. Through the twilight coming from the window, she watched her husband undress. His silhouette gleamed as he stripped from his dinner jacket and pulled his shirt over his head. The outline of his broad shoulders made her insides flutter—he was the epitome of masculinity. How did she get so lucky? She often pinched herself, married to such a handsome man.

Marlene reached behind her back to unzip her dress, letting it fall off her shoulders. She stepped out and lay it over the chaise. Slipping into her smocked chemise, she ran a hand along her hair, removing the beaded clip and putting it on her dresser. The effects of the wine lingered. Their evening alone had been so enjoyable, she hadn't wanted it to end.

And according to her husband, it wasn't going to.

As the cool fabric of her nightgown warmed against her skin, Marlene desired nothing more than to slip into the comfort of her bed and find out just what he had in mind.

One more thing, she thought. *Check on Erich*. She tiptoed to the crib as she did every night, his little face the last image she kept before she closed her eyes.

The bed was empty.

Marlene blinked and squinted through the dark. Were her eyes playing tricks on her?

She reached into the crib to where a lumpy blanket lay rustled in the corner, but when she pressed it, the blanket flattened to the mattress.

That's odd, she thought.

It wasn't panic that seized her throat at first: more a genuine confusion. Erich always slept in his crib. Then again, it was unusual for her and Gerald to be out so late. Maybe the change in routine prompted different sleeping arrangements.

He must be in Lara's room.

"Erich's not in his crib," she whispered to Gerald, who was crawling into bed. He looked startled, confused.

"He's not?"

"No. I'll check the girls' room."

Creeping down the hall, she turned the knob on Lara and Lena's door and pushed it open. On the right, Lena slept soundly, her yellow blonde hair spread around her face like a lion's mane. Marlene looked to the left. Lara's bed was empty, its covers pulled up tight and flat.

In that instant, she knew.

Dread jolted through her body like a lightning bolt. She clenched the doorframe to keep from crumbling to the ground. When she regained the air that had been sucked from her lungs, Marlene flung on the light and ran to the bed. Lena bolted upright, blinking rapidly.

"What's going on?" she said, alarmed and confused by the sudden frenzy.

"Where are they?" Marlene shrieked.

"What? Who?"

"Lara! And Erich!"

Before Lena could respond, Marlene ran from the room and collided with Gerald in the hall.

"They're gone!" she cried.

"What? No!"

The hallway was dim, but Gerald could see the color drain from Marlene's face. She put her hands over her mouth, afraid she might lose her dinner. Gerald pushed past her to Lara's room to confirm for himself, letting out a guttural "No!" upon seeing his daughter's empty bed.

By then, their screams had woken the rest of the children, who flew from their rooms, frightened and dazed.

"What's going on? What's happened?"

"Lara and Erich," Marlene said, her lips quivering. "They're gone." Tears rolled down her face. Gerald stared straight ahead, his jaw clenched. A blood vessel pulsed under the skin on his neck.

"I don't understand," Lena said. "What? Gone where?"

"She took him."

"Why? Where?"

Marlene looked to Gerald. He closed his eyes. There in the narrow hallway, the truth would finally come out.

"There's something you all should know," he said. "Something that we've been keeping from you." He paused. "Lara is Erich's mother."

"What?" the children gasped in unison. "No. What are you saying?"

"It's true."

"But, but..." Gloria sniffed and Miriam wiped a tear from dripping onto her pajamas. They couldn't grasp the severity of the situation, but something told them that if it was bad enough for their mother to be crying, it must be dire. They looked at their mother, bewildered.

"Your father is right. Erich is Lara's son." Marlene bowed her head.

Bettina, ever the logical one, shook her head. "But you had the baby. You were pregnant. We saw it."

"No, darling. I wasn't. It was a lie."

"Why?"

"To protect her. To protect all of us."

"I don't get it," Karl said.

"It's okay, darling." She reached out to pull him into a hug. "It's all very complicated, and I promise we'll explain it to you. But right now, we need to figure out where they went."

A strong voice broke the silence.

"I know." Felix stepped forward. His parents spun to face him.

"You know where they went? How?" Urgency hung on their words.

"I saw them leave. I tried to stop her, but she wouldn't listen."

Gerald stood face to face with Felix. "Did she say where she was taking him?"

"To be with Rubin."

"Rubin?" Lena shouted.

A fresh set of tears sprang to Marlene's eyes. Their greatest fear had been realized. Gerald turned suddenly and ran down the stairs.

"Where are you going?" Marlene yelled after him.

"To look for them!" he replied from below. "Maybe I can catch up to her!"

Felix darted into his room to grab a jacket, and still wearing his night clothes, ran after Gerald.

"I'm coming with you, Father!"

Before Marlene could protest, she heard a door slam, a car start, and then all was quiet. She looked back at her children's terrified faces as despair overcame her, buckling her knees. The children surrounded their mother, linking their arms around each other and melting to the floor into a puddle of worry and tears.

* * *

Gerald and Felix returned two hours later, defeated and weary.

When Felix said he didn't know *how* Lara was getting back to Austria, they'd figured their best bet was to check the train station. The car was barely in park before the men flew into the station, Felix checking the terminal and platform and Gerald inquiring with the ticket booth as to whether anyone had seen a young woman with a baby. Their search came up with nothing. In a last-ditch effort, they drove around the city in desperate hopes of stumbling upon Lara and Erich wandering the streets.

Nothing. Gerald knew they were gone. He turned the car toward home, focused on forming a plan. This was no longer an interception. It was now a recovery.

The house was quiet when they entered. A light from the living room drew Gerald in, and he found the children asleep, their bodies curled up on couches and chairs, while Marlene sat, awake, with Gloria's heavy head in her lap. She wordlessly searched Gerald with eager curiosity.

He shook his head. His shoulders deflated.

Sliding out from under Gloria's limp body, Marlene joined her husband and son in the kitchen. It was nearly three o'clock in the morning. Her eyes were bloodshot from crying and exhaustion.

"Nothing at all?"

"Nothing. No one admits to seeing them."

"How are we going to find them, Gerald?"

The three looked to each other, but no answers came.

FIFTEEN

The minute they crossed the imaginary line separating Switzerland and Austria, Lara felt lighter.

Home. Home!

Perhaps it was her imagination, but Lara swore the sky looked clearer. Certainly the air smelled fresher. Was that the shape of a heart she saw in the cloud formations above? She told herself yes, yes it was.

Everything would be better now. She was back in the country she loved, the place she had missed for two years. And she was with the father of her child. The three of them would finally be a family. Her spirits were so high she thought she might float right out of the car in a miraculous act of levitation.

As they drove, Lara peppered Rubin with questions: What had he been doing since they'd last been together? How was Salzburg? Had he thought of her as much as she'd thought of him? The need to make up for lost time consumed her, and Lara wanted to know every little detail. Before he'd get a few words out, she was already hurtling the next question his way. She was frenzied with hunger for him: a rabid animal foaming at the mouth.

Rubin found Lara's rambling amusing. He answered her questions with short responses: The city she knew was no longer—Gestapo patrolled the streets and many families lived in fear. Gone were the days of frolicking in the parks and strolling the sidewalks for leisure.

She should have been nervous about this revelation—she was about to enter a hostile zone—but irreverence pushed those worries to the back of her mind. They were above all that. Rubin would keep her safe. She felt invincible, in a way, the euphoria of being together feeling like a shield of armor.

"So what have you been doing?" she asked again, realizing he hadn't answered.

"Oh you know, odd jobs here and there."

"Such as...?" She was genuinely curious.

"Oh just boring things. Labor. Transportation. Nothing that would interest you, really." Was he blushing? "Forget about me, let's talk about Erich. I want to get to know him. Tell me everything!"

"Okay, what do you want to know?"

"Well, what about his temperament? He seems like such a good baby."

"Oh yes. He is. Really only fusses when he's hungry."

"How often is he hungry?"

Lara giggled. Rubin really knew nothing about babies. "I suppose he gets hungry just like you and I, silly." She playfully smacked Rubin's arm. His response was not one of amusement. Brow furrowed, his eyes grew dark.

"I'm just teasing," Lara said.

128

"And I'm just trying to learn what it's like to be a father."

"Sorry, I shouldn't have poked fun. I'm so happy you're taking such an interest in Erich." Then, to stroke his visibly-fragile ego, "I just know you're going to be a great father."

He softened at her comment. They rode quietly for another minute until Rubin continued his string of parenting questions.

"What does he like?"

"Well, he loves his toys—balls and little wooden cars. He'll sit and play with them for hours. We have blocks that he likes to stack too. That is, until he decides it's more fun to knock them down. It's really so cute, Rubin. It's like you can see the wheels in his head turning—always learning new things. Oh, and he loves strawberries. Especially the tiny ones that are super sweet. But he's not a fan of having his diaper changed. Too squirmy, too curious. He doesn't want to stop what he's doing to get cleaned up."

Lara was rambling again. She could talk about Erich all day. And why not? She knew him better than anyone in the world—the way he smelled right after a bath, the way his little feet turned in when he tried to walk, and how he rubbed his earlobe when he was tired. There were no secrets between them—except the freedom to live openly.

But that was over now.

"What about when he cries? How do you comfort him?"

What a thoughtful question, Lara thought. She momentarily pictured Rubin soothing an inconsolable Erich, the boy calming instantly in his arms. Father and son, connected through nurture and nature.

"I usually rock him. Or rub his back."

"Okay, good to know."

As they neared Salzburg, familiar sights—the landmarks of home—came into view. It had only been two years, but the city felt like a distant memory from her childhood—as if time and events transformed her into a new person.

Up ahead, Lara saw the fractured structure of a tall, white building. Stone crumbled at its base, leaving behind the remnants of what was once an impressive work of architecture. It looked like a bomb had exploded. As they got closer, she realized what it was: the Jewish synagogue.

"What happened?" Lara gawked at the destruction pushed into piles off the street. Passersby navigated around the rubble without a second thought.

"Kristallnacht," Rubin said. "You were already gone when it happened."

"Who did this?"

"Nazis. Took out thousands of Jewish establishments."

"But that's awful!" How had she not known? Did her parents really shelter her that much from the harsh realities happening in Austria?

Rubin didn't respond.

Despite the dim light of early morning, Lara made out many places she'd once frequented. Shops, markets, and schools glided by outside her window. But then another storefront with smashed windows, boarded up with wood covered in offensive slurs. The sign on the awning burned to an ashy skeleton.

Again, Lara felt the twist of revulsion deep in her gut. These were someone's livelihoods. Gone.

They passed St. Peter's Abbey and the domed marble Cathedral. High on a hilltop she saw Hohensalzburg, the famed 11th-century fortress looming above the city. Her father had once taken her and her siblings there to tour the grounds.

The areas of carnage made her uneasy, but not enough to outweigh her elation at being back in the country she loved. Lara closed her eyes and whispered, "There's no place like home."

Home. The word struck her.

"Can we drive past my family's house?" she asked Rubin.

"Are you sure you want to?"

"Yes. I would love to see it again."

"Okay then." He turned the steering wheel and navigated in the opposite direction.

They drove outside the center of the city, taking less-traveled country roads lined with faintly greening trees. After a while, a stucco wall the shade of fresh sage grew along the side of the street. Lara perked up in her seat, stretching her neck to see beyond it. The wall marked the beginning of her family's estate.

They moved forward. When the green wall turned into a stone pillar and then a magnificent swirling gate, Rubin stopped the car in front.

Lara stared through the wrought iron rods to the regal house that stood behind the wide, circular drive. Impressive in size and grandeur, the three-story mansion had never lacked splendor.

Lara regarded her childhood home—Oh, how she'd taken it for granted! A lump formed in her throat.

The pistachio exterior looked the same, yet something was different about the home she once loved. It was sad, worn. Time and neglect were not kind to the estate which had, at one time, boasted opulent landscaping and an aura of perfection. Now, moss grew along cracks in the walls, and most of the bushes were overgrown. Lara's heart sank to devastating depths at the sight of her beloved home in such a state of disarray.

"It's been empty since your family left," Rubin said, reading her mind.

She closed her eyes and pictured the open foyer and grand staircase. Lara had marched up and down those stairs more times than she could count, and she could still feel the smoothness of the banister under her fingers. She envisioned the ballroom, framed in artwork and gilded mirrors, where her father hosted parties complete with dancing and women in elbow length white gloves. Guests at the Weiss home were always dripping in luxury.

"I have so many memories here," Lara said, her voice trembling with nostalgia. "We left so abruptly; I didn't get a chance to say goodbye."

Erich fidgeted in Lara's lap. She stood him up on her thighs so his hands were pressed against the cool glass of the car window.

"You see, Erich? Such a beautiful home, isn't it? That's where your Mama grew up."

The boy tapped the glass with his fingers, then plopped back down onto her lap. He was getting squirmy, his little legs tired of sitting and aching to move. Lara tried to stand him up again, but he whined. A pang of desperation shot through her body.

She wanted to scream, *Look! This is important! Don't you understand what this place means?*

But he was just a baby. A baby whose home was another country, and to whom this house meant nothing.

After a few more moments without speaking, Rubin cleared his throat.

"We should probably be going," he said.

"Oh, yes. Of course," she replied, stealing one last glance at the spot where she'd spent most of her life. "Thank you for bringing me here."

As the car pulled away, Lara fought back tears and pushed the memories of the house from her mind. Looking forward, she tried to convince herself there was a new home that awaited her—a new future with Rubin and their child that would be just as blissful.

* * *

Rubin pulled the car into a private lot next to a tall brick building. Lara counted the columns of windows, stacked identically on top of one another: six stories. A handful of other cars parked haphazardly along the gravel.

"Here we are!" Rubin said brightly.

"Where?" Lara looked out the window, confused. She wasn't expecting to stop anywhere before going to Rubin's house.

"My apartment." He pointed to the building. "This is where I live."

Here? She wanted to say. Instead, the corners of her mouth turned down in mild revulsion.

Feeling embarrassed for her reaction, Lara tried to conceal her surprise. What did she expect? She was stupid to have assumed Rubin owned a large home.

Lara pinched the web of skin between her thumb and forefinger as a distraction. *Stop acting so entitled!* Of course he had an apartment. He was young and single—it made sense.

As she exited the car, holding Erich close to her side, Lara adjusted her expectations of what their home would look like. She erased the vision of a chandelier hanging in the foyer and lots of space for Erich to eventually run. In her mind, the image of a house morphed and shrank to a small apartment.

That's okay, she convinced herself, *perhaps this is just for the time being. We have the rest of our lives to grow together—including getting a bigger house.*

The main door sat atop three steps, framed with a wobbly metal railing. It was cherry red, and Lara noted that at least the door seemed cheerful.

Rubin led them up several flights of stairs to the third level. Doors lined the narrow hallway. The carpet on the floor was stained and threadbare down the middle from years of foot traffic. Lara felt dirty walking on top of it, even with shoes on.

She carried both bags and Erich, surprised that Rubin didn't offer to help. He walked slowly, glancing at each door they passed. Finally, they came to a solid brown door—the last on the left—marked "15" in tarnished brass. Rubin pulled a small, gold key from his pocket and inserted it into the slot. It fit, but when he tried to twist, it wouldn't turn. With one hand on the key and the other on the knob, he jiggled it and tried again.

Lara watched, perplexed. *Gosh, he must be nervous,* she thought. Finally, after removing and reinserting the key twice more, all the while looking more and more embarrassed, Rubin turned the key in the opposite direction. The door flew open.

"Ah, there we go," he said, looking flustered. "Darn key." Then, putting on a smile, he ushered her through the doorway. "Home sweet home."

Odd, Lara thought, *that he didn't know the proper way to unlock his door.* She followed him, carrying her two bags with one arm, her son with the other.

The tiny apartment entered into a small kitchen with a sink, range, and slim refrigerator. A stain the color of cinnamon tinted the sink basin like a mudslide in summer. Lara wondered when the last time it had received a good scrub.

She took in the space. The walls were bare, and she noticed a strip of wallpaper peeling near the cabinets. With no windows, the room had a dark feel to it despite the light cast by the floor lamp on the far side of the living room.

Lara looked around. To the right of the kitchen, the apartment opened up into a modest living room with a boxy couch, chair and two end tables. It was tight and cramped, furniture covering every available inch. A musky smell wafted in the air, and she so wished there was a window to open to let in a fresh breeze. Lara guessed she could cross the entirety of both spaces—if you could even call them two separate rooms—in a total of six steps.

"It's not much, I'm sorry," Rubin said. "But it's a nice place, nice neighbors."

She swallowed her presumptions. "It's just right," Lara assured him. Now was not the time to be unappreciative.

Rubin led her through another doorway, to the back of the apartment where she found one bedroom and a small bathroom with a stall shower. Taking in the close quarters, she pretended not to see the patch of disintegrating ceiling where water had filtered through the plaster. She imagined it falling on her head the first time she went to wash herself.

"You can put your bag here," Rubin gestured to a petite dresser next to the bed.

Lara lowered Erich to the floor, but when she let go he started to cry and clung to her like lint on wool trousers. So she picked him back up and slung him on her hip. Her arms ached from carrying him through the night.

"Thanks. I'll unpack later."

She imagined hanging her items in the closet amongst his, the fabric of their clothes brushing against each other in such an intimate way. How unusual it felt to be in the home of a man—a home that was now hers, as well. The apartment was a stark contrast to the grand surroundings of her father's old house just minutes away, but she willed herself to find happiness just being in Rubin's presence.

Nothing else mattered so long as they were together. Things were just things. Real wealth was measured in love.

In the living room, Lara sat on the edge of the couch and let Erich climb on her lap for a few minutes before he felt comfortable enough to be put down. She and Rubin exchanged awkward glances as Erich crawled around the floor near their feet. They'd once been so close, but now he felt like a stranger. Something about Erich's presence changed things.

"He's so curious," Rubin said, watching his son explore the room.

"Yes, he's a very smart little boy."

"He's my son, of course he's smart!"

Lara chuckled. Rubin's eyes were transfixed on the boy. His pride was palpable and her heart was happy seeing them together.

She licked her lips and felt the parched, taut skin of her mouth. Thinking back, she realized she hadn't drank any of the water from her father's flask. Her throat begged for relief—and the staleness of the air in the room didn't help.

"Can I have a glass of water?" she asked. "I'm so thirsty."

"Yes, of course."

Rubin stood and was in the tiny kitchen within three strides. He paused. His back to her, she saw his head swivel back and forth between the cabinets. He reached for the door on the right and opened it to reveal a stack of plates next to three nested bowls. Realizing his mistake, he swiftly shut the door and spun around to see if Lara was watching. She was.

"Oops, wrong cabinet," he said.

Nervous laughter followed, as he moved to the other cabinet and opened just a sliver before—happy with his choice—flinging it open the rest of the way and reaching for a drinking glass. He filled it with water from the tap and handed it to Lara.

"Here you go."

"Thank you." She guzzled the entire glass without taking a breath, and then let out a sigh. "Much better," she said.

She brushed off his clumsiness, attributing it to him being flustered to have them in his apartment, especially after living alone for the past few years. It was sweet, really. Hooked by the lovesick pull of a teenager, she found his nuances endearing.

They spent the rest of the day inside the apartment and Lara even took a midday nap on the couch with Erich. Her body was drained, both physically and emotionally, from the past twenty-four hours. Had it been less than a day since she was bidding her parents a final farewell? In her dream, she saw Felix's face, desolate, begging her not to leave.

She woke up in a cold sweat.

Lara tried to stay in the present—imagining her place in this new little life—but her mind continued to drift to her family. Whenever it did, she quickly tried to distract herself—from the pain of missing them, and from the guilt which lingered like a festering wound.

You're in Austria now. With Rubin. And your son. This was what you wanted.

Nearing five o'clock, Erich started to fuss.

"Getting hungry," Lara said.

Rubin went to the refrigerator and removed a piece of ham wrapped in butcher paper. He searched the rest of the drawers and then awkwardly turned to Lara.

"Sorry, I, uh, didn't have time to get anything before you came."

"Oh," she said, startled at the meager piece of meat on the table. Was this really all he had to eat? She was famished. How would this feed all three of them?

Lara was annoyed. They'd planned her arrival for weeks. Why hadn't he prepared more? She took a deep breath and counted to ten. Resigned to make the best of it, and fighting through gritted teeth to keep up the positive outlook she learned from her mother, she returned his stare with a smile.

"Well, that's alright," she said. "Here, I actually have some bread and cheese I brought from home—er, I mean, from Switzerland." She dashed to the bedroom where she'd put her bags and brought back the half-eaten loaf of bread and block of cheese. Setting them on the table with the ham, the two of them stood back and looked at the underwhelming meal before them.

"Looks great," she said. "I bet it will taste just perfect."

They sat at the small, two-person table, their knees bumping underneath. Lara served food onto both of their plates—which simply meant tearing chunks off the bread, and splitting the ham in half. Without any butter, the bread was dry and bland, but she chewed with a smile on her face anyways.

Erich sat on Rubin's lap while they ate. In just a few hours, the boy had warmed up to his father significantly, taking cues from Lara. With their heads stacked on top of each other, Lara could really see their resemblance. Everyone had always gushed how much Erich looked like Gerald—and he did—but that's because Rubin wasn't there for comparison. It was the eyes—squinty and deep-set.

In between bites of ham—she'd melted the cheese on top to offset the meat's dryness—Lara rambled on jovially about their new life together.

"First things first," she announced, trying to sound fun, "Shall I get some groceries tomorrow?"

Rubin speared a small bite of ham with his fork and fed it to Erich, making airplane noises like a jetliner making its descent onto the tarmac. He chuckled as the boy opened wide when the meat approached his mouth.

"Rubin?" Lara said again to get his attention.

His head shot up. "Huh? Oh, yeah, groceries. Sure." He returned his attention to Erich who expressed his satisfaction with the meal with a high-pitched "*mmmmmm*" after each bite.

"Okay." Lara hoped he'd offer input on what to buy—perhaps his favorite meals, or things he often craved. Maybe he didn't want to be bothered by such chores. She supposed that was part of a woman's job, to make those sorts of decisions. Lara folded the paper napkin on her lap.

She had a lot to learn about being a wife.

They finished in less than ten minutes. Lara's stomach growled audibly, begging for more. She stood to wash the dishes at the sink and made a mental list of items to pick up at the store. Baking soda, for one. The ruddy stain had to go.

After watching Marlene cook for two years, Lara had learned her way around a kitchen. She felt confident she'd be able to whip up meals that would satisfy a strapping man like Rubin. What she lacked, she'd eventually gain. She thought she might also pick up a cookbook while she was out—just in case.

The dishes laid upside down on the counter to dry. Lara joined Rubin in the living room. He sat on the floor with Erich, reading the boy a book, which Lara had brought in her knapsack.

Rubin spoke animatedly, giving each character its own voice, and Erich lit up at his energetic storytelling.

As the evening hours passed, fatigue took over. It was barely eight o'clock, but she felt like she'd been awake for days. Rubin, apparently unaware of her cues—multiple yawns, leaning her head on the edge of the couch—continued to play happily with Erich, who'd garnered a second wind.

She felt awkward going to bed first. Should she just excuse herself? Leave Erich there? It felt strange knowing there was a bed in the other room in which she and Rubin would sleep— together. Lara had never spent the night so close to another person.

She waited another ten minutes, but her eyelids simply would not stay open.

"I think I'm going to go to bed," she said. "I'm exhausted."

"Okay. I'll let you get situated. Be in in a few minutes." Rubin closed the picture book.

Picking up Erich, Lara walked to the bedroom and only then did it occur to her there was no crib for the little one to sleep in. He'd have to share their bed.

Still in his pajamas from the previous night, she laid him on the bed and changed him into a clean pair. Erich held onto his toes, legs in the air. A string of babbling made Lara chuckle.

"You sure don't seem tired at all," she said.

Lara slipped out of her clothes and put on a shapeless nightgown with a lace neckline. The contents of her bag spilled out onto the floor like lava. Normally, such a mess would have itched at her propensity for neatness and order. But she was just too tired to care. She'd unpack in the morning.

Lara pulled back the covers of the bed and slid in beside Erich. She stroked his hairline. The full-size bed would be tight for three people. How was this going to work? In her daydreams of their reunion, she hadn't considered Erich coming between them—literally—at such a private moment. She longed to get reacquainted with Rubin, and assumed the desire was mutual. But with a baby in the bed, the idea seemed unlikely.

The door opened. Rubin entered the room wearing nothing but his undershirt and boxer shorts. Her heart skipped a beat, seeing him like this. Where had he changed? Lara wondered why he had felt uncomfortable undressing in front of her. Was it Erich? Admittedly, part of her was glad—her thin, white nightgown left little to the imagination. She wasn't sure she would have been able to change in front of him either. At least not yet.

Rubin slipped into the other side of the bed, pulling the covers up over his waist. Laying on his side, his arm rested on top of his body, his bicep forming a mound like a little hill in a rolling field. Lara saw the outline of muscles through his shirt. A pulse flared between her legs. It had been so long since she'd felt such lust.

They lay face to face, their son between them. Erich looked back and forth, confused, and Lara suddenly felt bad for how disoriented he must be. The poor child had been ripped from the only home he knew—the parents he knew—and thrust into a new life with a strange man in a strange place. She pulled her son close to her and kissed his head.

"It's okay, little one. Go to sleep. I'm right here."

Erich yawned. He fought the heavy pull of his eyelids until they finally closed. Lara smiled as she watched her son drift off, thankful he felt safe within her arms. With Erich asleep, she and Rubin could finally give each other undivided attention.

Lara looked to Rubin. His mouth was parted and his eyes were still. He was comatose.

141

Disappointment crept back in. She'd hoped they'd spend the night staring passionately into each other's eyes. Whispering sweet nothings. But instead, she found herself the only one awake in an unfamiliar room far from home.

Lara shifted to her back and stared at the smooth, blank ceiling. This was not at all what she had imagined. Through the darkness, she reached a hand down to her stomach and felt a cramp, a knot buried deep in her gut. It wasn't hunger. It felt different.

It was doubt.

As badly as she wanted to sleep, Lara's mind ran wild with thoughts and questions. Each one left her more and more unsettled.

Why had Rubin behaved so strangely?

Was he happy to have her there?

How well did she really know this man?

And most disturbing of all: Had she made a terrible mistake?

SIXTEEN

Normalcy was like a piece of steak tied to the end of a string and held just out of reach. Marlene was the starving animal, jumping with all her might to reach it, and—unsuccessful every time.

She attempted routine for the benefit of the children. She walked the younger ones to school and picked them up, always with a smile. But when she returned home to an empty house—Gerald at work and no little baby toddling around—despair overcame her, and she spent many hours staring into space, wondering how this could have happened.

Was it all her fault? The whole façade had been her idea in the first place. Did her attempt at saving her family actually destroy it?

It had been two days since Lara and Erich vanished. Forty-eight hours—but that was nearly three thousand seconds! Three thousand times she didn't see Lara's beautiful face or smell Erich's sweet hair.

His presence was a fixture in the house, an anchor which held them all together. With Erich gone, Marlene found herself hearing phantom remnants of the little boy who stole her heart: A high-pitched squeal when she walked through the door, babble talk as he played, and even protests when something he wanted was out of reach.

They weren't real, but she heard them just the same.

In reality, the house was terribly quiet.

When Gerald and Felix had returned from their futile search, it was quickly decided the family must keep up appearances. There were so many unknowns, so many questions that needed answers, but what they could agree on was that unveiling their secret to the public was the last thing they needed.

So they carried on.

Gerald went to work the next morning, albeit in a much more distracted and somber state. Marlene went through the motions of making breakfast. Their daily routine continued, and Gerald instructed the children not to say a word about the previous night's developments.

That evening, with the youngest children in the other room, Marlene again asked the only question she had left.

"What are we going to do, Gerald?"

It was the only thing on their minds. It consumed them. They never found a clear answer.

"I don't know that there's much we can do," he said, unbuttoning the placket of his shirt. "But we cannot let this get out. We need to stay calm and think rationally."

"So we're just going to let them go?"

"What do you want me to do, Marlene?" he snapped at her, frustrated by the hopelessness of the situation.

"I don't know, but I just can't accept that they're gone for good." She dropped her head into her hands. Gerald placed his tie on the dresser and came to sit next to his wife.

"I know," he said. For the first time, her words made the unthinkable seem possible.

"We never should have forced her to live a lie. This is our fault." Marlene leaned her head onto his chest and gave herself over to hot and angry tears. Gerald bit the inside of his cheek to keep from crying. Nonetheless, he felt the hot trail of a tear roll down his face.

Their hands were tied. Calling the authorities would reveal the truth about Erich's identity—a scandalous discovery. Following Lara into Austria was also impossible. The Weisses were fugitives, considered by many to be traitors. They couldn't risk Gerald getting detained. Both he and Marlene knew it.

Gerald wiped Marlene's tear-stained cheek.

"At least they're together," she said with a sniff, searching for a silver lining. "I pray the Lord will protect them."

Her words were meant to ease their heartache, to soften the blow. But nothing she said could dispel the unspoken truth hanging heavy in the air: they might never see Lara and Erich again.

SEVENTEEN

A slap on the face jolted Lara awake. She jumped and her eyes flung open. Blurry at first, her vision focused to see Erich staring back at her with a toothy grin. He let out a string of gibberish and patted Lara's face again.

"I'm awake, I'm awake," she mumbled. Then, when she'd had a moment to adjust to the light, she said with a laugh, "Well good morning to you, too."

It came flooding back at once. *Fled. Train ride. Crossed the border. Nazis. Apartment. Rubin.*

Rubin.

It wasn't a dream. They were really together.

She propped herself up to greet him. Peering past where Erich sat smacking his palms together, she saw that the bed was empty. Rubin wasn't there. The covers were now folded over neatly, as if he'd slipped out without rustling them a bit.

So much for an early morning kiss to start the day.

Lara took in her surroundings in the clear morning light, noticing new details she'd overlooked the day before. An orange glow filtered into the room through the small window that looked out over the street—the only one in the entire apartment. She searched for a clock to tell her the time but there was nothing on the bare walls of the bedroom. If she were to guess based on Erich's typical sleep schedule, it was probably somewhere around seven o'clock. The boy adhered to a strict routine—imposed mainly from Gerald's need for order and consistency—including bedtimes and waketimes. It was very rare for Erich's internal clock to deviate from his typical schedule.

But then again, there was nothing typical about the past two days.

Lara swung her feet over the edge of the bed and stretched her arms overhead. The sleeves of her nightgown slid down her forearms. She rolled her wrists in the air, and then dropped her head from one side to the other. The mattress was firmer than Lara was used to—the soreness in her neck was proof. She had a lot to get used to.

"La La?" Erich said as Lara stood.

"I'm right here," she assured him.

Her moniker was all he could manage at such a young age, and Marlene had commented on the connection to music and singing, which Lara held so dear. She loved hearing him call to her in his angelic voice—*La La, La La, La La*—but it occurred to her now that she ought to correct him.

"I'm mama now," she said, putting her hand on her chest and looking Erich in the eyes. "Mama. Can you say it?"

"La La." He pointed to her.

"No, Ma-Ma. You try. Mama."

"La. La."

147

She gave up. It would take time for Erich to make the connection. But did that mean he'd have to forget Marlene altogether? Lara didn't want to erase the rest of her family members. She just wanted their roles to be true.

A sudden thought crossed her mind. Would Erich ever know her family? Had her decision severed the tie forever?

"La, la, la, la," Erich said.

"Silly boy," she said, flinging him back against the pillows and tickling his ribs. He cackled. "Let's go find your daddy."

Lara picked him up and walked to the living room, expecting to see Rubin. Maybe he was an early riser. Perhaps he'd be waiting with a cup of steaming coffee. Maybe there would be fresh flowers in a vase on the table.

She was wrong.

The room was empty, the apartment quiet. Where she'd envisioned a bouquet, she found a note with three short sentences.

Went to work. Will be back later. Stay inside.

The final two words were underlined with a thick, dictating stroke.

Disappointment deflated her attempts at optimism. Rubin's words were so curt, the note so impersonal—nothing like the secret correspondences they'd shared. Where was the emotion and tenderness he'd shown in his letters?

Lara glanced above the sink to a wood-framed clock with intricately carved hands. Six fifty-three. Her estimation of the time hadn't been too far off. *Children are so resilient,* she thought, pleased that even in a new environment, Erich was able to get a good night's sleep and wake close to his normal time.

Disheartened that he'd left her alone on her second day there, Lara tried to put herself in his shoes. It was unlikely he could take time off just to get her adjusted, she reasoned. But even that argument planted misgivings, as she realized she still didn't have a clear understanding of what he did for work at all.

"Well, I guess it's just you and me today, kiddo," Lara said, giving Erich a kiss on the forehead. The boy wriggled in her arms so she lowered him to the floor and he crawled away. She put her hands on her hips and looked around the apartment.

Now what?

Her belly let out a rowdy gurgle. Lara was so hungry her stomach nearly folded in on itself. She found a small egg carton in the refrigerator, with three perfect brown ovals inside. The rest of the sad shelves were bare, with the exception of a bottle of milk that, upon closer inspection, had curds floating on the surface. Lara removed the glass lid, took a whiff and dumped it down the sink.

"I guess we won't be having milk," she mumbled.

Stay inside.

His note was clear. A command if nothing else.

Rubin had originally agreed to her getting groceries, and the sounds coming from her stomach told her she needed food—real food—soon. Surely he didn't want Erich to go hungry. Maybe his note meant not to wander around the city *other than* the necessary trip to the market. Lara didn't want to upset him. But she didn't know when he'd be back. Could she go quickly?

Torn, she decided it was best to abide by the note and stay in the apartment. A proper wife follows her husband's lead.

Lara was famished, but resolved to make due until Rubin returned. There had to be a good reason he didn't want her to leave. Who knew what Salzburg was like now? She had been gone for two years during a tumultuous time. Perhaps Rubin knew something she didn't about being outdoors, especially with Nazis patrolling the streets.

Thinking this, Lara's annoyance turned to gratitude. He was protecting them.

"We can be resourceful, right?" she said to Erich, the forced pep in her voice failing to convince even herself.

After a breakfast of scrambled eggs mixed with water—the result much less fluffy and much more bland—the two played on the floor. Lara read Erich the same book Rubin had read the night before. As much as she loved books, it was the only one she'd brought with them. She made a mental note to purchase some new baby books when she went out. At the last page, she closed the book, but Erich, unsatisfied, frowned and flailed his arms.

"I'm already tired of this one, bud," she said. "I've got another story instead." She recited a fairytale she remembered from her youth about a maiden who encounters a witch that offers her three wishes. Erich watched and listened before becoming distracted, and Lara abandoned the story midway through. No sense finishing if no one was listening.

With Erich exploring the contents of a wicker basket on the bottom shelf of the end table, Lara turned her attention to the atmosphere of the apartment. It was sorely impersonalized. Not a photograph to be found, not a single indication of warmth. It was as if the place had barely been lived in. *Welcome to bachelor life*, she told herself.

Lara glanced back to the clock. Eight-fifteen.

It was going to be a long day.

She scanned the room. From her spot on the floor, she noticed a layer of dust coating the surface of the end table where

Erich had now picked apart the handle of the basket, leaving a little pile of debris.

"Well, I guess I'll make myself useful," she said aloud to no one.

Still in her nightgown, Lara tied her hair back with a ribbon and got to work cleaning the apartment—starting first with dusting. Next, she scrubbed the floors with a shoddy sponge she found under the kitchen sink. The stove had splashes of crusted food, and Lara gagged as she scraped the surface new.

Each rag came up filthy, leaving her more and more appalled by the state in which Rubin lived. With no sound in the house aside from the babble of a baby, she filled the void with her favorite songs—many of which had been taught to her by Marlene. Her delicate voice echoed through the cramped space, melodic as an angel's.

In the end, she was satisfied. The apartment received a much-needed facelift, and she imagined how pleased Rubin would be when he returned. If keeping a clean house was any measure of a wife's ability, she was determined to exceed expectations.

As the afternoon dragged on, Lara found ways to keep herself busy. She was determined to make a good impression in her role as a homemaker, and she thought back to her own family's culture as a cue of what she should and should not do. Marlene was the epitome of quality wife material: beautiful, kind, supportive. Could she live up to that standard? There were so many assumptions and expectations, it was enough to throw her brain into overdrive. The constant thinking—what else was there to do?—made her tired.

"C'mon little one," Lara said to Erich. "I'll lay down with you for your nap." She worried he wouldn't fall asleep alone on the big bed, but her body also craved reprieve, and so the nap served a dual purpose.

Erich fell asleep in a flash, leaving Lara to daydream. With pleasant thoughts of Rubin, she drifted off beside her son, her arm draped over his little body.

But those dreams quickly turned dark.

She saw her mother and father returning home from their anniversary dinner to find her and Erich gone. Their faces contorted in agony and their legs buckled as they realized what she'd done. Her mother wept. Gerald, consumed with grief, fled in his car, driving it off a bridge into the ice-cold water below.

Lara woke in a sweat, her breath rapid. *It was just a dream*, she repeated. But deep down she knew the pain was true. The thought of her parents living with such despair broke her heart. How could she have done such a thing? To the people who loved her most?

She felt sick and conflicted. She'd made a choice, for the sake of herself and her son, and, as her father once told her, she needed to live with it.

In the end—after excruciating mental gymnastics—Lara convinced herself that her parents would move on. The other children would fill in the hole left by her and Erich's absence.

Wouldn't they?

Careful not to wake Erich, Lara rolled off the bed and looked around the room for a distraction from her disturbing thoughts. Her knapsack sat on the floor in the corner, still full of the few items she'd brought from Switzerland. It only had room for a few pieces—a dress, the nightshirt she wore currently, undergarments, and Erich's essentials. She hoped Rubin would be able to get them some new clothes soon.

With nothing else to do and the waiting threatening to drive her mad, Lara figured now was as good a time as any to unpack. She'd wanted to ask Rubin where she should put her things—it was his apartment, after all, and she didn't want to come off as presumptuous—but she decided since there wasn't much, she'd just find room, and hoped he wouldn't mind.

Lara knelt at the foot of the bed, her feet pressed together underneath her. She took each garment from the bag, gave it a shake and folded it just so on her lap. When she was done, a neat pile of only nine items stood barely a foot tall.

Moving to the little walnut dresser, she pulled open the top drawer and found it empty.

He must have left this one empty for me, she thought.

Lara opened the next drawer just to check.

Empty.

Then the next, and finally the fourth.

All empty.

Not a single item filled the drawers. What? Why have a dresser if you don't put anything in it? She swiveled to look around the small room. A closet! That must be where Rubin kept his clothes. In three short steps, she stood in front of the hinged door. With a shaking hand—why was she nervous?—she reached out and folded the door open to the side.

Her heart dropped. The closet was empty. A single metal bar attached to either side of the wall stood bare. The sight struck her as odd—a clothes rack with no clothes, like a flagpole with no flag. What's the point?

The room began to spin as terror set in. Lara felt herself becoming lightheaded. She sat on the bed and put an unsteady hand over her mouth.

What was going on? If this was Rubin's home, where were all his clothes?

The uneasiness she'd felt the night before returned, only this time it grew from a paltry worry to an overwhelming fear. It didn't make sense; there was no other hidden closet that held Rubin's belongings. As she tried to regain her composure and clear her mind to think straight, she heard a door shut.

"Lara?" Rubin's voice rang through the small apartment.

Startled, she jumped off the bed, shaking her hands to stop the tingling. A mirror stood propped against the wall atop the dresser. She examined her reflection, noticing the color had drained from her face. She pinched her cheeks and smoothed her hair behind her ears and pressed the front of her dress flat. Did she look frightened? Glancing over her shoulder, she saw Erich was still, thankfully, sound asleep on the bed. She walked to the living room, closing the bedroom door behind her.

"Oh, there you are. Hi," Rubin said, removing his hat and flinging his coat over the back of the dining chair.

"Hi."

"I hope you got my note this morning. I didn't want to wake you. Sorry I couldn't stay, I had to go to work."

"That's okay. We managed." She stood several feet from him, unwilling to the close the distance. Could he sense something was off?

"Where's Erich?"

"Asleep," she said quietly. "He takes a nap in the afternoon."

"Oh yes, I was going to ask you about his schedule. It's all so new to me. I feel like I have so much to learn." He smiled and pulled out the chair to sit. He motioned toward the other chair. Lara tentatively sat across from him.

"So," he continued, "Tell me what I need to know."

"About what?"

"About Erich. Like, when does he nap?"

"Nap? Usually every day after lunchtime, unless he's very tired, and then sometimes he takes two naps, one in the morning and one in the afternoon."

"I see. Okay, good to know."

"And you said he'll eat pretty much whatever?"

"Yes, as long as it's cut small enough."

"Gotcha."

"Speaking of food," she said. "There wasn't much to eat here today. I would have gone out for groceries but your note said to stay inside."

"Right. Sorry about that. I thought it was best if you didn't venture out quite yet."

"Why?"

"Don't you think people might be looking for you? I mean, your parents could have put out notices about your disappearance."

"Oh, I guess I hadn't thought of that."

"Probably better to stay indoors. Just trust me, Lara." He looked at her sideways, his tone authoritative, as though his being one year older made him that much more wise and worldly.

See? He's just protecting you. It made her think of all the times he promised he'd take care of her. Now he was. But that still didn't explain the sick feeling in her stomach.

"Okay, sure. I understand," she said quietly.

He stood and strode toward the sink, filling a glass of water.

"There was still a little food that you brought from home, right?"

"Yes, we were fine. I made some eggs. And there were a few apples left. I guess I was just expecting to be able to go to the market. I would have loved to have made a nice dinner for you."

"Well, I brought some things home we can eat." He placed a brown paper bag on the table and pulled out two chicken thighs and a basket of string beans.

Again, hardly enough for the three of them.

"Looks delicious. Thank you," she managed.

Sensing a shift in her demeanor, Rubin stepped toward her with outstretched arms. Lara stood still, stiff as a board, as Rubin wrapped his arms around her, pulling her in tight to his chest. She breathed in the smell of him—the same smell that once made her knees go weak. If smug had a scent, it would be Rubin.

"I missed you," he said. "I thought of nothing all day but getting home to you."

She couldn't meet his gaze.

"Rubin," she began nervously, "where are all your clothes?"

"My clothes? What do you mean?"

"Yes. I went to put my things in the dresser and closet, but they're both empty."

His face went blank, a deer in headlights. A cool frost covered his eyes. *Damnit!* His mouth creased, and she was sure she sensed anger in his expression.

But the look was fleeting. As quickly as it came, it disappeared, and he was as warm again as she always knew him to be.

"Oh, I should have told you!" he laughed, as if his dismissal should banish any worry she might feel. "I sent it all out for cleaning before you came. You see, I wanted everything to be just perfect for your arrival, including my clothing. I admit, I'm not the best at keeping a clean house and tidy clothes. I'm sorry

156

about that, Lara. I wanted to impress you, but the clothes got delayed. But don't worry, it should all be delivered back here tomorrow."

She opened her mouth to question his explanation, but before she could get a word out, he quickly leaned down and pressed his lips against hers. Caught off guard, her eyes opened wide and her neck stiffened. His eyes were closed, his hands running down the sides of her face to her collarbone. He trailed the line of her bodice. When his fingers reached the mounds of her breasts, her body took over, and she gave in to the pleasure. Her body softened in his arms. They kissed passionately, as memories of their love floated through her mind.

I must be going crazy, she told herself. *There's nothing to worry about. He loves me. I need to trust him.*

That evening, they ate by candlelight, at Lara's suggestion—an idea she'd had to try to restart the rocky outset of their reunion. Rubin continued to ask more questions about Erich—his likes and dislikes, as well as the ins and outs of caring for a baby. Lara answered his inquiries with a renewed sense of energy and hope. Her heart swelled; Rubin genuinely cared about their son and wanted to be the best father possible.

It was so new for all of them. She felt foolish for expecting a seamless transition. With a deep sigh of relief, she promised herself she'd relax and let the kinks naturally shake out.

Across the table, Rubin and Erich took turns making goofy faces. The boy belly laughed so hard he could barely catch his breath. Lara's shoulders bounced with happiness.

Soon, another day was gone. Dusk settled as the sun dipped below the lofty structures of the city.

Crawling into bed later, Lara buried the doubt that had plagued her during the day. She gave Erich a gentle peck on the head and closed her eyes, resounding to wake up with a fresh sense of peace.

EIGHTEEN

The screech of an owl startled Lara awake. The sound, high-pitched and shriek-like, was so powerful, she would have bet money the bird was actually not outside, but flying around in her room. Laying on her side facing the window, Lara blinked her eyes several times to strain through the darkness. No darting shadows, no flapping wings. The owl was definitely outside (but of course it was). She sealed her eyes again, desperate to return to the pleasant dream from which she was so rudely jolted.

Another screech—a loud, barking call of warning known only to flying nighttime predators. Her eyes flashed open again. Lara wondered if the sound was disturbing Erich. She rolled in place, turning away from the window to face Erich and Rubin.

Nothing but the flat plane of mattress extended to the other side of the bed.

Lara stretched her arm out along the surface of the sheet, searching for the little boy's body. The darkness, devious and sly, must be playing tricks on her eyes. She reached long. The bed was cool to the touch—unlike her side, which radiated heat from her body.

Jerking upright, she whipped back the covers, as if the two were hiding underneath.

But this was no illusion, the blackness had not fooled her. Erich was gone. And so was Rubin.

Lara ran to the living room and flipped on the light, scanning the space with wild eyes. What did she expect? That Rubin and Erich would be in the kitchen making a sandwich in the middle of the night? She wanted to believe there was a reasonable explanation, but her gut told her otherwise. A cold sweat prickled the surface of Lara's skin, and her heart picked up speed, like a song's tempo reaching crescendo. Shallow, quick breaths made her lightheaded. As she stumbled to the table, her consciousness dangled on the edge of fainting.

"Rubin!" she cried out. "Erich!"

Frantic, Lara swept through the apartment, opening the small hallway closet door, checking inside the shower. They weren't there. Coming back to the living room, she looked to the clock. It was half past three in the morning. There was simply no explanation for their absence at this hour.

With a thought, she dashed back to the bedroom and yanked open the top dresser drawer where she had placed Erich's few belongings the day before—a handful of clothes, diapers, a book and his beloved stuffed toy. The drawer was cleared out.

Terror seized her. She stood frozen, her eyes transfixed on the empty drawer hanging open. Not only was *he* gone, but his things were gone too.

"No," she said, shaking her head. "No, no, no."

How could she not have heard them leave? What kind of mother doesn't realize her child is being taken right from under her nose? Rubin must have been purposefully quiet. The realization made her sick to her stomach.

Lara felt like she was floating above herself, watching from high up as a terrible nightmare unfolded. It couldn't be real. It must be a dream. *Wake up!* her brain screamed. She dug her nails into the skin on her forearm, leaving little crescents and a stinging sensation that traveled up her arm and down to her fingers. A pinprick of blood formed a bead near her wrist.

She was very much awake.

Lara backed slowly out of the room. Nausea churned, and she raced to the bathroom where she wretched last night's dinner into the toilet. Balled on the floor, shaking and confused, a voice in her head finally shook Lara to her senses.

Get help.

But where? Who? She hadn't left the apartment since they'd arrived two days prior, and wasn't even sure what part of Salzburg she was in. It was the middle of the night. How could she find help now?

Hopelessness kept her anchored to the clammy tile. Then Erich's innocent face flashed in front of her eyes and her maternal instinct kicked in.

With a surge of focus and energy, Lara sprinted to the door and darted into the hall. It was dimly lit—two bare bulbs suspended from the ceiling emanated a sickly orange. Lara remembered the look of the corridor from when she'd first arrived. She guessed there were at least eight doors she could try.

It was the middle of the night, but she had no other option. Rushing to the first door on the left, Lara pounded on it with her fist. No one came. She moved onto the next impatiently, giving little time for anyone inside to wake, let alone answer her banging. Again, nothing.

At the third door, she added a choral of pleading cries.

"Help!" she yelled. "Please, someone help me!"

Her hands hammered the wood. Subconsciously, it occurred to Lara that her father would be appalled at her lack of manners. But this was no time to be polite. She pounded harder. With every second that passed, desperation grew until tears flowed from her eyes, drenching the neck of her nightgown.

"I need help! My baby has been kidnapped!"

Mid-knock, the door flew open. Lara faltered forward, nearly falling into a middle-aged man in blue striped pajamas. His hairline was receding, and a few strands—which were meant to comb over the thinning top—flopped out to the side comically. He squinted into the dingy hallway.

"Oh!" Lara exclaimed. "Thank you! Please, I need help. My son has been kidnapped." She talked wildly with her hands.

"What?" the man asked, looking bewildered, having been woken from a deep sleep.

"They're gone! I woke up and they're gone. He took him!" She rambled incoherently between sobs, and the man struggled to follow.

"Took him from where?"

"The apartment down the hall. Two doors down." Her chest heaved as she spoke.

A woman—Lara presumed was the man's wife—emerged in the doorway, her tawny hair pinned in soft rollers around her head. She looked panicked at the appearance of a surprise visitor at this hour.

"What is going on?" she asked, holding a frying pan and raising it up, ready to swing.

"It's fine, Ottie. Put the pan down, for God's sake."

Lara repeated herself again, making no more sense than the first time.

"I'm confused," the man said. "What were you doing in that apartment?"

"It's my boyfriend's place. His name is Rubin. He's my son's father. And I think he kidnapped him!"

"Number 15?"

"Yes!"

"Sweetheart, you must be mistaken. Are you sure it's 15?" the woman said. "That apartment has been empty for months. No one lives there."

Lara stared at them in horror.

"But that can't be true." She took a step back. "Rubin told me he got the apartment last year. He said he knew the neighbors."

Ottie looked to her husband and then back to Lara, concern spreading across their faces.

"We've never heard of a man named Rubin," she said.

Stumbling backward, Lara hit the wall. Her vision narrowed, the outer edges turning white and tapering into the center before she had a chance to grab onto anything for support. She was blind. But she certainly wasn't deaf, as a primal wail pierced her ears.

Guttural and terrifying, it took a moment before Lara realized the sound was coming from her.

NINETEEN

Somehow she got to the dining table in the center of the neighbor's apartment. Had they dragged her in? Did the man carry her? She had no idea. All she knew was that her body felt paralyzed and her brain like it was sifting through a heavy fog that rolls in from the sea in springtime.

"We need to call the police," the woman said, placing a glass of water on the table in front of Lara. The girl's elbows propped on the edge of the faux cedar, and her head hung heavy in her hands. She focused her eyes on a chip in the laminate where the seam met.

"No," Lara muttered. "Please. You can't. I'm not supposed to be here." She didn't raise her head.

"What do you mean?"

Finally, she met their eyes. "I ran away from home. My family doesn't know where I am." A quiet cry escaped from her lips. Saying the words out loud intensified the guilt she'd been feeling for days.

The husband and wife looked at each other. Ottie's face filled with horror, the man's remained unreadable. Ottie stepped toward Lara and placed a hand on her back.

"There, there, dear. We'll get it figured out. What's your name anyways?"

"Lara," she croaked.

"Well, I'm Ottie and this is my husband, Elias." She pointed in his direction. "Okay, Lara. Listen, we need to call the authorities if they're going to help find your baby." Her voice was calm and level, as though she was conditioned for crisis control. She spoke to Lara like she would an inconsolable toddler.

"No, I'll get in trouble. My father will get in trouble. I shouldn't be here!" Lara's sobs intensified. Ottie looked to her husband again, who stood with his back against the refrigerator, taking in the scene. He'd fixed his hair—the flyaway now swept neatly across his bald spot.

Ottie held her hands up, shrugged her shoulders, and mouthed: *What should we do?* He shrugged back.

"What do you mean your father will be in trouble?" Ottie asked, trying to pry more information Lara, whose tears were forming a stream down the length of her table.

"We had to escape. We don't live here anymore."

"Escape? Who did? And why?" The woman lowered her face near Lara's. Her questions spewed in rapid succession as if she could sense she was getting closer to critical information that would solve the mystery of why a young woman barged into their apartment in the middle of the night.

"My family. The Nazis were trying to recruit my father. So we fled. Climbed over the Alps and sought refuge in Switzerland."

Ottie's eyes exploded open and her mouth hinged open. Elias, who hadn't moved from his spot nor said a word during the entire interrogation, straightened. Lanky and quite tall, the vertical stripes of his pajamas only exaggerated his height. He took a step forward, suddenly interested in Lara's last comment.

"Are you...Lara Weiss?" he said, his voice no more than a whisper.

Lara lifted her head, revealing swollen, red eyes.

"Yes."

"Oh my gosh," Ottie gasped. "You're Doctor Weiss' daughter?"

"Yes," she said again.

Elias hurried across the room and pulled open the top drawer of a roll-top desk in the corner. He rifled through its contents before pulling out a small, bound notebook.

"What are you doing, Elias?" Ottie asked, standing.

The man didn't respond. Instead, he hastily flipped through the pages of what Lara could see appeared to be an address book. Coming to the page he was searching for, he trailed his finger down the list of names and finally stopped on one near the bottom, stabbing it with his pointer.

"Elias?"

Ottie huffed. Unable to wait for his response, she turned her attention back to Lara.

"We know of your family's story," she said, her voice low. "News of your escape was posted all over Austria. I prayed for you, hoped you had made it to safety. Now I see that you did."

Lara stared into the woman's eyes. Ottie's words got lost somewhere between Lara's ears and brain. She couldn't register what was being said. People knew about her family?

Elias, who had rejoined them at the table with the notebook in his hand, looked up from the page as though a lightbulb had sprung to life in his head. He opened his mouth to talk, but Ottie interrupted.

"Lara, why are you here?" she asked. "Why did you come back to Austria?"

"I came back with my son. To be with *him*." She pointed toward the door.

"The man you said was your boyfriend? The one who lives down the hall?"

"Yes."

"I didn't know Doctor Weiss had a grandson," Ottie said, confused.

"No one knows." Lara looked down and twisted the fabric of her nightgown.

"What do you mean?"

"No one knows Erich is my son."

"But...I don't understand."

Lara took a deep breath. "It would have been scandalous," she explained. "So my parents pretended he was theirs, and I went along with it until I couldn't take it anymore. I came back because Rubin said we could be a family. He said he loved me." The crippling ripple of consequence overwhelmed her, as Lara realized how foolish she'd been. Her shaky voice turned to poignant weeping. Ottie scooted her chair closer to Lara and wrapped her arm around the girl's heaving shoulders.

"Okay, okay, let me think," Ottie said. Elias raised a finger as to speak, but was cut off by Lara who sat upright, flinging the woman's arm from around her.

"I need to get home," Lara said with sudden urgency, as though everything was suddenly perfectly lucid.

Startled, Ottie's hands flew up like a scarecrow. "Home? You mean back to Switzerland?"

"Yes. Right now." Lara stood, the chair screeching across the hardwood floor. Her eyes were frantic but unflinchingly sure. "My father will know what to do."

"But, but...what about your son?"

"He's safe. I don't think Rubin would hurt him."

Ottie stared in utter shock and confusion at the resolution on Lara's face.

"But he kidnapped him!"

"Rubin tricked me," Lara said, suddenly seeing her situation clearly. Her voice cracked as she spoke. "He didn't want me. Never did. But when he heard we had a child, he convinced me to come back. And I was naïve enough to believe him. All along, he just wanted Erich." The lump in her throat threatened to rise again, but she swallowed it back down. "I must go. I've got to get to my father."

Lara paced the short distance between the table and the door, her hand on her head, her breathing short and fast. She muttered to herself. "But how? Train? No. Can't walk. So far..."

The pajama-clad couple watched her, dumbfounded. Lara choked on the words, as the impossibility became real. She knew she couldn't simply walk back across the border. And even in a car, she would be stopped and questioned.

"How did you get here in the first place?" Ottie interrupted Lara's train of thought.

"Rubin met me near the border. He drove us back."

"But weren't you interrogated upon entry?"

"No. Rubin got us through without question. He had an armband."

"A Nazi armband?"

"Yes," Lara said, lowering her gaze, embarrassed. "It had a black swastika. He said it was from before. He said he wasn't part

168

of them anymore. I can't believe I fell for it. There were so many signs..." her voice drifted off and Ottie could see the distress on the girl's face. The kind woman felt bad for her, understanding how easy it was to be blinded by love. She'd been young once, too.

"Nevermind that," Ottie said, standing to face Lara. She put her hands on Lara's shoulders and gave them a little shake. "That's in the past. Nothing we can do to change it. We need to figure out what to do now."

"We'll help you," Elias' deep voice announced, finally tired of waiting for his turn to speak. Ottie turned so both women faced where he sat at the table.

"You will? But how?" Lara said.

"Well if you two would have let me get a word in, I would have told you." He rolled his eyes at his wife, and she in turn, pursed her lips, dismissively. "I know a man," Elias continued. "He travels between here and Geneva every week for work. Drives a truck carrying cargo."

Lara's eyes scrunched in confusion. "I don't—"

"You can hide in his truck," Elias said. "He's a good man. I know he'll do it."

"Yes, of course!" Ottie exclaimed. "That's the perfect idea. When is his next trip?"

"I'll have to call him. That's why I got the phone book. I'll ask, and we'll set it up."

Lara's body refused to relax. They seemed so sure, made it seem easy. But would it really work? Could she really get all the way home without being discovered? It was a risk, but what was the alternative? Her options were pretty bleak.

And even more than that, could she leave knowing her son was somewhere here without her?

169

I have to trust them, she thought. Her jaw softened, and she realized she'd been clenching it tight.

Lara looked to her rescuers. "Okay."

Elias picked up the phone that hung on the wall, and placed his forefinger in the dial, turning it sharply.

"Come, Lara," Ottie said. "Let's go sit. It's more comfortable." She led Lara to a gray couch next to the end table where Elias had found the address book. Patting the cushion with her wrinkled hand, she urged Lara to sit.

"Why are you helping me?" Lara asked, her voice—she could hear it—sounding like a child's.

Ottie took Lara's hand in hers and looked her straight in the eyes.

"Your father is admirable," she said. "And highly respected by many Austrians—ourselves included. Don't forget there are still some of us who didn't side with the Germans after the Anschluss." She gave Lara a warm smile.

Elias clicked the phone back onto the cradle. He turned to the women on the couch. Their gazes met, Lara's expression filled with hope. His words were brief but were exactly what she wanted to hear.

"Tomorrow night."

TWENTY

Lara was a woman divided. Half of her—both physically and mentally—felt one way, while the other countered. Emotionally, she seesawed between despair and determination, and her body, drained and energized, clashed against itself.

But the clearest fissure, the split most painful, was that of her heart—half of it beating firmly in her chest, but the other half—her son—somewhere unknown.

She prayed he was safe. She prayed he wasn't scared.

Ottie offered Lara food, but Lara couldn't eat. Mostly, she sat in a daze, praying the hours to hurry up. A handful of ladies' magazines were stacked neatly on the coffee table. Lara studied the cover of the top issue—the image of a woman wearing a neatly tailored vest and skirt. It reminded Lara of Marlene. She yearned for her mother's comfort.

The waiting was unbearable. And at any minute she thought she'd abandon the plan altogether, fleeing Ottie's apartment on foot to search for her son. Isn't that what any good mother would do?

But she stayed and waited. Until it was finally time.

* * *

Elias pulled into the remote parking lot behind a large brick building just as the sun dipped behind the horizon, casting the city in a cool dark blue. A single streetlight hung overhead, giving just enough glow for Lara to take in her surroundings. The gravel lot was wide, with wire fencing marking its property. It felt industrial, cold.

From the back seat, she peered out the window at the rows of freight trucks, either coming or going from their deliveries. Lara didn't know exactly what the trucks carried, or what products the building manufactured. All Elias said was that the man transported "goods"—the type of goods, she had no idea. Could it be dangerous? It didn't matter. Her only focus was getting home and getting help.

"Hans said he'd be leaving at nine," Elias said to Lara. "We'll wait here until we see his truck pull out."

Lara nodded. Her mind struggled to stay focused, having been awake for over twenty-four hours. The anticipation fueled her adrenaline, but the interim downtime made her eyelids fight to stay open. She looked at the bag on the seat next to her thigh. After formulating their plan—last night? This morning? She'd lost sense of time—Ottie had convinced Lara to lie on her couch to get some sleep.

It was useless.

Instead, Lara went back to Rubin's fictitious apartment and gathered her few belongings back into her sack. In a strange way, it comforted her, knowing Rubin had cared enough to take Erich's necessities. That her son had a few pieces of clothing and his beloved stuffed toy with him, wherever he was, eased a fraction of her worry.

Now in the car, she stared out the window, as she and Elias sat in silence, waiting. Finally, a set of glaring, yellow headlights came alive across the lot. They flashed twice—on, off, and on again. A signal. Lara and Elias watched the box truck pull forward, but instead of turning out of the parking lot to the road, it continued straight toward them.

"This is him," Elias said. "Get your things."

She slid her arm through the straps of her bag and drew them up to the flat of her shoulder. With her fingers clasped on the door handle, she watched the truck approach. It pulled alongside their car and stopped, dwarfing them in its shadow.

"Ok, this is it. Let's go." Elias opened his door and Lara followed suit. They met at the front of the car. Elias pointed to the back of the truck without saying a word. They hurried toward the double doors, quickening their pace as the red blaze of the truck's brake lights illuminated their silhouettes for anyone who might be watching.

Elias slid open the bolt lock and pulled the handle. The right-hand door flung open.

"In you go," he whispered. Lara stared into the darkened cargo bed. *Don't be scared*, she told herself. Tentatively, she placed a foot on the metal step and hoisted herself into the back of the truck. The air inside was warm and musty.

Lara turned to face Elias, emotion rising from her core.

"Be safe," he said.

"Thank you, Elias. Thank you so much."

173

He shut the door without another word and gave it a double tap, signaling to the driver that the package had been deposited. A second later, the truck lurched forward. Lara stood wide-legged and reached for the side wall to steady her balance. Her eyes struggled to adjust to the pitch-black darkness.

As the truck rumbled forward, gaining speed, Lara felt around to get a sense of her surroundings, curious with what she'd be riding for the next several hours. Reaching out, her fingers traced the outline of what felt like a burlap sack. To her right, another large bag had the same rough texture. The air smelled dry, like the baking aisle at the grocers. She detected a faint hint of wheat. Her eyes adjusting, she pulled open the top of one of the sacks, feeling the small uneven seeds. *Grain*, she thought, thankful that at least she wasn't traveling with anything jeopardous or vile.

Lara slid her back down the side of the truck until her bottom hit the floor. Her knees pulled into her chest, and she tilted her head up to stare at the metal ceiling. *Safe.* She said a silent prayer of gratitude for the kindness of Ottie and Elias, strangers who had opened their door—literally—and given her a chance at redemption.

Lara's body bounced and jolted with every divot the truck hit. Just as they'd reach a smooth stretch of road, a sharp turn or hole in pavement sent her toppling. Sleep was impossible. The journey would be several hours. But despite being exhausted on all levels, she could not allow herself to succumb to dreams, even the good, hopeful kind. She didn't deserve such relief. She must stay alert.

A tear flowed down Lara's cheek, coming to rest in the corner of her mouth, and she could taste her own salt. It tasted like sin.

Erich.

174

Where was he? Was he crying for her?

The only comfort she allowed herself was the belief that Rubin genuinely cared for the boy. She'd watched their interactions. Everything else may have been a sham, but the love for his son was real. Rubin wanted Erich, not her. His motive for luring them back to Austria was clear. The thought crushed her into a heap of bitter resentment.

Still, Lara found some relief knowing Erich was in the care of someone who loved him. *He's okay,* she convinced herself. He wasn't with her, but he was okay. The thought was the only thing keeping her from hurling the door open and jumping into oncoming traffic.

Deep in her thoughts, Lara didn't notice the truck had stopped moving until she heard muffled voices just feet away.

"Identification?" a gruff voice said. Then, after a pause, "What's your purpose for crossing?"

"Transporting dry goods," Hans, Lara's trusted driver, said. It was the first time she heard his voice. She still hadn't seen his face.

"Orders are to check all vehicles with enclosed spaces."

We must have made it to the border, Lara thought. She pictured the same SS officers she'd encountered with Rubin. Were the same armed patrolmen stopping them now?

"Just a bunch of bags of seeds and grain," Hans said. His voice remained level, and Lara was thankful for his composure.

"Orders are orders. I'll need to check the back."

Lara's pulse quickened and, she sprang up, feeling her way further back into the truck, winding and climbing over the bags. She clamored over a stack, pushing one to the side, and dove behind just as the door of the truck swung open. The glow of a flashlight filled the inside of the truck.

The officer slowly scanned the truck from left to right with his light. Lara hunched down as the circular beam traveled close to where she hid. It reminded her of the night her family fled Salzburg, when all nine of them crouched behind garbage bins and bales of hay as they made their way through the villages toward the mountains. The parallel between then and now was eerie, and the hairs on her arms stood on end at comparing the two. There was only one significant difference: this time she was alone. No protective father or comforting mother for guidance. She'd felt safe with them—now, not so much.

The ray from the flashlight crossed the front of the bag where she hid. Lara held her breath, making herself small, scared to let even a wisp of air from her lips. Squeezing her eyes shut, she pictured Erich. This was for him. She had to be as still as possible.

"What'd you say was in the bags?" the officer's gruff words penetrated the silence.

"Grains," Hans replied. "Mostly wheat. Some corn."

"Hmm."

Lara couldn't see anything, but she didn't like the tone of the officer's voice.

"You don't have any jewels in those bags, do ya?"

"Jewels? No. Like I said, it's all dry goods from a farm a couple hours back."

"Well, we've heard that story before. Seen lots of fellas like you acting all innocent, but really trying to pull one past us."

"I'm telling you officer, I don't have jewels—or anything else—in this truck."

"Gonna have to see for myself, I'm afraid."

Lara heard a click, and then the violent rip of fabric. The officer plunged his pocket knife into the burlap, slashing it open.

Mustard-colored kernels spilled from the opening like blood from a wound.

"Hey! I'm supposed to deliver that!" Hans protested.

"Quiet!" The officer barked his commands. He tore open another sack and Lara heard the tiny grains ping off the aluminum floor.

"Please, Sir! I won't get paid if my shipment is ruined!"

"Jürgen, leave it be." Another man's voice rose through the dark, calm and steady.

"Ah, I'm just havin' a little fun," Jürgen said as he slashed a third bag. As the wheat cascaded to the floor, a plume of dust rose in the truck. Lara put her hand over her mouth to keep from coughing.

"C'mon. That's enough."

"You're goin' soft on me, Walter." Jürgen stepped back from the door, sheathing his knife. He turned to Hans, who stood helplessly watching his precious supply trickle over the tailgate to the gravel below. "You're free to go."

The two officers turned toward their booth, chuckling cruelties.

"Bastards," Hans muttered, as he pushed handfuls of grain back into the bags.

"What did you say?" Jürgen's voice boomed from a yard away.

"Nothing. I didn't say anything."

Jürgen was on him in three long strides. The barrel of his pistol whipped Hans above the right eyebrow.

"Don't you ever speak that way to a German officer. Next time, you won't be so lucky."

Lara didn't dare move. She wished she could help Hans, but fear kept her frozen. The sound of footsteps leaving told her the officers were gone. Hans said not a word. A minute later, the door slammed shut and she once again found herself surrounded by pitch blackness.

TWENTY-ONE

The minutes felt like hours as the truck pushed forward into Switzerland. They had to be nearing the drop-off point. When Elias had arranged for her secret passage, Hans agreed to take Lara as far as he could without deviating from his route.

"I'll help," he'd said. "Happy to. But I can't drop her off on her front doorstep. If I'm not on time, it'd draw suspicion."

"That's fine," Elias said. Then to Lara, "You might have to walk a bit."

"I'll manage," she said.

Hans filled in the details. "I'm heading directly to Geneva, so you'll have to find your way north to Zürich."

Without another option, she agreed. "Okay."

Now, bouncing along with the movement of the rig, Lara thought about reuniting with her family. How would she explain everything to her parents? Would they accept her back, or shun her as a dishonorable pariah? Her stomach twisted at the possibility.

Remorse and shame took up permanent residence in her brain—making themselves cozy and not showing any signs of leaving. All she could do was pray for forgiveness.

Pushing the doubts to the back of her mind, Lara refocused. There'd be no chance for redemption if she didn't make it home at all. *Let's take it one step at a time.*

The truck slowed, the tires rolling to the brim of the road. As it jerked to a stop, Lara braced herself against the burlap. Her heartbeat quickened again. Was this her stop? Or had they been intercepted by more patrollers?

She crouched lower and bit her bottom lip. The back door opened. Outside, the crimson tail lights blended with the night sky to create a maroon hue, which illuminated the silhouette of a man. His arm held the door ajar.

"Psst," a raspy voice hissed. "Girl!"

Lara peeked her head above the bag.

"Come on," Hans said. "Time to go."

Lara stood and was relieved to see, not a Nazi officer, but a short, stocky man in overalls. She grabbed her bag and pushed through the sacks of grain until she reached the exit. Hans extended a hand to help her down. As her feet hit the gravel, she looked around. They were on the side of a back road. The headlights of the truck illuminated farmlands in either direction.

"Where are we?" Lara asked. Without any identifying landmarks, she couldn't be sure she was even in the right country. Had Hans taken her where he'd said? It occurred to her that she'd taken him for his word—but could he be trusted? Hans could have driven north or south instead of west. She could be in Italy for all she knew.

"Lucerne," Hans replied. "I went out of my way as much as I could, but I'm afraid this is as close to Zürich as I can get. You're about twenty miles south."

Lara relaxed her tightened shoulders. He seemed genuine. But then again, she didn't have the best track record for detecting fraud.

Lara shook her head, and Hans continued. "We're on a side street, but if you take the next turn up ahead, it will lead you back toward the main roads. Head due north, and when you reach the lake, follow the bank and it will take you directly to Zürich."

She nodded along with his directions even though fear was setting in. She'd never been out on her own like this in an unfamiliar place. Twenty miles? It would take hours to get home. And what if she took a wrong turn or got lost?

"How do I know which direction is north?"

"See that star?" He pointed to the sky where one star burned brighter than the rest.

"Yes."

"Follow it. It will lead you north. Once the sun comes up, that will reinforce you're headed in the right direction. Remember, the sun always rises in the east."

"Okay."

Hans watched the nerves tighten in her head. "Just be careful, will ya? I'm sorry I can't get you closer."

"Thank you," she breathed. "I'm so very thankful." She was lucky to have gotten this far under such circumstances, and she knew it.

Hans tipped his cap and hurried back to the driver's side door. He hopped in and shifted into gear. Lara stepped off the berm into the grass, laden with dew. As the tires spun, a cloud of dust rippled where Lara stood, and she shielded her face from breathing it in. The truck drove off into the distance, its taillights shrinking to red pin pricks.

She was alone.

Anxiety crept up through her limbs. Lara looked left, then right. Nothing stirred. It was a ghostly feeling. Paralyzed in the moment, Lara considered melting to the ground. If only she could wait until morning—everything seemed easier in the daylight. But she had no idea of the time. Was dawn in two hours or six?

Erich.

She was wasting time. A rush of adrenaline took over. Step by step, Lara walked, moderately at first, before quickening her pace to just short of a jog.

The speed-walking was a full-body exercise, forcing her to switch her bag from shoulder to shoulder when the muscles started to burn. Every so often, a burst of energy hit. She'd run several yards before slowing to a walk and catching her breath again. It was awkward, trying to run with the burden of extra weight, as well as shoes built much more for fashion than function. All the while, only one thought kept her going: the quicker she got home, the quicker she could get help.

Along a stretch of heavy brush, a branch snapped to her right. Lara whipped her head around, fearing the attack of a wild animal. Heart in her throat, she jumped to the other side of the road. The sense that she wasn't the only living thing prowling the night sent a chill down her spine. And with nothing sharper than a hair pin to use in self-defense, she pushed away the fear and walked on.

Lara took several short breaks to rest her legs and quench her dry mouth. Sweet Ottie had filled the girl's flask before she left— feeling a motherly instinct to send Lara off as prepared as possible. The water was heavenly on her tongue, its coolness hydrating her shaky lips. Lara's body was weak, and she wanted nothing more than to curl up in a ball and wish this nightmare away. But her brain commanded otherwise. And so somehow, someway, she got back up and took another step forward.

This walk-run-walk pattern continued up dimly-lit streets lined with fields and woods. She passed through small villages but never saw a soul. Houses were dark, curtains drawn. Inside, people slept soundly, without a thought of crooked lovers or kidnapped babies.

Her legs ached and her chest tightened from the labor of heavy breathing. Every time she stopped to rest, the thought of Erich's face propelled her forward. With each step, she was that much closer to home.

After nearly four hours, she guessed, a shimmer of white flashed through a row of sparse trees. *The lake*, she thought. The sight of the water told her she was going the right way. Long and skinny, Lake Zürichsee narrowed to a point at Zürich.

Lara followed the grassy bank, mesmerized by the pale band of silver that reflected off the water. Moon-bleached stones lined the edge where the ripples met the Earth.

As the lake rounded out at the northern tip, Lara knew she was getting close. She'd been to the lake with Marlene and her siblings a handful of times. The children had fished, the little girls squealing at the slimy scales of their catches. The lake was a stunning representation of Mother Nature. Now, Lara thought the scenery was even more beautiful under the cover of night.

With the lake behind her, trees and vegetation gave way to the outskirts of the city. From there, Lara knew the way. The Weiss home sat near the city's center, just a couple blocks from Main Street. *Just a little bit further*, she urged herself. The realization infused her with a renewed vigor, and she picked up her pace to run along the darkened sidewalks of Zürich. Her arms swung. Fresh tears filled her eyes. She was almost home.

The sky faded from black to indigo, a moody ombre that indicated morning was coming. Lara ran past the courthouse. Its massive pillars supported a pitched roof, where a turret clock sat at its center. She squinted to read the curved hands—just after five o'clock. Her father, always an early riser, was probably getting ready for work. Lara imagined her younger siblings sleeping peacefully in their beds, and felt a sudden pang of envy. She missed her own bed: its familiar softness, the safety it provided.

The house came into view as she rounded the corner. Box lanterns framed either side of the front door, their flames flickering in the murky morning hours.

Lara sprinted up the front steps with surprising momentum for someone whose legs had been working overtime through the night. She reached for the knob on the front door. It was locked. Maybe someone was awake. Peering through the narrow window next to the doorframe, she saw no movement inside.

The key, she remembered.

Her parents hid a spare key under a patio stone in the back garden for the older children who walked home from school. Gone were the days of butlers answering the door. When the family settled in Switzerland, they had to adjust to new household dynamics—one of which was not getting locked outside without a key.

Lara dashed off the steps two at a time and circled the side of the house, coming to the little courtyard below her window on the second floor. It was framed with rose bushes, her mother's favorite. Crouching beside the round stone engraved with a large

"W" in a swirly script, Lara lifted the edge. Underneath, a small brass key.

The back door entered directly into the kitchen. Before she even slid the key into the knob, Lara noticed a light coming from inside. Her heart raced, knowing someone—her father, most likely—was awake on the other side of the wall. Lara turned the key and the door sprung open. The rich smell of freshly-brewed coffee hit her face, bringing her already-awakened senses to full tilt.

It smelled like home.

A cupboard door shut and there stood Gerald, mug in hand and shock on his face.

"Father!"

"Lara!" They exclaimed as they ran into each other's arms.

"Oh Father, I'm so sorry. I made a terrible mistake," she wept, clutching the fabric of his shirt in her fists. Gerald held her tightly, stupefied by her sudden appearance. "I never should have left. Please forgive me." Her tears soaked his collar.

"You're back," he whispered, stunned. He stroked her hair. "Thank God."

But, wait—something was missing.

Gerald pulled back from her grasp, straightening his arms and gripping Lara's shoulders. Grim-faced, their eyes met.

"Where's Erich?" he asked, a distinct alarm rising in his voice. She didn't respond, but her tears and look of defeat was enough to cause him panic.

"Lara!" He shook her shoulders. "Where is Erich?"

"Gone," she managed between sobs.

"What do you mean gone? Where? What happened?"

"Rubin took him."

"Rubin?"

"Yes. We went back to Austria to be with Rubin." She sniffed and took a deep breath, trying to regain her composure. "He said we could be a family. So I went. I took Erich. But right away I knew something wasn't right. I knew it and I ignored it. And now look what's happened. I'm so sorry, Father."

Gerald's eyes were wide in disbelief. Erich was gone? And here in front of him stood his daughter, taking the blame. He pulled her back into his chest and ran his hand down her hair.

"What's going on?" A frantic Marlene flew into the kitchen, tying the belt of her robe around her waist. At the sight of Lara, she dropped her hands and rushed toward them. "Lara! Oh, thank the Lord you're home." She wrapped her arms around the girl and kissed her head.

Consumed with relief, it took Marlene a moment to realize the absence of her precious grandson. "Wait, where's Erich?" Her eyes darted between Lara and Gerald, decoding the agony on their faces. "No," she said, bringing a hand to her mouth. "Tell me it's not true." Her face crumpled and she dropped her head into her hands.

"I'm so sorry, Mother. It's all my fault."

"Rubin kidnapped Erich," Gerald said. "He's somewhere in Austria. Or God knows where."

"We can find him, right?" Lara looked up to her father with hopeful eyes. "That's why I came back. I knew you'd know what to do, Father."

Gerald looked to his wife, her face twisted in uncertainty. When he didn't immediately respond, Lara returned to panic.

"You can help, right Father? Can't you call the authorities?" Hysteria rose in her voice. "Father, please. We have to get him back!"

"I can't just call up the Austrian authorities, Lara, you know that," Gerald snapped. He paced around the island in the center of the kitchen, hands on his hips. "I'm a traitor to them. They don't care about us. The last thing they'll want to do is help our family."

"But he's my son. And he was kidnapped from me!"

"He's Rubin's son, too. The police will say he has the same right to be a parent." Gerald ran his fingers over his scalp. "Plus, it doesn't look very good that Rubin never even knew Erich existed. We lied, Lara. That's not going to help our case."

"But—"

"There's no buts, Lara." Her father's voice elevated, his look severe. "No one in Austria will want to help us."

"That's not true. There are people there who have resisted German occupation. Loyal Austrians. I met some. That's how I got home."

He wanted to scream at her, to discipline her for her foolishness. How could she be so naïve? *Look what you've done!* he wanted to cry. But when Gerald looked at his daughter, he knew she'd already imposed a lifetime of punishment on herself.

Lara bowed her head, overwhelmed with shame. What had she done? If they didn't get Erich back, she wouldn't be able to go on living.

Marlene stood against the wall, biting the skin around her thumb. Pools of water filled her eyes. "We've got to think of something," she said. "Gerald? There's got to be some way."

They stared at each other. Lara's eyes pleaded for a miraculous answer she knew wasn't possible. Her father was angry, and his temper wasn't something she wanted to be on the receiving end of. Could he look past his disappointment? For the sake of Erich?

The silence was unbearable. Gerald stood still, turning scenarios over in his mind. Then, as if a joint decision had been made, he spoke, adamantly.

"I'll go."

Marlene stepped toward him. "What? But Gerald, you can't. You'll be arrested."

"We have no choice. I won't be able to live knowing I didn't at least try."

It was pointless to argue. When her husband set his mind on something, he didn't easily sway. Gerald's strong will was one of the things Marlene had initially fallen in love with, and while she'd worked to soften his exterior, she knew the inner workings of his mind remained steadfast.

Lara felt guiltily relieved. She thought she should object—refuse to let him go, proving her love and devotion. But deep down, she was glad. Wasn't this exactly what she'd hoped would happen? Her father, strong and invincible, whisking in to save the day. She was nothing without him. Just a reckless, foolish girl.

Marlene laid her head on Gerald's shoulder without a word. It was settled. Extending an arm out toward Lara, Marlene welcomed her daughter into the fold. Together, the three of them stood in a silent embrace.

But there was a fourth presence in the kitchen: Regret.

Regret for the choices they made and the decisions which brought them to this point of disaster. It circled them, nudged them. They didn't fight it.

TWENTY-TWO

"**W**hen?" Marlene sat on the edge of her bed watching her husband pull clothes from their closet and stuff them into a large leather duffle bag. In the corner, Lara stood like a child in punishment, hands clasped in front of her stiff body. Her eyes followed Gerald back and forth across the room.

"I'll leave around midnight. Better to drive through the night—less conspicuous. Should be early morning by the time I get to Salzburg."

"Shouldn't we wait another day? Make sure we've figured out the best plan?"

"There's no time, Marlene."

Suddenly unsure, Marlene bit her nails. "I just don't know if we've thought this through. There's so many possible consequences. What if you're arrested? How do you even know where to find him?"

"I'll find him."

He zipped the bag as he said this, and the gesture paired with his declaration sounded so convincing.

Of course you will, Lara wanted to shout. The idea that her father *wouldn't* find Erich was almost inconceivable. She put blind faith in his ability. Like most fathers to their children, Gerald was invincible, a hero. Only Marlene's hesitation caused Lara any inkling of doubt.

"Maybe we should try to locate him first? That way you're not searching all over Salzburg or beyond," Marlene tried. "Couldn't you reach out to someone for help? You still have so many connections in Austria, Gerald."

Gerald whipped his head up to face her. Marlene's eyes pleaded. His severe look made her take a step back.

"The Austria we knew is no longer," he said, coolly. "You know that, Marlene. Our grandson is in a hostile, unpredictable place. And I'll be damned if I'm going to wait another day to try to find him. I don't care if it's a German-controlled state or not. I'm going."

Lara's skin tingled. It was the first time she'd ever heard her father refer to Erich as his grandson. The moment was bittersweet. Finally, the acknowledgement she'd craved, but under all the wrong circumstances. Lara wanted to leap into her father's arms, but guilt rooted her to the floor.

You did this, she told herself. *See the pain on his face? It's your doing.* Not even her father's intense determination could hide the sobering truth.

Gerald and Marlene faced each other in a standoff—one Marlene knew she'd lost before it even started. There was no changing his mind. Realizing this was happening today, whether she liked it or not, Marlene shifted the conversation to more productive arguments.

"How are you going to get across the border?"

"Don't worry about that. I'll figure something out."

"And then what? You're just going to waltz into Salzburg and drive around until you see a blonde-haired man with a baby?"

"I have a plan, Marlene." His firmness put a halt to her line of questioning. Grabbing her hands, he pulled her to him. Marlene took in his crystal blue eyes—the same ones she had fallen in love with years ago. His tone softened. "The less you know, the better. I'll be okay. I promise." Gerald cupped her face in his hand. They couldn't stay angry at each other for long.

"Oh Gerald, I'm so scared." She inhaled a sharp breath.

"Shhh. It's okay. I need you to be strong. For the children."

Lara bowed her head and hot tears dripped onto the carpet as she watched her parents embrace. She wished she could melt through the wall and disappear from the intimacy of the moment, knowing full well if it weren't for her decisions, their family wouldn't be in this situation. Shame made her stay. She deserved to feel all the pain.

Gerald grinned, his thin lips pressed together. It was a cover, surely—a façade to hide his nerves. But then again, they were good at façades.

He ran a finger down the bridge of Marlene's nose and tapped its soft tip. Marlene managed a smile.

* * *

The children woke one by one and lumbered downstairs, gasping at the sight of Lara sitting at the kitchen island, Marlene at her side. They ran to her, arms wildly reaching. Each reacted slightly differently, yet all expressed the same unbridled love of siblings.

"Lara! You're back!"

"Where were you?"

"Why did you leave?"

"Oh Lara, we missed you!"

Joy and relief...but then:

"Where's Erich?"

Lara listened with large, liquid eyes. Hearing the same questions over and over multiplied her guilt six-fold. How could she have done this to her family? She was lower than low. Would they ever forgive her?

With each barrage of questions, Marlene swooped in with her inherent softness.

"Don't worry, children," she said. "Erich will be alright. Your father will find him and bring him home. Until then, we'll lift him up to the Lord. He'll protect Erich, protect us all."

The little girls nodded, even though they couldn't possibly understand. For that, Marlene was thankful—their naivete served as a blessing. Father would fetch Erich and all would be well. Of course! Was there really any alternative?

But the older children could read between the lines. And the tension in the room was palpable. They studied Lara's body language and noted their parents' grim expressions. Even Marlene's cheerful disposition seemed phony—and *that* was enough to worry them.

Felix reached a hand to Lara and gave her a knowing squeeze. He wrestled with his own grief. Could he have prevented this? Picturing the night Lara left, he kicked himself at letting her go so easily. *You should have been more forceful—what kind of man are you?*

By the time all the children awoke and gathered in the kitchen it was nearing nine o'clock. "Let's get some breakfast," Marlene said, hoping to re-establish some sense of routine. At the stove, she fried eggs and placed each on atop a piece of brown toast.

"Mmmmm," Gloria announced.

Lara considered her sister. How wonderful the simplicity of childhood. A younger version of herself wanted nothing more than to grow up. Now, she'd give anything to make the harsh realities of the world go away.

As ravenous as she was, Lara couldn't stomach the smell of the food. She retreated to the den and curled up into the corner of the couch. The normalcy of it all was unbearable. Nothing was normal. She feared nothing would be normal ever again.

The rest of the day progressed in a haze. From his office, Gerald called the Chief Medical Officer to tell him he would need to take a temporary leave, effective immediately. His request was met with concern, but he assured his superior it was a family matter that would be solved soon. They conceded with full confidence.

Marlene phoned the schools. She informed them that the family was taking a short vacation and that the children wouldn't be present for several days.

"I'll arrange for them to make up their work," she said over the phone. The children were smart, they would catch up easily. It was a provisional explanation, one that would do for the time being. The teachers didn't question, for what was Marlene if not pure and trustworthy? Marlene knew she'd have to come up with alternate arrangements should her husband be gone longer than they hoped.

"But I have a group project this week," Bettina complained, aghast at tarnishing her perfect attendance record and subsequent model student status.

"You'll survive," Lena said.

"I'm sorry, darling," Marlene added. "We just can't risk it."

"I won't say anything. I know how to keep a secret."

"I'm sure you do, dear. But it's better if we all just stay put. Hopefully it will only be a few days."

Bettina huffed. The other youngsters celebrated, happy to stay home—the girls content to continue making clothes for their dolls, and Karl thrilled to be excused from gym class. But Lena and Felix, older and wiser, took no pleasure in either scenario.

"How are we supposed to go on like nothing's happened?" Lena whispered to her brother.

Somehow, they did.

Atyellow dinner, Marlene prepared potato goulash—a family favorite—but the lumpy cream mounds went untouched. No one had an appetite. Instead, they sat awkwardly at the table, pushing food around their plates like a bunch of toddlers being forced to eat their vegetables.

Fear pulled itself up to the table like one of the gang, its nasty air sucking the liveliness from the room. There was no sense in trying to pretend. They were scared. Worry seeped from the radiators; their spirited home was no more.

As the evening hours ticked away, the family gathered in the living room—a silent gesture of camaraderie before the inevitable. The children huddled around their father, grasping onto whatever piece of him they could touch. Gloria and Miriam sat on his lap, each taking a thigh and leaning into the solid block of his chest. At his feet, Bettina and Karl wrapped their arms around Gerald's legs, laying their heads on his kneecaps. Lena and Felix sat on opposite sides, bookending their father and trying to sniffle to only themselves.

He was their protector. And he was leaving.

Across the room, Lara and Marlene sat on the smaller loveseat, their legs touching. Marlene let the girl's body sink into her own, helping to absorb the weight of her sadness. Her husband and children were entwined into a ball of arms and legs and melancholy faces. Miriam sniffled.

No one spoke. There was nothing to say. The room was quiet except for the low tick of the grandfather clock, which loomed over them from the corner.

Eventually, little eyes drooped and limbs grew heavy. The children fell asleep where they sat. Marlene gave a subtle nod, and Gerald carefully slid from the couch. The youngest girls took up the space he'd left, the crowns of their heads bumped up against each other.

When he moved, Bettina, Karl, and Lena roused. They looked around, groggily.

"Is it time?" Karl asked, his eyes barely slits.

"Yes, darling," Marlene said. Karl frowned, looking to his father.

"No tears," Gerald said. "Off to bed. Everything will be okay. I'll see you soon."

The three middle children climbed the stairs to their rooms, looking back every few steps. When they were out of sight, Gerald turned to Felix. Tall and strong, the boy stood straight with his chest puffed up. He attempted a brave face, though his quivering chin gave him away.

"Can't I come with you, Father?"

"No, son." Gerald shook his head. "I need you to stay. You're the man of the house while I'm gone."

"But I can help you. I don't want you to be alone."

"I'll be fine. You must stay."

Felix's body physically deflated, like a balloon pricked by a pin. Gerald knew how much the boy admired him and craved his respect. "Well I'll at least see you off, then."

Gerald agreed to this much.

With the younger children in bed, Marlene packed some food and a canister of water into her husband's bag. How exactly he was getting to Salzburg, let alone where he planned to stay, she didn't know. He insisted it was best to keep her in the dark on the details. Would he be gone two days or two weeks? She packed as much as she could fit, just in case.

They met at the bottom of the stairs—her from the kitchen, him from gathering his bag in their bedroom. As he descended, Gerald slipped his second arm into a wool suit coat, buttoning the front all the way up. The velvet green lapels folded over, tacked down with gilded pins from his service to the government.

The two clapped eyes on each other, a single look saying a thousand unspoken vows.

You are mine, I am yours.

I've never loved another. I'll never love another again.

Come home.

The clock struck ten, an ominous foreboding. The foursome—Gerald, Marlene, Lara and Felix—in an effort to delay the inevitable, avoided eye contact. Felix stifled a cough. Finally, deciding that waiting any longer would just bring more pain, Gerald dipped his head.

"I'm ready."

They walked him to the front door where he swung the duffle over his shoulder. Gerald pulled Lara in tight and kissed the top of her head. Her eyes were recessed and hollow. To Felix, he extended a hand and shook it with the authority of a military captain, but the tenderness of a father. The children took a step aside, giving Marlene room to come forward. She reached up and traced the line of her husband's thick brow, letting her finger glide down the curve of his face.

"I know God will bring you back to us," she said. "Both of you."

"I love you, Marlene."

He pressed his lips against hers. Marlene squeezed her eyes shut, praying that if she wished hard enough she'd open and everything would vanish into the smoke of a nightmare. But when she released, there he stood—the man who had expanded her heart to a love she never knew existed. He was resolute, the weight of the world on his shoulders. She bit her lip to stop from crying.

Gerald took a final glance at his family, then briskly turned and jogged to the car waiting at the curb.

He didn't look back.

TWENTY-THREE

Gerald drove in a trance. Eyes fixed on the illuminated road, he watched as the city limits of Zürich faded from view. Soon, the swelling silhouette of the great Alps surrounded him. A soaring border between the countries, the mountains stood like a fortress, guarding who passed through. He sped east, planning to circle Liechtenstein and enter Austria to the north.

The rugged contour of the peaks rose from the ground, scraping the sky. The sight of them transported Gerald back to the time he'd led his family over the crests on foot. The journey felt like yesterday: lush green hills merging into rocky paths, where single file on hope and prayer was the only way to proceed. He'd been nervous—much like he was now—but determined not to show it.

Seeing the mountains in this moment brought back all the overwhelming emotions of their escape two years ago. Like déjà vu. Only now, his motive was reversed—instead of crossing the mountains to flee adversaries, he was crossing to meet them head on.

Gerald pressed on, ignoring the menacing cliffs and their provocation. They whispered to him, warning of the threat that laid on the other side.

After close to two hours, the border came into view. A small, dingy checkpoint booth sat at the side of the road. Above it, a rickety overpass supported a sign in bold, black lettering.

Sie kommen nach Ostmark

You are entering Ostmark

Gerald cringed at the renaming. Who did the Nazi's think they were? Austria would always be Austria—nothing else—in his mind.

He clenched his jaw tight, feeling the resentment swelling. *It's just a name. Don't think about it,* Gerald told himself. It was not the time for pride. He had to get this right, or else the rest of his plan would be worthless.

As the car inched forward, a young officer stumbled from the booth looking dazed, clearly not expecting traffic. He pointed a flashlight in Gerald's direction. A shiny pistol was clipped to the officer's belt, and the man—was he even eighteen?—brought his hand to the holster as he approached the driver's side of the car.

Straightening in his seat, Gerald cleared his throat, and rolled down the window.

"Good evening," he said with a smile.

"What are you doing out at this hour?" the officer asked, tipping his nose in the air.

Gerald laughed inside. *Oh, the confidence...*

With years of authority and influence behind him, Gerald had no trouble in the art of persuasion. That the guard was merely a boy only made it easier.

"On official business," he responded, touting equal clout. Intimidation was a tactic he'd mastered long ago, and he planned to use it to his advantage.

If getting past the SS required a bit of acting, Gerald had the script ready. He'd play the part.

The officer eyed the pins on Gerald's jacket. "I'll need to see your identification."

Taking the folded paper from Gerald's outstretched hand, the boy skimmed the card. When his eyes widened—as Gerald expected they would—he jerked his head up.

"I'm sure you recognize my family name," Gerald said smoothly, speaking before the boy had a chance. It was time to set the plan in motion. "I'm here to report for my medical position. Admiral Von Schreiber is expecting me."

The officer's hand holding the paper trembled in midair. He glanced over his shoulder to the booth, where Gerald knew there'd be a radio with backup on the other end. One call and he could be taken into custody. He had to keep the boy at the car.

"I'll need to make a call to verify this." He turned toward the booth.

"No!" Gerald shouted, making the young officer pivot back. Then regaining his calm demeanor, "Can you imagine how angry your superiors would be at being woken up after midnight? I imagine that could be just cause for punishment. You wouldn't want to be thought of as incompetent, would you?" A glint of ego twinkled in his eye. The smugness would easily have infuriated the boy if he weren't so frightened.

The officer second-guessed himself. His face reddened. Realizing the insult disguised within Gerald's forwardness, his eyebrows furrowed.

It was exactly as Gerald had planned. He registered this reaction, and pleased, he continued.

"Come now, officer...what's your tag say? Wagner. Officer Wagner, do you really want to hold me up and make me late to meet with the head of the Wehrmacht?"

Tension tightened between them as the young man considered his options. Signal for help and risk discipline? Or stand back and make a massive mistake? He was damned either way.

The boy thought. Lifting his chin again, he handed the identification card back through the car window.

"I'll be making a call at first light to make sure you've arrived where you say you're headed," he said haughtily, as though the decision to let Gerald pass was his alone.

"You do that, son."

Gerald grinned as he rolled the window up and flew through the checkpoint, leaving behind a budding Nazi soldier who didn't realize he'd just been duped.

TWENTY-FOUR

Despite his outward confidence, Doctor Weiss was on edge. He would have been lying if he'd said his heart didn't beat significantly quicker as he passed into German-occupied Austria. His car window down, the fresh breeze dried the film of sweat on his forehead.

Getting past the guard at the border was one thing. The rest of his agenda was another.

It was pitch black as he navigated the streets toward Salzburg. The road threaded the Alps, and despite the daunting task before him, Gerald felt a sense of ease just knowing he was back on his beloved homeland's soil. As the city grew near, daylight broke the horizon—the florid orange ball spreading spectacular rays in every direction. Gerald passed a few cars, early-risers starting their day with the sun.

The desire to visit his former home brought a full-body ache. He wished so badly to see the grand green house. Temptation whispered in his ear, but Gerald remained focused. He was there with one goal. No time for distraction.

Gerald shook the mansion's image from his mind and instead pictured another glorious place. It wasn't to where Rubin and Erich were—that, he didn't know. He was driving somewhere else. Somewhere he knew he could seek refuge until more information was available. Until he could determine his final destination.

The car navigated the tight streets of Salzburg until it came around a bend and a familiar crimson dome rose high in the sky. Atop a small crest in the city, the Nonnberg Abbey looked down majestically over the community below. Its exalted presence was a beloved fixture for the people of Salzburg, made only more noticeable by its bells chiming every hour.

At the sight of the ancient Benedictine convent, Gerald found himself lost in nostalgia. One of the most significant times of his life was spent within its walls. His wedding to Marlene—just two years earlier—was held in St. John's Chapel at the abbey. It was the only logical place Marlene could think to hold such an event. After all, she'd developed a fondness to it, feeling a kinship with the nuns, and especially the Reverend Mother. On her breaks from teaching in the nursery, Marlene often tip-toed into the sanctuary and took in its splendor. It would be a lie to say she hadn't—on more than one occasion—pictured herself marrying there.

Gerald's mind wandered deeper. He pictured his wife walking toward him, preceded by his eldest daughter. A vision in white, Marlene captured the attention of everyone in attendance. She'd walked with grace and poise, the cathedral train of her dress trailing behind her along the stone aisle. The ceremony was magical.

It was one of the happiest days of his life.

Coming alongside the abbey, Gerald put the car in park. He looked around. Not a soul in sight. Relieved, he released the tension from his jaw. He'd made good time.

Gerald pulled the brim of his hat low on his forehead, casting a shadow over his eyes. He grabbed his bag and left the car, walking swiftly along the path that took him to the rear of the building. The lesser-used trail offered more coverage. A heavy iron gate at the entrance sealed the outside world from the spiritual realm on the other side.

Gerald tried the gate, but it was locked. *Why wouldn't it be*, he told himself. To the side, a teardrop handle on a chain hung at eye level. He pulled down on it, sending a trill through the air. Would anyone come? He guessed the abbey didn't receive many visitors at five in the morning.

Nervous and impatient, he shifted his weight from foot to foot. He looked to his left and right, then rang the bell again.

From a distance, a figure emerged, small at first, then growing in size as it approached. The nun, he could tell now, was clad in black from head to toe. Her feet were invisible beneath the flowing fabric, making her appear to float rather than walk. She tucked her hands inside her habit, as customary. Her wimple, a tightly creased white wrapping, framed her face so all he could see were her pinched cheeks and pursed lips.

She did not look friendly. Gerald worried he might have drawn the short stick from the nun pool.

"May I help you?" the woman said, prickly, when she reached the gate. She stood perfectly still. Only her lips moved. She didn't even blink.

Gerald slowly lifted his head to meet her gaze. Their eyes locked. And as he reached up to take off his hat, she gasped.

"Doctor Weiss!" she exclaimed in hushed shock. His was a face she'd never forget. But how could she? Especially after she'd used people she knew from the outside world to help hide the Weisses on their way across the border.

She'd spend the rest of her days repenting.

Before Gerald could say a word, the nun fumbled a large metal keyring from inside her habit. Her hand shook as she slid the brass key into the keyhole on the gate. With a twist, she pulled the heavy passage open. Gerald slipped through sideways. Behind him, the nun locked the gate, then hurried to where he hid in a shadow along the near wall.

"Come. This way." She didn't ask the purpose of his visit, but something told her it couldn't be good.

There was no question of where to take him. A flash of black, the nun nipped along the cobblestones, the fabric of her habit waving with the movement of her body. They moved briskly. Gerald was grateful for her urgency.

At the top of a flight of steps, the two passed along another corridor, and finally reached a small wooden door marked with a large, gold Crucifix.

She knocked gently. After a second, a strong female voice replied. "Come in."

The nun opened the door and pulled Gerald in behind her, closing it quickly. On the far side of the room, behind a dark cherry desk and silhouetted by the glow from the beveled window, stood another woman. An ornate cross pendant hung from her neck on a gilded chain.

"What is it, my child?"

"Reverend Mother," the nun said, "we have a visitor." She stepped aside, revealing Gerald. He gripped the brim of his hat with both hands below his chest and raised his head.

"Doctor Weiss!" The holy woman dropped the Bible from her hands. She strode across the room to see him closer, as if he might be a mirage. Extending her hands to him, Gerald took hers. He noticed the gold band on her right hand—a symbol of her commitment to God.

They stood at arm's length, her mouth agape. The lax skin on her aged face curved into soft lines. He remembered her round cheeks and kind eyes so well.

"Whatever are you doing here?" she said.

"I need your help, Reverend Mother."

"He was at the back gate," the younger nun chimed in. "I was just as shocked to see him as you are."

"Thank you, Sister Birgit." The Reverend Mother motioned toward the door, excusing her from their company. "Thank you for bringing Gerald to me. Please, let us speak in private."

Sister Birgit knit her brow, disappointed at being dismissed. "Yes, Reverend Mother." She bowed her head and left the room in a pout.

When the door clicked shut, Gerald didn't give the Abbess a chance to speak.

"I need your help."

"What's wrong? How did you get here?"

"I snuck in under the cover of darkness. Came straight here. I need somewhere to stay. Hopefully not for long."

"Of course you may stay here. But Doctor, why? Where is Marlene? Is everything okay?"

"No. I'm afraid everything is not okay." The intensity in his eyes made her knees go weak.

Gerald told her everything—about Erich, about their secret, about Lara's disappearance and subsequent return. She listened without a sound or expression. When he finished, the Reverend

Mother stood and walked to the large window behind her desk. Outside, the city below came alive with the activity of morning.

A bell chimed, cutting through the silence. The Reverend Mother studied the marbled windowsill, tracing her finger along the grey veins. Her face was pensive, and Gerald wondered what the woman was thinking. Would such a righteous woman be able to understand the complexities of secular life? Could she accept the choices they'd made?

Maybe, maybe not. But more importantly—regardless of approval—would she be willing to help him?

Gerald waited for her response, arms at his sides as if pleading, *Please! I'm in your mercy! Say something!* Finally, she spoke.

"You've been through a lot." Then turning back to face him, "You are safe here within our walls. But I cannot protect you out there."

Relief filled his body, and he let out a sigh. She would help. She would not turn him away.

"I know," Gerald said. "But I have a plan."

"What are you going to do?"

He stepped forward with bold conviction. "I need to get word to someone as soon as possible. Today, if possible. Can you send a telegram for me?"

"Yes, of course."

"Thank you."

"Doctor, where do you think the baby is?" Her tone was one of concern.

"I can't be sure. But I'm hoping I haven't burned too many bridges here for help in finding him."

"This city is a very different place now, I'm afraid. Terrible things are happening every day. Hitler's regime is unleashing hatred like I've never seen before."

"I know. But the resistance exists. I'm just hoping the sentiments of those people still align with mine."

They gave each other a knowing nod. The Mother Abbess went back to her desk, opened the top drawer and pulled out a sheet of cream paper.

"Here," she said. "For your telegram."

"Thank you." Gerald perched on the upholstered armchair in front of the desk and leaned over onto its smooth surface. He printed hurriedly.

Markus,
There is an emergency and I need your help. Meet me where my wife once lived. Speak to no one.
Gerald

The message was cryptic enough for Markus to understand, but vague enough for others to disregard. Folding the sheet in half, he addressed the front to his longtime friend, Markus Baumgartner.

"Thank you again," he said, as he handed it to the Mother Abbess who had, while Gerald wrote, called for a courier. A minute later, the note was whisked away, taking with it Gerald's sole strategy of recovering his grandson.

With the message in transit, Gerald slouched in the chair. His hands covered his eyes.

Another step closer.

The Reverend Mother regarded his state. "You must be exhausted," she said. "Let me show you to a room where you can rest."

He didn't object.

They left her office and he followed the formidable woman through a foyer to another long hallway lined with doors on either side. The sound of their footsteps echoed off the high ceilings. *(Is this what Marlene meant when she described them raising their voices to the Lord?)*

As they turned a corner, Gerald noticed two robed figures huddled at a distance. The nuns' heads nuzzled together and they spoke in a low murmur. At his appearance, they flew toward him.

"Oh, it's true!" the shorter of the two gasped, clapping her hands together. Her blue eyes stretched with astonishment and a friendly smile spread across her face. Excitement made her practically bounce as she talked. "Sister Birgit said you were here, but I didn't believe her! How is Marlene? We miss her so. What a dear she was. And those darling chil—."

"Sister Magda," the Reverend Mother cut her off, "Gerald is quite tired. Let's not overwhelm him with questions."

"Yes, yes of course. Forgive me, Mother." She stepped back and regained her composure.

"Shouldn't you two be in morning prayers? Even the most welcome surprises need not lead us astray from our routines."

Gerald pinched his lips into a small smile, as the women, scolded and embarrassed, floated off in the other direction. He continued to follow the Mother Abbess until they came to a modest room with a single twin-size bed, perfectly made with a plush, fleece blanket tucked into all four corners. A bible, burned with red edges, sat on the nightstand. Above the headboard, a crucifix hung on the wall.

"This room is unoccupied," she said. "Please, rest. Only sleep can bring a clear mind."

"Thank you, Reverend Mother."

With a dip of her head, she left him alone. Gerald took in the sparseness of the space. Marlene had once told him her own bedroom, in a tiny two-bedroom house not far from the convent, was comparable to the nuns' rooms at the abbey. He pictured her in that room, in a house he never saw with his own eyes. What a wildly stark contrast to their life together!

The bed called to him, and he lowered himself onto the thin mattress. For a while Gerald could do nothing but think. Scenarios scrolled through his mind like the slow, hellish reel of a slideshow, one right after the next. Would he find Rubin and Erich? And if he did, then what? How would he get the boy back? His stomach curled with dread.

A dull ache at his temples told Gerald a headache was looming. The Reverend Mother was right: he needed energy to stay focused.

Lying back onto the stiff surface, he folded his hands on top of his chest. His eyes, the last things to relax, finally closed. Within seconds, Gerald fell into a deep sleep where his dreams centered on the glory days of a country he no longer knew.

TWENTY-FIVE

A soft knock at the door roused Gerald from sleep. His eyes flew open, as his consciousness remembered where he was before his sight even had a chance. What time was it? How long had he slept? He checked his watch. Eleven o'clock. He'd been asleep for nearly three hours.

Another knock, this time a little louder.

"Yes?" he said, scooching up to sit with his back against the headboard. The door cracked open and a face framed in white appeared around the edge of the door.

"Sorry to disturb you, but I brought you some soup." It was the same eager nun from earlier, the one who had excitedly asked about Marlene and his family.

"Oh, thank you. Please, come in."

She carried a tray and placed it on the small side table next to the bed. In the center, a shallow bowl filled with clear broth let off steam that wafted in a visible mist. Accompanying the soup, atop a napkin, sat a hard roll—its crusty surface serving as a shell for the soft interior. Gerald's mouth watered.

Stepping back from the table, the nun stared at Gerald with an earnest smile that hinted she'd get no greater satisfaction than to watch him eat every single crumb.

"Thank you," he repeated, unsure of what else to say to fill the awkwardness.

"I'm Sister Magda," she blurted. "I knew Marlene when she worked here. Such a sweet girl. I always had a feeling she had a bigger future than volunteering at a convent. And sure enough, I was right, wasn't I?" She laughed and then continued her long-winded declaration. "When she confided to us about her feelings for you, it was clear. And those children! Oh, how dear. I knew Marlene felt a special connection there. Not surprised, really. She has such a wonderful maternal nature. I'm just so delighted that she found her true calling. God always shows the way—He never leads astray."

Gerald nodded along with her rambling, and when she finally finished, he managed to sneak in a few words.

"That's very kind of you to say."

"I sense that you're not here under joyful circumstances," she continued, her tone turning sober. She spoke quietly as though they weren't the only two in the room. "It's not my place to pry. Just know that we're happy to have you. And I will pray for whatever trials you may be facing."

"Thank you, Sister."

She pressed her palms together and bowed her head, then slipped from the door as quietly as she'd come.

Gerald turned to the lunch before him. Thankful for a warm meal, he ripped a chunk off the bread and dipped it into the broth. The doughy center soaked it up like a wet sponge and it practically melted in his mouth. He took another sip with the spoon. The hot liquid soothed his throat and sent a balmy wave through his body. With each spoonful, he felt the effects of the food entering his bloodstream. It was bland, and a bit on the watery side for his taste, but he was in no position to complain. Hunger does not discriminate against nourishment.

He tipped the bowl to his lips and swallowed the last remaining drops. Refreshed and energized, his thoughts returned to the mission at hand.

There were still so many uncertainties: Did the telegram reach Markus? Would his friend be able to help him? Gerald ran through viable scenarios—best case down to the worst possible outcome. Logically, he considered whether he'd be able to jump through the hurdles he faced. Ease, unfortunately, was not on his side.

The afternoon wore on and Gerald remained in the little room alone. He sat. He paced. At times the minutes crawled impossibly slowly. Gerald's body fought against the adrenaline fueling him to search for Erich. Other stretches of time flew by in an instant, as he became lost in his thoughts and plans, only to look down at his watch and realize two hours had passed.

The empty bowl on the table taunted him. His stomach gurgled. *Feed me!* Gerald wasn't used to such meager portions, especially since Marlene often prepared enough food for an army.

Marlene. He missed her already.

On the floor next to the bed, Gerald noticed the bag he'd brought from home and remembered the food his wife had packed. Grabbing an apple, he wiped the waxy skin against his sleeve, then bit into its juicy flesh.

Being in such a state of limbo was torture. His mind played tricks on him, tempting him into second thoughts. Had he made a mistake by relying on the help of someone else? Was he wasting time waiting around, when he could be out there searching for Erich? He could leave at any time—no one was holding him prisoner.

There were no right answers. In the end, Gerald had no choice but to trust his gut. And his gut told him to wait a little longer.

As the bright light of the day faded into the dim glow of evening, another knock came to his door. Gerald jumped up from the bed, hungry for news—or food, whichever it happened to be.

It wasn't Sister Magda or Sister Birgit. This time, the Reverend Mother's face appeared. He impatiently searched her expression for an update.

"You have a visitor," she calmly announced. The woman pushed the door open and in its frame stood a short, slim man with dark hair and a neatly trimmed painter's mustache. He wore a gray houndstooth suit with a deep burgundy bowtie. Atop his head, a homburg hat was fashioned with a wide grosgrain ribbon and finished with a downy feather. The look was smart and refined, if not mildly garish.

"I had hoped I'd never see you again," the man said with smooth sarcasm as he stepped into the room.

"Markus." The men embraced. "I knew I could count on your brains to figure out my little riddle."

"Quite clever, but I must know. What on Earth is going on, Gerald? I'm hesitant to even ask. Something tells me you're not just here for a visit."

"I'm afraid not."

214

The Mother Abbess shifted in the doorway. "I'll leave you two to talk," she said, and shut the door.

Markus, a man who struggled to take anything seriously, wiped the smile from his face.

"What is it, Gerald? Tell me."

"I need your help, Markus. My family needs your help. We're in a bit of trouble. You have connections."

"You know a lot of people with connections too, Gerald. Why me?"

"I can trust you. You're a loyal friend. Unfortunately, that can't be said for all Austrians anymore."

Markus nodded in acknowledgement.

"A lot has happened in the two years since we left," Gerald continued.

"Yes, I know. The Nazis are taking over this place. It's bloody awful, Gerald. SS everywhere you look. They're rounding up Jews left and right. We keep hearing about these camps..."

"No, Markus. I mean a lot has happened with me. My family." The correction stopped his friend in his tracks. Soberly, Gerald continued. "I know things are bad. All of Europe knows. But that's not why I'm here."

"What's going on, Gerald? Now you're starting to frighten me."

"I need to find Rubin."

"Rubin? You mean that weaselly kid who Lara always hung around? Why on Earth?"

"He kidnapped my grandson."

"Your *what*?" Markus's mouth hinged open, knocking his chin against his neck. Dumbfounded, his upper body pitched forward.

"My grandson. Lara's baby."

215

Markus blinked several times, his jaw still agape. "But, but how?"

"Rubin is the father."

"Wait, wait, wait," Markus pumped his arms in front of him. "Back up a minute, Gerald. Let's start from the beginning. What in God's name happened between the time you left Austria and now? What happened to my wholesome little family?"

Gerald dropped his head and sat down on the bed. Markus was right—so much had happened, it was hard to remember a time before their lives revolved around secrets and lies.

He patted the mattress, motioning for his friend. Markus followed, coming to sit side by side with Gerald. Over the next fifteen minutes, Gerald retold the entire story: Lara's pregnancy, the coverup, living as if Erich was his child, Lara's disappearance and return, and finally his journey over the last twenty-four hours that brought him to the abbey.

Markus stared, astounded. "Unbelievable," he whispered.

"Oh, believe it. It's all real," Gerald said. "Now, I need your help. I must find Rubin. The more time that passes makes me worry he'll take Erich even farther."

"But what do you want me to do?" Markus asked, perplexed. "I'm a publicist, Gerald, not a high-ranking official. I work in the entertainment business, for crying out loud."

"You know people, Markus. Important people. Rich people. Plus, you're a schemer." Markus beamed at the off-handed compliment, as Gerald continued. "It's not like I can just call up acquaintances here in Salzburg or wander around town until I find him."

"Okay..."

"So you'll help me?"

"Yes of course I'll help you, Gerald. What do you take me for?"

"That's the Markus I knew." Gerald wrapped his arm around Markus's shoulder, giving his friend a playful shake. They sat, co-conspirators with a mission to plot. In a low voice, Gerald laid the groundwork.

"Rubin was under the command of Hans Rainer. He was loyal, even before Rainer became Gauleiter." The thought of his nemesis being named as the head political figure of Austria under Hitler's command made Gerald cringe. "But loyalty runs deep with those cronies," he continued, "and I have a feeling Rainer would repay Rubin's loyalty."

"Are you saying you think Rainer is helping Rubin hide Erich?"

"That's exactly what I'm saying. Or at least, what I'm thinking. We need to get to Rainer and figure out a way for him to give up the boy's location."

"But how?"

"You're a charmer, Markus. Think of all the antics you've pulled over the years. You've been pulling the wool over people's eyes since you were ten! Don't you remember fooling that teacher into thinking you were someone else? She bought it completely.

"Well," Markus snickered, "it was pretty clever, if I do say so myself."

"See? Now we just need to come up with something that will trick Rainer."

They thought, each staring at the ceiling as if stargazing, focusing on nothing, searching for a stroke of brilliance. At last, Markus whipped around, pointing a finger in the air.

"I've got it!"

Gerald faced him, anxiously waiting to hear.

"I think it will work," Markus mused aloud. "I mean, it should, if we play our cards right."

"Tell me, for God's sake!"

Markus clapped his hands together. "A television show."

"A television show?"

"Yes, a television show. Highlighting Nazi officers. I'll say it's a new way to spread the German message. Give viewers a chance to see inside the lives of the men who are leading 'their great country.'" He made air quotes with his fingers, but his mouth turned down in a look of disgust. "You know those Hitler-followers are all full of themselves. Bunch of self-righteous narcissists. They'll love the idea of even more self-promotion. Heck, I bet they'll throw viewing parties just to see their faces on screen."

"Okay, that may be true, Markus," said Gerald, "but I don't see how this helps me track down Rubin and Erich."

"Patience, Gerald. I'm just getting to the good part."

Gerald's eyes rolled.

"I'll set up a meeting with Rainer to explain the project and once he's on board, I'll ask for the addresses of the officers I want to interview. Rubin Pichler has risen in the ranks a bit since you've been gone, so it won't be unusual for me to request his participation."

Gerald nodded along, finally seeing the big picture. "And once you give me the address, it will be me who shows up on his doorstep instead of a camera crew," he said, the idea sinking into his head.

"Exactly."

"Markus, I always knew you were a genius."

Markus stroked his mustache with his thumb and forefinger. "Well, Gerald, they don't pay me the big bucks for nothing."

TWENTY-SIX

Marlene placed the serving dish on the center of the table. It was her favorite; bright yellow with a hand-painted floral motif. She liked to think it offered a lightness, an optimism to the meal. But now, as she rotated it just right, her reflection bounced off the bowl's highly-glossed surface: troubled and pale.

The hearty, comforting fragrance of beef and tomatoes floated around the room. It was the kind of aroma Gerald always commented on when he got home from work: "I smell something pretty tasty!"

Only today, of course, he wasn't there to give his typical compliment.

Next to the yellow dish sat a platter of steamed vegetables—green beans and zucchini Marlene picked from their backyard nursery. Gardening reminded her of her time at the Abbey, where she and the nuns tended the crops in their little courtyard.

It was something she did for herself—a way to keep in touch with her roots.

"Dinner's ready!" Marlene called through the entryway of the dining room. The well-known sound of feet followed—she often thought her growing brood sounded more like a cavalry—and the children entered, taking their seats around the table. Marlene took a chair at the far end. She looked down each side of the table at the somber faces of her children.

"Cheer up, my darlings," she said. "We mustn't dwell in our worry. That will do us no good. Besides, I've made one of your favorites tonight." She pointed to the dish, which sat prominently on a flat pedestal.

"Goulash," Bettina said. "Father's favorite." The reminder doubled their melancholy to the point Marlene was sure their frowns couldn't dip any lower. She'd planned the meal to raise their spirits—it wasn't just her husband's favorite, it was a dinner of choice for them all. What she hadn't considered, however, was that the children would connect the beloved supper to the one person missing from the table.

Across the length of the table, the chair opposite Marlene's sat empty. Gerald's absence weighed heavily on the house—when they were all together, and especially when she was alone. Nothing felt right without him home. Everything was wrong. Add to that the fact that they knew he was very likely in harm's way, and the mood took an even more grim turn.

"Your father would want us to eat, and to enjoy this delicious meal," she urged them with a smile. "Come now, eat up."

The children picked at the food on their plates. It was hard to work up an appetite when their stomachs were in knots. After an hour, when Marlene accepted that no amount of begging would make them eat, she tossed her napkin on the table.

221

"Well, I'm certainly not going to force you," she said.

There was still a great deal of food left in the dishes—much more than a typical evening, where the children ate freely and plentifully and asked for seconds. *Ah well,* Marlene thought. *Leftovers. I suppose I won't have to cook again tomorrow.*

After cleaning and putting away the dishes, the family gathered in the coziness of the den. Lena snuggled on the couch under a shearling blanket, tucking her legs beneath its long, curly wool. Felix drew the blinds, closing them in from the outside world.

"Why can't we go for our evening walk?" Gloria asked.

Marlene responded gently. "It's best we stay inside for a while."

"Yeah," Karl added. "Remember? No one knows where Father is. What if someone brought it up and you slipped."

"I wouldn't!" Gloria said defensively. Marlene smoothed the girl's hair and said, "We know, dear."

Everyone was on edge. Normally carefree and jovial, the family had become a pack of highly-strung snapping turtles, eager to take each other's heads off.

Miriam, Karl and Bettina kneeled around the low coffee table, playing a dice game. Gloria, still brooding, climbed onto Lena's lap while she read a book. On separate chairs, Lara and Felix sat quietly, staring off into space.

Marlene's heart ached at the sight of her children so distressed. They were shells of themselves. How could she liven their spirits?

"Lara, why don't you get your guitar?" she suggested. "A few tunes will cheer us all up." Gloria's face lit.

"I don't feel like singing," Lara said softly.

"Well, you don't have to sing. Just play."

222

"Mother, please."

"I don't feel like singing either," Lena added, looking up from the book in her hand.

"Oh, alright," Marlene resigned. Music had always been her go-to for every emotion—joy, despair, confusion. Yet she understood how her children felt—maybe this was one situation that music couldn't fix.

When the littlest girls started to yawn, Marlene shuffled them upstairs for bed, despite their insistence at not being tired. She sat cross-legged behind them on top of the lofty spread. Brushing their long, wavy hair, Marlene admired both of her daughters for the striking beauty each possessed: one kissed by the sun, the other as dark as a raven's feather.

"Mother?" Miriam said, pressing against the bedpost with hands and feet for resistance.

"Yes?"

"Will father bring Erich home?"

"I hope so. I believe so."

"But how do you know?"

"No one knows anything for sure, Miriam. All we can do is have faith that God will protect and guide him." She stroked the girl's cheek, then continued brushing. Moving on to Gloria, Marlene divided the girl's locks into three handfuls and braided the pieces down her back.

"Mother?"

"Mmhmm."

"Do you really think singing makes people feel better?"

"I do."

"I know the others didn't want to sing, but do you think the three of us still could?"

Marlene smiled softly at her daughter's sweet innocence.

"Of course we can. What would you like to sing?"

"You choose."

Marlene pressed a finger to her lips as she thought. She knew dozens of songs, but a select few always seemed to come to mind first. These ones, the ones she heard the nuns sing daily, held the most meaning. Remembering that long-ago time, her heart swelled as the voices of the abbey filled her ears. A single voice stood out among the rest—a voice of gentle authority and endless compassion. One that once gave her so much peace.

Marlene closed her eyes and began to sing, her angelic voice rich in tone and honeyed in melody.

After the first verse, she opened her eyes to see not only the girls, but all of the children—even Lara—standing along the perimeter of the room. A smile bloomed across her face as she continued the hymn. They watched her, mesmerized by the purity of her voice. Marlene stood from the bed. She walked to face the row of children, giving each one a personalized gesture: grasping and squeezing their fingers, running a hand down the side of their faces.

Marlene's voice rose in pitch and intensity for the culmination of the song. She swooped her arms up, welcoming the children to join in singing. All seven opened their mouths and belted the remaining chorus—about following your path and finding your dream—drawing out the final words of the tune in perfect harmony.

Marlene held the last note longer than the rest, then gasped for breath. She opened her arms and the children raced into them, forming a group hug in the middle of the room. Marlene felt the tension lift; the song had done the trick. Standing back, she beamed at the tender faces of her children.

"Better?"

They nodded.

"Alright then, off to bed." She patted Miriam on the bottom and the girl hopped up on the fluffy comforter. The rest followed Lara out and turned to their respective rooms. With contentment restored, Marlene tucked Miriam and Gloria into their beds, pulling the covers up tight around their chins.

"Goodnight, my sweet girls," she said, and gave them each a kiss on the forehead.

"Night, Mother."

Marlene made her rounds through the children's rooms, wishing them pleasant dreams.

"Tomorrow's another day," she told the boys. "We must stay positive."

At the far end of the hall, Lara and Lena's room was quiet. Inside, the eldest girls changed into their long cotton nightgowns. Lara hung her dress in their joint closet. As she did, her eyes fixed on a pale pink chiffon dress. She ran her hand along the gauzy fabric and felt the familiar smoothness of the ruched bodice. The dress had always been her favorite, its feminine cut and alluring movement making her feel sophisticated and beautiful. She'd worn it on many occasions, but one in particular stuck out.

Lara closed her eyes. She remembered the feel of the skirt spinning around her as she swayed with Rubin outside the boathouse on the grounds of her old home. She wanted him. He wanted her. The force pulling them together was magnetic. Like a mouse drawn to the cheese on a trap, there was no way for her to know the danger ahead.

That night was the first time they kissed, and Lara thought her heart might explode at that very moment. He'd been so charming; she'd been infatuated by his maturity, his charisma.

How little she knew.

Climbing into bed, Lara rolled to face Lena in the bed parallel to hers. The sisters stared into each other's eyes, a thousand unspoken truths between them. The urge to spill her darkest secrets was overwhelming. Lara wanted so badly to confess, to talk to someone. Would Lena understand? At the same age Lara was when she first met Rubin, Lena had matured over the past two years. Yet, Lara struggled to see her sister as anything more than an inexperienced child. How could she disclose the ways of a woman?

Lara shut her eyes, willing sleep that would fast forward the hours. She prayed she could dream away reality and wake up with Erich toddling toward her.

Lena's voice broke the silence and made her open her eyes once more.

"Lara? Why did you do it?"

The question hung in the air between them like a bomb, sparked and about to detonate. There was no need for clarification; they both knew what she meant.

Lara propped herself up on an elbow. "I loved him," she said, plainly. "I thought he loved me."

"But you knew better. I mean, you knew it was wrong to take Erich and run."

"Yes. I suppose love makes you do irrational things." Her voice trailed off. The girls were quiet for several minutes, as they lay in the darkness of their room.

"Lara?"

"Hmm?"

"What did it feel like? Love, I mean."

Lara smirked. Maybe her little sister wasn't so young after all.

"Do you have someone in mind?"

"Just tell me, Lara." Even through the dim light, Lara could tell her sister was blushing. Her answer came gently, after a pause of consideration.

"Well, at first it felt wonderful. Like the taste of the sweetest berries in the summertime. I had never experienced such a thing. It reminded me of all the times we studied classic art—you know, how each painting blended into the next with the same dull hues, until all at once you stumble upon a work bursting with bold color that awakens all your senses. It was kind of like that. So unexpected, and yet, it was as if I'd been waiting to discover it for years."

Lena marveled at her older sister. "It sounds so magical," she breathed.

"It felt pretty magical too. That is, until it wasn't." Lara paused in thought, then let her head fall down to the pillow. "I'm such a simple girl. How could I have thought it was all real?"

"I think real love is out there. Just look at Mother and Father." Lena reached a hand out across the gap between their beds. Their fingers met mid-air. "Don't give up on it, Lara. You'll find it someday."

Their fingers lightly locked together, the girls let the stillness of the room take over. Downstairs, the clock struck ten, and the house fell asleep.

TWENTY-SEVEN

Markus Baumgartner gave a few sharp raps on the door of Hans Rainer's office. Upon entering the military headquarters, he'd been shown to the second-floor suite by a pudgy junior officer whose sole job was to escort guests. The young soldier didn't think twice when told that Herr Rainer was expecting a visitor. Surprised and relieved by the ease with which he was taken directly to Rainer, Markus wondered if the officer's dim wit is what kept him in such a lackluster position.

As Gauleiter of Salzburg, a lofty position appointed by Hitler himself, Rainer was a powerful political figure with a particularly brutal reputation. He ruled under the thumb of fear and manipulation. Far from a daunting man, it was his tongue that wielded the power. With a word, he could make a man's life miserable—or end it all together.

Markus despised Rainer—as most Austrian loyalists did—and he had to remind himself the reason he was there.

I'm doing this for my friends.

As he was led to Rainer's office, Markus grew more and more disgusted. Nazi propaganda lined the walls of the hallways—posters of strong, able men and women with blonde hair and blue eyes: depictions of the chosen race. An illustration of the grim reaper, wiping out hordes of people who cowered at his feet hung next to the sketch of a long-nosed man in a top hat with a six-pointed star on his chest. The poster screamed in bold lettering: *Der ist schuld am Kriege!*

He is to blame!

The air of pure evil made Markus's skin crawl.

He knocked again and the office door flew open. Hans Rainer stood in its gape, his salt-and-pepper hair slicked back from his forehead. He looked older than Markus remembered, the war having apparently aged Rainer's sixty years quite noticeably.

"Herr Baumgartner," Rainer said as a crisp greeting. "I must admit I was surprised to see your name on my list of visitors today. What is it I can do for you?" His mustache moved while he spoke, but his eyebrows, high and arched, remained raised in fixed curves.

Rainer ushered Markus into the room and gestured for him to sit. Centered on the wall above a leather couch hung an oversized flag of the Third Reich, bright red and emblazoned with a bold, black swastika. The sight sparked a memory for Markus: his friend, Gerald, ripping down a similar flag from the balcony of his villa. He'd torn it in half, damning the German nationalism efforts and vowing never to fly the symbol anywhere near his home.

Markus sat cautiously on the sofa. "Thank you for fitting me into your full schedule, Herr Rainer. I know you are a busy, busy man." He eased in enough sarcasm to make Rainer

229

uncomfortable, yet not enough to be thrown out. Rainer would not take too kindly to swipes at his intelligence.

Markus couldn't risk being dismissed from this critical meeting due to mockery. *Don't get too cocky*, he reminded himself.

"I have a proposition for you," Markus continued. "A publicity project, if you will."

"Oh?"

"Yes. A brilliant idea, if I do say so myself."

Rainer rolled his eyes at his guest's self-admiration. "Get to the point, Herr Baumgartner. I don't have all day."

"A television show—or more like, a documentary feature—highlighting some of your top men. I would interview them, dig deep, show the civil side of these officers. Think about it! The public never gets to see the inside of the Wehrmacht, the people behind the uniforms. I think it could be great promotion for your cause, Herr Rainer. A chance to spread the Führer's agenda in a new way. Picture it: humanizing the Nazis. I can just see it now."

Markus waved a hand in rainbow-like fashion, as he stared off into the distance, painting a picture with his alluring words. Spinning a story was one of his many talents. Markus knew at the core—the deepest roots—of Fascist Germany was arrogance. He just needed to tap into it and sell the scheme in the right way. Appealing to a narcissist should be easy.

"And who are you expecting will participate in this little project of yours?" Rainer asked.

"Why, you of course! We're starting at the top. That is, unless you think the Führer himself would want to be included." Markus chuckled, but quickly wiped the grin from his face when he saw Rainer was not amused.

"You flatter me, Baumgartner. I assume you have others in mind?"

"Yes. I'd like to sit down with a few of your most patriotic—the most loyal men, with the most passion will be best for the screen. I was thinking Himmler, Schneider, maybe a few others from the Schutzstaffel. But I'd also like to include younger voices, as well. You know, those rising through the ranks. There's that promising officer, Rubin Pichler."

He tried to sound casual in his suggestion, eyeing Rainer from the corner of his eye to gauge the man's reaction. Rainer remained stone faced, but Markus could see the wheels turning.

"Pichler would be good," Rainer finally said, tapping his chin. "Determined chap. Plus he's got the looks for television. From what I hear, the girls can't get enough of him."

"Oh I'm sure," Markus said, flatly. Then, clapping his hands: "Well, sounds perfect. That's just what we need. So I'll go ahead and write up the contract and we can get started on this right away. We'll have it on air in no time." He reached for his portfolio pad.

"Hold up a minute, Herr Baumgartner," Rainer smirked. "Why should I trust you? It's not like you've been a vocal supporter of the Third Reich. Something about this smells off."

The hairs on the back of Markus's neck stood on end. He was so close, he couldn't let this plan crumble at the last moment. He crossed his leg and sat back into the deep leather cushions.

"My dear Herr Rainer, you know me too well," he said, making his voice charming, smooth like syrup. "It's true, I may not be shouting 'Heil Hitler' from the rooftops, but I know how to make a good buck when I see an opportunity. And this, this has the potential to be quite a money-making production. Plus, it doesn't hurt to stay in your good graces, am I right?"

Seemingly satisfied, Rainer studied Markus for several seconds before announcing his decision.

"Alright. You may proceed with your film, or whatever it is. Just remember, Herr Baumgartner, I've got my eye on you."

"Just where I like the eyes, my good sir, just where I like them." Markus stood and extended a hand to shake on their agreement. Rainer didn't move.

"Right." Markus dropped his arm awkwardly. "I won't bother you with setting up a location for our shoot. In fact, I'd like to speak with these men in their home environments. More of a relatable approach, I think. I'll just need addresses. And I'll take care of the arrangements. One less thing to clutter your busy calendar."

Rainer's eyes narrowed at the comment. He stood and walked to his desk where he jotted down the names and addresses for six different Nazi officers. Markus clenched his fist at his side to keep it from trembling. Rainer passed him the list.

"Wonderful," Markus said. "My deepest gratitude, Herr Rainer. I foresee this being a truly extraordinary project."

Rainer nodded and opened the door, indicating their meeting had come to an end. Markus tipped his hat and sped through the door before Rainer had a chance to demand a customary salute. Rainer, ever so skeptical, watched Markus go, the heels of his shoes tapping on the floor as he went.

Shoving the paper into his jacket's inside breast pocket, Markus made little eye contact with the passing guards as he returned to his car. His hands shook as he took the wheel and sped toward the abbey.

"A fine acting job, if I do say so myself."

When the complex was out of sight behind him, he glanced in his rear-view mirror and, with a smirk, winked at his reflection.

TWENTY-EIGHT

"I got it!" Markus burst through the door to the small room where Gerald waited eagerly for his friend's return. The Reverend Mother followed in his wake of excitement, shutting the door behind her so the three of them stood a foot apart, taking up much of the room's space.

Pulling the folded paper from his coat like a golden ticket, Markus handed it to Gerald. He fervently scanned the names until he found the only one he needed: Rubin Pichler.

"Bingo," Gerald said. "Markus, I knew you'd pull through."

"Did you ever doubt?"

Gerald gave his friend a strong pat on the back. He reached for his hat and duffle.

"Hold on, you're going now?" Markus said.

"What do you want me to do, Markus? Wait around another day? I need to find my grandson, and I'm not willing to waste another minute."

"No, of course not. I just mean...I...well, I just hope you're..."

"I'll be fine, Markus." He put a hand on the man's shoulder. "Thank you for what you did. You're a loyal friend."

"But of course. I'd do anything for you and Marlene. You know that."

Gerald pinched his lips appreciatively, then turned to face the Mother Abbess.

"I can't thank you enough, Reverend Mother." He bowed. "We are once again indebted to you."

"The Lord commands me to give shelter to those in need, my child. But you know your family will always hold a special place in my heart. May He keep you safe and see you through back to the arms of your loved ones." She raised her right hand and made the sign of the cross through the air in front of him.

Gerald picked up his bag and started toward the door. But before he could leave, Markus grabbed his arm, stopping him in his tracks.

"Wait, Gerald," he said discreetly from the corner of his mouth. "Here, take this." He held out an object wrapped in a dark green cloth. Unfolding one side, he revealed the metal barrel of a handgun. "I keep it in my car. Never know when you'll need one, right? Take it. Surely you'll need it more than I would."

Gerald stared at the weapon, then back to his friend, a mischievous look on his face. Slowly, he opened the top of his bag and tilted it toward Markus. Inside, the glint of a cool, silver pistol stood out against the soft folds of his clothes.

"No need, Markus. I've come prepared."

TWENTY-NINE

It turned out that Rubin's apartment wasn't far from the abbey at all. As Gerald drove toward the address, he realized the close proximity. Could his grandson have been this close the whole time?

He turned onto Schwarzstraße, an unassuming road lined with identical buildings that gave it a regimented feel. A group of Nazi officers marched down the other side of the street, their feet moving in robotic fashion, single arms extended in salute. They passed the window of Gerald's car. Being only inches away from the soldiers made him feel dirty.

Gerald searched the stone buildings for numbers indicating his location. When the numbers neared his target, he slowed the car to a crawl.

The address alone was the only piece of information he had as to Rubin's whereabouts. Lara, having been inside nearly the entire time, and then leaving in the dark, wasn't much help. The only thing she had been able to recall about the location of

Rubin's phony apartment was that it was a tall, brick building with a cherry red door. But that didn't matter anyway—Gerald was looking for a real apartment, not a fake one.

Looking around, Gerald saw nothing but stone the color of dried cement. No red door in sight.

"Bastard," he whispered through clenched teeth.

He looked again at the address written on the paper and then back to the ordinary apartment building in front of him. They matched. Five stories high with rows of windows and little other ornamentation, the building was like the other hundred in the city—one you'd drive past indifferently, without thinking there was a kidnapped child inside.

This was it.

Or was it?

What if Rainer had seen right through Markus's ploy? Could he have purposely given him a false address? Was Gerald about to walk straight into a trap?

He shook the thoughts from his mind. *Focus*, he thought, reminding himself he wouldn't know anything for sure if he remained in the car.

The only parking was on the street, so Gerald positioned the car along the curb and made a beeline directly to the front door without looking around. It was unlocked, and for a split second Gerald wondered what he would have done if there would have been a doorman.

Hi. I'm looking for a kidnapped child?

He checked the note again. *Flat 7,* Rainer's slanted script read. Gerald climbed the stairs two at a time until he reached a door on the third floor marked with "7" in chipped blue paint. A ceiling tile hung down in the distance.

This was not the type of apartment building that had a doorman.

It was clear Rubin was not living in the lap of luxury. He was just a dumb kid following a heinous crusade. The realization gave Gerald a twisted sense of pleasure. That is, until he remembered his grandson was likely behind the door.

The hallway was quiet and through the wall he heard the faint cry of a baby. Erich! Gerald's heart jumped into his throat at the thought of the boy just feet away. Was he hurt? Was he scared? The urge to burst through the door overwhelmed him. A vein pulsed from his forehead.

Gerald was happy to hear any noise at all, even if it was crying. Having worried that perhaps Rubin had already fled with Erich to a new spot, or even out of the city altogether, he had no Plan B if he would have found the apartment cleared out. But it was a Saturday, and they were home. Gerald wondered what Rubin had done with Erich the past two days while he worked? Had the baby been left alone all day?

Stay calm, Gerald thought. He took a deep breath for composure. *Concentrate.*

First, he needed to determine how he would actually get into the apartment. It wasn't as though Rubin would open the door and welcome him in. And even if he did, then what? Grab Erich and run?

He didn't have time to reason, let alone formulate an answer for each question that assaulted him. Another cry came from inside the apartment.

That's it, enough thinking.

Standing a bit taller and puffing his chest, he knocked purposefully on the door.

"Coming!"

Gerald's eyes widened in surprise. It was the voice of a woman, high pitched and frazzled, like the sound of a mother trying unsuccessfully to comfort a fussy child. For a second, he considered perhaps he was at the wrong apartment. *Damnit! Rainer tricked me!*

Another wail from the baby and instantly Gerald knew it was Erich. He could feel it in his gut; he knew that cry well. This was the correct flat—even if someone else lived there he wasn't expecting.

"I'm coming," the woman's voice called again, getting closer. The lock clicked and the door opened to reveal a petite woman wearing a pale blue house dress tied at the waist. Her light blonde hair was pulled into a low twist at the nape of her neck, revealing high cheekbones and eyes the color of robin's eggs. She looked young; Gerald thought she couldn't be more than eighteen.

She reminded him of Lara.

"May I help you?" she asked, smoothing the skirt of her dress and brushing a wisp of hair from her face. The baby cried out again, and the woman looked back over her shoulder then to Gerald with impatience.

"I'm looking for Herr Pichler," he said, trying to remain cool and steady. "Is he home?"

"Yes, but I'm afraid it's not a good time."

"Oh, I won't be long." Gerald began to feel nervous that he would have to force himself past her. Despite the gun in his waistband, he didn't want to have to get rough with anyone. "I've come a long way and would just like to say hello."

She looked at him curiously. "I'm sorry, I missed your name. Who are you?"

"Oh, just an old friend."

The crying stopped, and Gerald heard a faint shushing sound coming from inside the apartment.

"Okay," the woman said after a moment's pause, visibly annoyed by the surprise visit. "Come in. Rubin's in the living room."

He followed her through the doorway and with each step Gerald's heart raced faster until he thought it might bolt right from his chest. The home was small yet comfortable—dishes on the counter and shoes stacked near the door gave it a lived-in feel. Gerald noticed a framed poster on one wall with a headshot of Adolf Hitler and an inscription that read "Blut und Ehre." *Blood and Honor.*

The admiration made Gerald's blood run cold.

"Who was it?" a harsh voice echoed from around the corner.

Before the woman could answer, she ushered Gerald into the living room. Rubin stood on the far side of the room bouncing a red-eyed Erich in his arms, clearly doing a poor job of consoling the child. The men locked eyes—Gerald's angry, Rubin's shocked.

"Weiss!" Rubin yelled. In one swift move, he dropped Erich to the couch and pounced toward Gerald. Agile for his age, Gerald swerved, and Rubin stumbled to his knee. He rebounded quickly, ready for another go.

"Give him to me," Gerald demanded. He continued to move backward around the open room, as Rubin dove for him again.

"Never. He's my son."

"Dada!" Erich squealed at the sight of Gerald.

"What is going on?" the woman shrieked as the men faced each other in a standoff, their hands up, their bodies on guard. "Rubin? What's happening?"

Gerald seized the opportunity. "Oh, so she doesn't know?" he taunted. "How you kidnapped a child from his mother?" Rubin's face burned and he gnashed his teeth. Gerald continued, assaulting Rubin with his words. "What? Did you just show up one day with a baby and pretend everything was normal? Like you just plucked him from the street? And you were just going to be one happy little family? Everything about you is a disgrace." Gerald continued to press him, as they circled the room.

Rubin's body shook and he bared his teeth like a predator. "You have no right to be here," he growled. "This child belongs to me. He's got German blood and he'll be raised under the eye of the Führer."

"Ha! There's nothing German about him. His parents are Austrian. You're Austrian, boy! Or have you forgotten?"

Gerald could see the rage pulsing in Rubin's neck. His last comment—the power of identity—had been the blow that pushed Rubin over the edge. He clenched his fists and made another lunge toward Gerald, this time getting a chunk of Gerald's shirt in his grasp. The two men tumbled to the ground, Gerald falling onto his back and Rubin straddling him on top. They wrestled, each taking turns throwing swings—some missing and some making contact. The woman screamed and backed into a corner.

"Quiet, Hannah!" Rubin snapped at her. She clapped a hand over her mouth. Perched on the edge of the couch, Erich cried, a look of terror on his poor little face.

"I'm taking him back," Gerald said through gritted teeth. Rubin's hands were at his neck, and Gerald swung a punch toward his opponent's head, landing his fist against the boy's jaw. A trail of blood ran from the corner of Rubin's mouth.

"He's staying here," Rubin seethed, releasing a hand to wipe the blood from his face. When he did, Gerald took advantage and flipped Rubin to the ground, taking back the upper hand. He pressed Rubin's arms into the floor with all of his might and used his knee as a wedge against Rubin's groin. Rubin grunted, struggling to break free.

"You should burn alive with all the other vermin at those camps," Rubin spat. "Traitors are just as filthy as Jews."

Gerald resisted the urge to spit in Rubin's face.

"I don't want to hurt you, Rubin. Just give me the boy." His words were sharp against his teeth.

"Never!"

Gerald lifted him by the collar and slammed him back down, smacking his head against the ground, hard.

From the corner, Hannah shrieked. "What should I do, Rubin?"

"Get my gun!"

Gun.

At that, Gerald scrambled off Rubin and stumbled past an overturned chair. He needed to get out of there—fast—before things got any uglier. Coming to his feet, his body surged with adrenaline and his hands shook. Erich sat cross-legged on the couch, whimpering. Snot ran from his nose and his eyes were bloodshot from crying.

"Dada," Erich said again, reaching out his pudgy arms as Gerald moved toward him. Scooping the little boy into his arms, he pressed Erich's head into his body.

"No!" Rubin yelled, charging Gerald from behind. "He's mine!" Rubin jumped onto Gerald's back, forcing Gerald to put Erich back on the couch. The force of the attack knocked the wind from Gerald's lungs. He managed to turn, facing Rubin, and their arms interlocked. They tussled in a standing position, whipping each other's upper bodies back and forth, panting and

241

grunting in each other's ears. Rubin lurched to the right, and the men knocked over a table lamp, the ceramic base shattering against the hardwood floor.

"I got it!" Hannah's voice pierced the room as she flew around the corner. She gripped the handle of the pistol with shaking hands, pointing the barrel directly at the rivals.

As Rubin turned, Gerald reached around and squeezed his arm across Rubin's neck, locking him in a chokehold. He could feel Rubin's Adam's apple thumping against the crook of his elbow. Both men faced Hannah, only now, it was Rubin whose body was in the direct line of fire.

"It doesn't have to be like this, Rubin," Gerald wheezed into Rubin's ear. "Give me the boy, and no one needs to get hurt."

"He's. My. Son." Rubin could barely muster the chopped words through his constricted airway. He gripped Gerald's forearm, pulling down to release pressure.

"I'm not leaving here without him."

"Over. My. Dead. Body."

"I don't want to hurt you, Rubin. Just give up!"

"No!"

Gerald squeezed his throat tighter, and Rubin gagged, his hands frantically tearing at Gerald's sleeve.

"Don't you remember what I told you that last time we were face to face? You'll never be one of them."

Rage flowed through Rubin like lava.

"Shoot. Him." His wild eyes focused on Hannah.

"What?" she cried. "I can't!"

"Do. It!"

Gerald fumbled his free hand to the waistband of his pants and unclipped his handgun. He didn't want to do this. He just wanted his grandson.

Raising the gun, he aimed. A deafening shot rang through the apartment.

THIRTY

A man lay dead on the floor. A pool of blood, so dark it was almost black, spread around his torso and filled in the grooves of the boards. Lifeless eyes gaped wide at the ceiling. His mouth hung open in a limp oval.

"Oh my God!" Hannah screamed. Her face completely drained of color. She dropped the gun and it hit the floor with a clang. Flying onto hands and knees, she crawled to the body in the middle of the living room.

"Rubin! Rubin!" she sobbed loudly. She shook his shoulders and his head bobbed from side to side. The hem of her dress soaked up the blood like a sponge, turning the blue fabric a grisly shade of purple.

Gerald was alive.

He patted his chest, feeling around for signs of injury. There was blood on his hands, but it didn't belong to him.

Gerald, whose lower half had landed underneath Rubin after the gunfire, pushed himself away in shock. He kicked Rubin's body off his legs and scooted back against the floor, smearing a red trail. Shock set in. As his senses came back, the woman's wails, deep and guttural like a wild animal's, filled his ears. She bent over the body, her head on Rubin's chest.

Then, a new sound: the high shrill of a child. Gerald swiveled toward it. Erich, who had tumbled from the couch, now sat clutching onto its skirt, which brushed the floor. He trembled with fear.

Erich.

Without another thought, Gerald fumbled toward the boy and grabbed him. Standing, he realized his legs were like that of a newborn, wobbling unsteadily with each step. They needed to get out of there—fast. Hannah's cries would draw attention at any moment. Should he do something? Stay and explain what happened? It was his word against hers. Who would they believe: a traumatized young woman, or a well-known fugitive?

The answer was simple. He had to go.

Gerald hurriedly stepped over Rubin's body and rushed toward the door, Erich holding on for dear life.

"He's dead! You killed him!" Hannah shrieked, as Gerald's hand gripped the knob. He turned to face her.

"No, *you* killed him."

"I panicked! I was trying to shoot *you!*"

Gerald glared at Hannah for a fleeting moment, feeling sorry for her, before whisking through the door with Erich. He ran down the hall, clutching the baby to his chest. Hannah's voice followed him: "I'm calling the police!"

He leapt down the stairs, one foot barely touching the step before hurdling over a handful more. Erich's little body bounced along for the ride. He'd stopped crying, but the look of horror hadn't left his face, and his tiny fingers clutched Gerald's collar.

"It's okay, it's okay," Gerald soothed. "Shhhh...it's okay. I've got you."

As they descended, Gerald glanced behind him and listened for Hannah's cries. They could no longer be heard from the ground level, and he breathed a small sigh of relief. The police would arrive at any moment, but his car was right there—he was so close! Bursting through the exit of the apartment complex, Gerald rounded the corner and flung open the car door. Scooting Erich toward the middle of the seat, he climbed in behind the wheel. Bile burned his throat.

"It's alright, Erich," Gerald said, out of breath. "We're going home. Home to Mama." The boy just stared, confused, his bottom lip quivering.

The tires peeled against the pavement as Gerald pressed hard on the gas. He circled the block, taking the turn so fast that the momentum made Erich fall into Gerald's side. Another right, then a left, and they were headed toward the westbound highway. Gerald's hands gripped the steering wheel so tight his knuckles turned white.

Relax, he thought. *We did it. We're going to make it.*

His heartbeat sounded as thick and loud as a bass drum at the rear of a parade. Rubin was dead. Was it his fault? He dismissed the feeling of culpability.

As the car merged onto the single lane road that would lead them toward the border, Gerald's pulse slowed. He took a deep breath and shook the numbness from his hands. They had a ways to go, but each kilometer that passed felt like a hundred closer to home.

The Austrian countryside opened up to fields and trees, sprinkled with small towns where women hung clothes on lines in their front yards. The beauty of his homeland astounded him.

He missed it—that is, missed the Austria that once was. Now, this land that was occupied by leaders of hate and ugliness, felt like a strange place, one he did not want any part of.

Gerald was thankful they wouldn't have to pass through many populated areas before reaching the border. Innsbruck was the largest city they'd encounter before the final stretch of Austrian territory. Had word reached the local law enforcement there? Would officials be on the lookout for him?

He repeatedly checked the rear-view mirror to make sure they weren't being followed. As they passed other drivers—unsuspecting bystanders out for Saturday drive—Gerald feigned anonymity. He pulled his hat low and stared straight ahead. *Nothing to see here!* Inconspicuous as possible, he pressed the gas and sped past.

Erich sat on the vinyl seat, his head drooped to the side, his eyes struggling to stay open. A few minutes later, the rhythm of the car's movement lulled him to sleep. Gerald shifted Erich with one arm so that he was nestled, his little feet, covered with blue fuzzy socks, against Gerald's thigh. So peaceful, so innocent.

Gerald was struck by the lengths one would take for someone they love.

Is this how Lara felt when she made her choice?

A sign stood erect on the side of the road. Forty kilometers. With luck, they'd be across the border and nearing Zürich within two hours. Gerald let his mind wander to their reunion, waiting for them back at home. He imagined the chorus of cries, the happy tears, and Lara—his darling Lara—reunited with her son. The thought turned his eyes into hot, salty pools.

He'd only been gone three days, but he physically ached for Marlene—her touch, her smell, and the security he felt in her arms. They were two halves of a whole.

Gerald was lost in the heartwarming daydream when the sound of a shrill siren in the distance brought him back to present. Barely audible at first, it grew louder, and he again glanced in the mirror to find its source.

His insides clenched.

Two police vehicles approached at great speed from behind, red flashing lights swirling on the hoods of their cars. The patrols weaved around the other drivers on the road, and continued in a direct line toward Gerald's black car.

Damnit.

Easing off the accelerator, Gerald brought it to a more permissible speed, and again gripped the steering wheel with both hands. His heart beat in his throat.

"How did they find us?" Gerald muttered. No one—aside from Markus and maybe the Sisters at the abbey—knew what car he was driving. Had Hannah followed him and seen him drive away? She couldn't have. He'd been so fast, and when he'd left the apartment, she was still in such a state of shock.

The police were closing the gap. They showed no signs of slowing down. The sirens blared, and Gerald noticed several cars pulling off to the side of the road to allow more room for the authorities who were clearly in a hurry.

"Damnit. We're so close."

His foot remained steady on the gas. Curious, his eyes darted around the car's interior. Could he hide Erich? Put him down on the floor and cover him from view? Where was his gun?

Get real, Gerald, he thought. *You don't stand a chance against four armed policemen.* His thoughts quickly turned from determined to defeat.

This is it. It's over.

248

Marlene's face flashed through his mind. He would never see his beautiful wife or loving children again. Would she ever find out what happened to him? And what about Erich? Where would he be taken? What would become of his grandson?

Gerald's throat constricted and a wave of nausea rose from his stomach. Everything inside him tensed.

The cruisers were nearly upon him. He looked in the rear-view mirror and watched as they passed the last vehicle between them. Through the windshield he saw two men in the front seats, wearing the telltale gray uniform of the Schutzstaffel, their visor caps wrapped with silver cording and marked with a skull. Heated conviction on their faces.

Gerald closed his eyes, resigned. Any second the cars would be on his back bumper, forcing him off the road.

But then the sound of the sirens began to shift, growing louder in his right ear. And when he opened his eyes again, he was shocked to see both police vehicles passing him. They whizzed by in a flash, never even glancing in his direction.

Gerald let out a powerful exhale, as he realized he'd been holding his breath. Like the fading music at the end of a song, the sirens waned as the patrols sped forward and out of sight.

How was it possible? He looked to Erich, still asleep on the seat, unfazed by the squeal of the sirens. Bringing a hand to his chest, Gerald felt his heart through his skin.

They weren't after him—or at least, they hadn't located him yet. Gerald had no doubt Hannah had phoned the police the minute he'd fled. They were probably scouring the countryside for him, deciding which route he'd take to freedom.

The car passed a distance marker. Only five kilometers to the border.

"We're almost there," he said to his sleeping grandson. "We're almost there." If only he could will the car to go any faster. Still rattled from the near disaster, he couldn't shake the sound of swirling alarms from his mind. His brow furled. Were they getting louder? Gerald checked the mirror and saw another military vehicle with a spinning red light coming up behind him.

Not again. He gripped the wheel. But just as before, the jeep zoomed past at double his speed.

"Where are they going?" he wondered aloud. "There's nothing ahead but the—"

His heart dropped. The border. That's what was ahead.

Of course, he realized, feeling foolish he hadn't thought of it sooner. *They're blocking the border.* It didn't matter if they caught him en route. As long as they sealed the border, he'd be trapped.

They were only a few miles out. What could he do aside from run straight into an ambush?

His mind swirled. There had to be another way. Suddenly, the light bulb went off. He knew what to do.

Gerald slammed his foot on the brake and made a wide U-turn in the middle of the road. Dust flew up behind the car into a light brown cloud. Beside him, Erich stirred. The boy stared at his grandfather from where he lay.

"Hello, darling," he said. "We're getting closer, okay? It's alright. We'll be home soon." He patted Erich's soft belly.

Speeding in the opposite direction, Gerald retraced his route for several kilometers until he came to a crossroad that would take him south. He navigated off the highway and onto a maze of back roads covered in loose gravel. The cliffs of the Swiss Alps followed in his wake.

At once, a keen sense of familiarity flooded him. *I've been here before.* Pulling down a narrow dirt road, he came to a farm at the base of the mountains. A large wheat field was the only thing separating them from the towering ridges above.

Shifting the car into park, Gerald slung his pack over his shoulder and tucked the gun into his waistband. He turned to Erich and took a cleansing breath. This little boy for whom he'd risked his life—and for whom he'd do it a thousand times more.

"I've taken this journey before," he said, hoisting Erich to his hip. "And now we'll do it again."

251

THIRTY-ONE

It was the fifth day. The fifth day since Gerald left to search for Erich. The collective sense of trepidation grew with each passing hour. Lara thought surely it would consume her entirely if it lasted any longer.

There'd been no contact; not a word from her father. No reassurance that he'd found her son. Nor news of the contrary—that he'd been arrested. She wondered if he'd even made it into Salzburg without being detained. Did his lack of communication mean he was sitting alone in a cold jail cell? No, she reassured herself. Surely if her father had been arrested, they would have heard. Still, their policy—no news is good news—only offered so much comfort. Her mind swirled with scenarios, each one more dire than the last.

Lara hadn't slept well in over a week, and her already thin frame had shriveled to nearly skin and bones. Marlene tried to get her to eat, offering to make her favorite meals. She pushed food in front of the girl, and even suggested sugary treats, which were usually limited, to pump up her daughter's calorie intake. But Lara refused. A creamy cake on the counter did nothing. Her appetite was lower than low; it was non-existent.

"How can I eat when I have no idea if I'll ever see my father and son again?" She'd cried enough to fill a sea.

"We must keep up our strength," Marlene gently insisted. "And remember, the Lord only gives us what He knows we can handle." When Lara didn't respond, Marlene sulked from the room, defeated, leaving the tray of food, which she'd find again in the morning, untouched. The other children tried their best, but there was an undeniable strain in the house. Each day darkened with ominous uncertainty.

On the fifth morning since her husband left, a sunny Tuesday with warmer-than-usual temperatures, Marlene bustled around the kitchen preparing breakfast for the children.

"Doesn't this sausage smell delicious?" she asked, hopefully. Her positivity felt forced—even she knew it. It was everything in her power to get out of bed and on with the day each morning. The covers held her tight, begging her not to go. She'd have loved nothing more than to sink into her blankets and her sorrow and stay curled up on her husband's side. Marlene had been sleeping there—inhaling his scent—since he'd left.

The thought of losing not only her treasured grandson, but also the love of her life, caused a physical ache deep inside her body, which was only intensified by the dark solitude of the evening hours. Every night she buried her face in Gerald's pillow, letting her tears form a wet and widening circle.

Then the sun would rise again, beckoning for her to summon the strength of another day. She'd put on a happy face, even though it was just a mask to hide her pain. She greeted the children's faces with a smile and hug, saving her tears for the nights when she was alone in her room. In the mornings, there'd be icy tracks of salt on her cheeks, which she'd wipe away with the pad of her thumb.

Marlene placed breakfast on the table. "Looks glorious, right?" The children nodded quietly, their faces drooped in sadness. Marlene sighed. Her naturally positive disposition couldn't break their worry. But she certainly tried.

"Where's Lara?" she asked as she placed a piece of sausage on each child's plate.

"Maybe she's not up yet," Miriam suggested.

Marlene frowned and finished scooping a spoonful of eggs onto their plates. She couldn't help the apprehension she felt whenever Lara was the only one "missing." After all, the last time that happened, she really had been gone.

Leaving her dish empty, Marlene wandered through the kitchen toward the stairs and climbed with light feet. At the top, she stopped and listened for any rustling that might suggest Lara was awake. A soft whimper stopped her in her tracks. But the sound wasn't coming from Lara's room at the end of the hall. It was closer. It was coming from Marlene's.

She pushed open the door to see Lara huddled in a ball on the floor near the base of Erich's crib. Her hand reached up, clutching onto the bottom rung. The rest of her body collapsed in anguish.

"Oh Lara," Marlene said, kneeling next to her daughter.

"I just can't forgive myself," Lara cried. Her shoulders shook and she sniveled against Marlene's shoulder when the woman pulled her into an embrace. "I miss him so much."

"Me too, darling. Me too."

"It's been five days. Don't you think we should have heard something by now?"

"I don't know, Lara." Marlene's eyes welled. "But I trust that your father is doing everything he can to bring Erich home. We must stay strong and not lose faith."

"But it's so hard."

"Yes, it is." A tear rolled down Marlene's cheek. Being this close to the crib, she caught wisps of the little boy's scent—a mixture of sweet talcum powder and musky cinnamon.

"How much longer do we wait?" Lara asked. "I mean, at some point, don't you think people are going to start asking questions? Then what do we do?"

Marlene stared at the girl. Her questions were valid, but not new—Marlene had lay awake for several nights obsessed with the same uncertainties. Now, like all those times alone, she couldn't offer an answer.

She held Lara's hands in her own, and the girl laid her head on her mother's shoulder. Two bowed bodies weighted by the crushing pressure of grief. Their hush left so many things unsaid. But really, what else was there to say?

At once, a door slammed downstairs, making the two women jump.

"FATHER!" a collective outburst echoed from the floor below. Marlene and Lara looked to each other stunned, their eyes expressing the same thought: *Gerald? Father? Home?*

In disbelief, they clamored to their feet and ran to the door, bounding down the steps and practically tripping over one another. Marlene turned the corner into the kitchen first and let out a gasp.

"Gerald!" Her husband stood in the middle of the room, six children clawing at him with hungry affection. Marlene could barely make out his face among the twist of bodies and limbs. He kissed their hair and hugged their heads into him. Lena's face was wet with tears. Felix's chin shook despite his attempt at composure.

When Marlene entered the room, Gerald glanced up. Their eyes met and brightened with relief. All the emotion she'd been restraining for a week poured from her exhausted soul. He was home!

Alive.

Whole.

Safe.

But as she walked toward him, she remembered the reason he'd been gone in the first place.

"Erich?" she asked with hopeful eyes.

The children parted, revealing the little boy in Gerald's arms. Bettina reached a hand up to stroke Erich's cheek and he smiled, as if the whole ordeal of the past few days had never happened.

"Erich!" Lara cried, pushing past Marlene and flinging her arms around both her father and son. Gerald passed the boy to Lara and she crumpled to her knees, squeezing her son against her breast. "I'm so sorry, Erich, I'm so sorry. Please forgive me," she wept.

The children watched awestruck at the wild abandon with which Lara grieved. They had never witnessed such a display of emotion, and the older ones placed a hand over their mouths to control their own happy tears.

Lara stood without releasing her grip on Erich, and faced her father who had his arms around his wife.

"Thank you, Father," she cried. She laid her forehead on his shoulder and sobbed. "I owe you everything."

"Shhh," he soothed. "We're home now. Everything is okay."

"I thought I'd never see you both again."

"I wasn't going to give up. Not in a million years."

"I knew the Lord wouldn't take you from us," Marlene said. "Oh, darling, I'm so glad you're safe."

The rest of the children linked arms and surrounded their parents in embrace. They stood that way for what felt like hours, until an innocent voice broke the silence.

It was Gloria, who tugged on Marlene's dress with a smile. "Can we finish breakfast now?"

THIRTY-TWO

The water in the bowl turned a marbled pink. Marlene dipped a rag and wrung out the tepid water before placing it gently on Gerald's palm. The gash had crusted over, leaving a raised mosaic of deep reds and blacks stretching from his ring finger to the pad of his thumb. It was superficial: not deep enough to need stitches, thankfully.

Marlene dabbed the wet cloth against his skin. He winced. Slowly and with care, she wiped the hardened scab remnants to reveal the wound below.

"It's a bad cut," Marlene said. "What happened?"

"Tripped in the middle of the night. Nasty rock broke my fall." Gerald flinched as she administered rubbing alcohol that Lena had fetched from the medicine cabinet.

"Where were you?"

"Don't know exactly." He flinched again. "Somewhere over the Alps."

"The Alps?" Marlene flung her head up in surprise as she wrapped his hand in a clean bandage.

"Yes. That's how we got home. Went over the mountains again."

Marlene gasped. She hadn't even considered it; she figured he'd come home in the same way he'd left.

"And the car?"

"Left it. It was the only way."

The memories of their escape two years prior came rushing back. Marlene pictured the contours of the trails—sometimes tight and winding—and how they'd open up to rolling fields of bright green grass.

"Took us three days," Gerald continued. "But we had no choice. The borders were on lockdown. We never would have made it through by car."

"But what about food?"

"I had a few things in my bag. Don't worry, I made sure Erich ate. The Reverend Mother gave me some fruit and bread to take, too."

"You were at the abbey?" Marlene exclaimed.

"Yes," he chuckled, realizing this was all coming at such a surprise. "Oh my love, I have so much to tell you. But first, we need to eat. I'm starved."

Marlene made a plate for her husband and Erich—there were plenty of sausages left. Gerald ate ravenously, finally able to stomach a full meal. Erich, happily sitting on Lara's lap, devoured every crumb. Their journey had left them famished. With little food to last the journey, Gerald had given most of it to Erich.

Their plates licked clean, Erich squirmed to be put down, but Lara held tight; she never wanted to let him go again. Only at his fussing did she allow him to shimmy to the floor and toddle to his basket of toys in the living room.

"So resilient," Marlene said, watching Erich. She interlocked her arm through Gerald's. "It's quite amazing what children can withstand."

"I just pray he won't remember any of this," Lara whispered.

"He won't."

The little girls, bored already with grown-up talk, retreated to the living room. Cradling and cooing over the dolls in their arms, they already felt a sense of normalcy with the return of their father. Marlene glanced in their direction and watched Karl engaging Erich in a game of peek-a-boo. Her heart nearly burst with happiness.

"I owe you an apology," Marlene said, reaching for Lara's hand. "For everything."

Lara stared, a flush of warmth coming over her.

"We shouldn't have put you in that position, with Erich I mean. If I hadn't suggested it, this all never would have happ—."

"No," Lara interrupted. "It was my choice to leave, Mother. I was foolish. I'm the one who owes the apology."

"Well, I can't help but blame myself for lighting the spark that started us down this path in the first place."

"We've all made mistakes."

"I suppose you're right. There's enough blame to go around." Marlene squeezed Lara's hand. The two exchanged a smile of understanding.

Felix and Lena joined the adults at the table, pulling chairs near their father, trying to soak up every drop of him.

"Looks like you're going to have to learn to eat with your other hand," Felix said to his father, pointing to Gerald's bandage.

"Ha! I guess you're right." The hearty laugh made him grimace. He brought his fingers to his jawline. The skin was tender to the touch, even through the thick gauze.

"You have bruises all over," Marlene said. "Gerald, I'm afraid to ask why. This can't all be from tripping over a rock." She lightly touched the black and blue marks on his face.

"No." He cast his eyes downward, miserably remembering the brawl at the apartment. Could he spare them the truth about the tragic outcome?

"Father," Lara interrupted his thoughts, "I need to know. How did you get Erich away from Rubin?"

He studied Marlene, the grave look in his eyes saying everything—this wasn't going to be an easy story to tell.

"It's okay, Father. You can tell me. I can handle it."

"I don't want to cause you any more pain, Lara."

"My heart has changed." Lara placed her hand on top of her father's. "I know now that Rubin was never the person I thought he was. I'm ashamed that I let him manipulate me the way he did. Please, tell me."

He took a breath, held it for a moment, and then released it into the air. He spoke in a low voice, not wanting the younger children to hear. Beginning slowly, he told them about crossing the border and how he'd convinced the guard to let him pass for official military business. He told them about his meeting with Markus at the abbey and the plan they'd conceived.

"Uncle Markus is so clever!" Felix said.

Gerald grinned. "Yes, he's a schemer all right," he said. "That's why I knew I needed his help."

He continued to explain how Markus conned Hans Rainer into revealing Rubin's address, and how he himself showed up at the apartment the following day.

261

"And he just let Erich leave with you?" Lara asked, bewildered.

Gerald paused and looked to his daughter, meeting her eyes with a solemn face. "No, my dear," he said. And when he didn't elaborate, the origin of his bruises became clear.

"Oh. I see," Lara said softly. The guilt returned, heavy as a stone in her stomach. His suffering was her doing—even if it hadn't been her hands delivering the blow. "But what if he finds us? What if he tries to take Erich back again?" Her voice teetered on the edge of crumbling.

"He won't be finding us, Lara."

"What do you mean?"

"Rubin is gone." Gerald closed his eyes and saw the barrel of the gun aimed straight at his face. The memory was jarring.

Lena gasped. Lara, stunned, was still.

"Gerald, tell me you didn't!" Marlene said, wide-eyed.

"No," he quickly assured her. "It wasn't me."

"But how?" Lara's voice shook and her eyes filled.

Gerald thought of his daughter and all she'd been through. Her fragile heart had suffered the pain of deception and betrayal from a man she loved. What good would it do to add another layer of agony with the revelation of Hannah? It would serve nothing more than to add insult to injury.

He wouldn't do it.

"Some things are better left unsaid," Gerald said quietly. "Let's just leave it at that, huh?"

It was more a statement than a question. There would be no elaboration. With those words—plain, yet resolute—the group understood that the details of that day were to remain with Gerald, alone.

* * *

That evening, as the family settled into the comfort of the den, serenity made its way back into the house. They were together—and that was enough. After a few hours, the past was gone, and only the present mattered.

Miriam, Gloria and Bettina formed a star on the floor with their outstretched legs, the soles of their feet pressed together. In the middle, Erich scampered from girl to girl, kissing their faces and giggling with the glee at their simple game.

The older children burrowed close to their father. Age and maturity gave them the gift of appreciation, and they didn't want to miss a moment away from him. Marlene, sitting next to Gerald, linked her arm in his. They intertwined their fingers, and she stroked his thumb. Her mind should have been reeling, but it wasn't. She was calm—filled to the top with gratitude and contentment.

At half past nine, Erich began to fade. He crawled toward Marlene and pulled the hem of her skirt to stand. With a wide yawn, he rubbed his eyes.

"Getting tired, little one?" she said, running her hand across the top of his head. "You've been through such an adventure."

Lara watched from where she sat and felt a twinge of sadness. Was it all for nothing? Would Marlene always be "Mother" to Erich? She was thankful for her son's safety—something that wouldn't have happened without her father. Lara was indebted to him. But was this her eternal punishment? Her heavy heart felt as though it would tear at the seams.

On the floor, Miriam turned to Erich, her face eye-level with his. "What a sleepy little boy," she said, leaning in to rub their noses together. Erich chortled and swatted at her face.

"Mother, are you going to take him to bed?" she asked Marlene.

Again, Marlene and Gerald glanced at one another, speaking the wordless language only spouses know. The look alone was enough—they both understood. Marlene gave the slightest nod and he reciprocated.

"No, darling," Marlene said aloud to everyone. "I'm not 'Mother' anymore. Not to Erich, I mean."

The children glanced around, confused. On the far side of the couch, Lara sat upright. She stared at her father. A tear fell and bounced off her cheek.

Was he really going to say it?

"Lara is Erich's mother," Gerald said. "And from now on, it's no longer going to be a secret."

Euphoric yet with a sense of disbelief, Lara stood, her thin legs trembling beneath her. The children parted, giving Lara a clear path toward her son. She bent and lifted him from the floor. Bringing his tiny face in front of hers, Lara stared into his eyes, blue as the summer sky. Side by side, there was no denying their likeness—Erich was her carbon copy.

Their faces nuzzled together, Lara let out an exhale that had been buried deep within her soul, burning for release.

"Mama loves you," she whispered. And with that, she turned to take her son to bed.

EPILOGUE

Five Years Later

L ara grabbed the long black case from inside the cedar chest and made her way out of the house into the mid-morning light. Across the gravel driveway, a man swung an axe, splitting a log down the center. She watched as he picked up another piece, placed it on the stump, and swung again, chopping it directly in the middle.

Something about the cracking noise—the metal blade tearing the wood in two, as well as the rhythmic grunt he made with each swing—comforted her. She felt protected, both by the strength of him and the warmth the logs would bring to their home.

Sensing her presence, the man looked up, shielding his eyes from the sun with a calloused hand. Lara waved.

"Hello, darling," the man called back. "Heading into the fields again?"

"We're going to have our music lesson outside today," she replied with a warm smile.

"Okay, be safe."

"Always." She blew him a kiss and he pretended to catch it in midair, then gave her a wink.

He returned to his work. From where she stood, Lara saw the lean outline of muscle in her husband's arms. She clasped the case tighter, feeling a pinch where the handle pressed against the gold band on her finger. She looked down at the wedding ring, engraved with a swirling pattern of interlacing vines. It fit so perfectly, as though it had always been there.

At times she still couldn't believe this life was hers.

As she walked up the narrow footpath toward the hills, she glanced over her shoulder and took in the sight. The house was far from glamorous, what with the clapboard siding and chipping cornflower paint, nothing like the sprawling mansion of her youth in Austria. An old farmhouse, it sat on a large plot of land just outside the city limits. Delightfully quaint with the charm of the previous century, it wasn't what she envisioned—as a child— her future home to be.

But it was hers—hers and Steffan's. And somehow that made it exactly what she always wanted.

They had met by chance. Nearly six months after her father had rescued Erich, Lara was accompanying Marlene to order a new bed for Erich—a small piece that would fit next to Lara's own, as the boy was quickly outgrowing the small crib. They browsed the store, debating which style would match best. But instead of focusing on choosing a design, Lara was distracted by the tall, young man loading dark, cherry boards into the back of a pickup truck. It was his rugged good looks and strong arms to which she was instantly drawn. Later, Lara learned he was an apprentice to one of the most skilled carpenters in Zürich, a man who crafted custom furniture for many of the prominent families in the city.

Among the headboards and boxsprings, they'd made eye contact and said hello, both flushed in the face. That first meeting turned into a request for a proper meal. And from there, the natural course of young love commenced. Steffan called on Lara at the Weiss' home, and while Marlene met the young man with giddy excitement, Gerald displayed a more restrained air of caution.

"I know what you're thinking," Marlene said in private before her husband even had a chance to speak. "You think he's beneath us because he's just a woodworker." Gerald stared at his wife, expressionless. Boldly, she continued. "Who are we to judge another man's passion and talent? And how could we deny our daughter a chance at love? *Real* love. Don't you think she deserves it?"

"Yes, but—"

"No buts, Gerald. Look at us. Who am I? I was a poor young woman with no means before I came into your life."

He considered her words, stubbornly. Marlene fixed her hands on her hips—she'd learned to hold her ground against his unbending nature.

After a moment, Gerald's eyes softened. "You're right," he sighed. "Thank you for always showing me the truth."

It was a lesson they'd both realized when their undeniable pull brought them together: Love is love, and there's little one can do to stop it.

From there, Marlene and Gerald gave their blessing to Lara and Steffan. The sweethearts spent hours together, discovering new places around the city. On the park benches, they sat just close enough to share one another's heat. Steffan was respectful, never pushy. Somehow, he sensed a fragility—one he didn't want to fracture.

After several weeks, Lara decided to open up about Erich's true identity.

"He's my son," she revealed one night as they strolled through the streets of Zürich. She waited for his reaction.

"The little boy I've seen playing in the yard at your house? I assumed he was your youngest brother."

"No. His name is Erich. And he's mine."

Steffan thought for a moment, then grabbed Lara's hand. He looked more deeply into her eyes than anyone ever had. "I'd love to meet him."

* * *

Lara watched as Erich ran ahead, through the tall grass that tickled his shins.

"Stop when you get to the rock!" she yelled, pointing right to where the boy was galloping.

"Okay, Mother!" He sprinted on, flapping his arms in the air. "Look at me, I'm a bird!"

Lara chuckled as he darted back and forth, dipping each of his wings toward the ground before turning in the other direction. After a few yards, Erich reached the rock and came to a stop, panting, bent at the waist with his hands on his knees.

Lara walked slower, allowing the small set of feet beside her to keep up. She looked down at her hand grasped tightly by five little fingers. It was the perfect day—light breeze, puffy clouds and the smell of nature all around.

"Come along, Trudy," she cooed. The girl with ringlets the color of cinnamon glanced at her mother and smiled. They wore matching dresses, which Lara had sewn from pale green calico. Trudy—Lara, in miniature form—had the same sharp eyes and delicate features, although her red-brown hair was Steffan's.

They eventually made it to their spot at the rock. Erich waited patiently, blowing dandelion fluff into the air before plucking another weed from the ground.

Lara delivered her instructions.

"Alright," she said. "Have a seat, Erich. Trudy, sit next to your brother. That's good. Okay, today we're going to learn a new song."

"Yay!" Erich cheered.

Lara flicked open the buckles on her guitar case and pulled out the beautiful instrument, light sliding along its silver strings. A cloud shifted, sending a ray of light toward them like a drop of golden sun.

"This is a special song," she said. "Oma taught it to me. In fact, Tante Miriam was your age when she learned it."

Erich smiled and clapped his hands in his lap. Trudy copied him.

With a strum of the strings, Lara played the first chord.

"Now, let's see where to begin. Ah, how about we start at the very beginning. It was, after all, always a very good place to start."

Did you know that reader reviews are the #1 way self-published authors gain visibility? In a world with incredible competition and mysterious internet algorithms, growing a fan base is a major hurdle. Authors count on reviews by the people who buy their books.

If you enjoyed this book, please take a few moments to write a review of it on Amazon and Goodreads.

I'd also love for you to follow my writing journey on Instagram @jennifercravenauthor. So many more stories coming your way.

Thank you!

ACKNOWLEDGEMENTS

For as long as I can remember, I've loved musical theater. I recall seeing *Phantom of the Opera* on Broadway as a young girl and being swept away by the pure emotion of the music. Likewise, there were many days I bypassed homework after school to get lost in *Fiddler on the Roof* on VHS in my grandmother's basement. Something about the songs...

You might be able to trace the inspiration of this novel, and truthfully, what drew me to this story was watching the film on repeat. To this day, it remains my all-time favorite. For that, I can thank my dad, who always seemed to be humming some tune or another. Now, decades later, he sings those beloved songs with my children.

I owe a depth of gratitude to my editor, Jill, for her brilliant eye and ability to make my words soar. That, along with her genuine interest in my work, makes writing that much more of a

ACKNOWLEDGEMENTS

pleasure. My early readers and launch team are also invaluable assets, to whom I'm so grateful.

Thank you to my family and friends for being my biggest cheerleaders—hounding me for details about my books even when I remain tight-lipped, and then singing my praises from the rooftops. Mom, Dan, Diane, Brian, Kelli, Gram, Torie, Megan, and many more...Your support means the world to me.

Finally, to my husband, DJ—thank you for helping me plot stories. I owe a lot of this one to you. And to my three littles, who put up with my marathon writing sessions, and share in my excitement over writing milestones, you'll never know the depths of my love.

Enjoy a selection of Jennifer Craven's debut novel, *A Long Way From Blair Street,* available on Amazon.

A Long Way From Blair Street

PROLOGUE

I n her dreams, Jeanne was always running. Running down a
cracked sidewalk with the neighborhood girls, giggling about
what penny candy they would choose that day. Or playing
tag with her three brothers in the backyard, keeping up and
matching their pace step for step. Even in nightmares—the ones
where she was being chased by a wild animal, or where a faceless
monster threatened to eat her up—Jeanne was running.
Unrestrained and able, with wild vigor.

Feet pounding on the pavement, arms swinging back and
forth, her body propelled her forward. She'd be exhausted from
the exertion. Bending at the waist and resting her hands on her
knees, she'd gulp in mouthfuls of air, letting the oxygen reach her
brain. Her energy nearly depleted—but never fully. Because in
her dreams, she always got back up and ran some more.

She was always running. Perhaps because she knew when she
woke up, it would all be an impossible hope.

CHAPTER 1

1932

B efore the sun breached the horizon, Jeanne Gildea's eyes were already wide open. She didn't dream last night, which was odd. But it was easily explained: she simply hadn't slept, anticipation keeping her awake and tossing all night. Today was a big day—the biggest—in her young life. It was the first day of school. Finally, it was her turn to join her older brother, Dick, at the big, brick elementary school a few blocks away.

Jeanne lifted her head, leaving behind a deep impression on the pillow. She propped her small frame up on her elbows and looked around the room. Her brothers were still sleeping. Dick was the only other one who would have to be up for school, as Joseph and baby Tommy had years before it would be their turn. She didn't envy their ability to stay home.

Jeanne liked sharing a room with her brothers. They spent their evenings whispering to each other after they were sent to bed, quietly enough so only their little ears could hear. Jeanne sang the alphabet, and Dick corrected her when she strung together L, M, N, O and P into one letter. She'd giggle. But never too loud. They certainly didn't want Mother or Daddy coming up to scold them. Even one-year-old Tommy knew that. The four siblings made a game of seeing who could stay up the longest, the next morning's bragging rights awarded as the sole prize.

Jeanne never won.

She was too tired. The abundance of energy her body burned throughout the day meant she couldn't fight the urge to sleep. After Mother helped her into bed each night, her tiny form would melt into the mattress, releasing the tension her underdeveloped muscles had used that day. At last, her joints came to a much-deserved rest.

But this morning, despite a fitful night's sleep, Jeanne felt a surge of strength. As the dark morning hours gave way to blue morning light, her thoughts turned to the day ahead. Adrenaline kicked in as she realized her first taste of independence was within reach.

"Pssssst!" she whispered in Dick's direction, an attempt to stir him from his peaceful slumber. His eyes fluttered open and he rubbed them, groggy, until she came into view—a mass of dark hair, cut into a short bob and blunt bangs, atop a skinny stem of a body. It took Dick a moment to remember the significance of the day, and Jeanne's eager smile was an unmistakable reminder.

Dick returned her smile, tossing the covers off his body and coming to a seated position. "C'mon," he said quietly. "I'll help you up."

He shuffled over to where she was sitting upright in bed, taking care not to wake the other two. Mother had chosen a dress for Jeanne to wear for her first day—the best one she owned, a hand- me-down from an older girl in the neighborhood. Jeanne reached for the ruffled collar of the garment that laid over the footboard of her bed. Gliding it over her head, she twisted in place so Dick could button the three ivory clasps in the back.

She fingered the little embroidered rosebuds on the bodice, and she felt a flutter deep in her belly. The dress made her feel special.

From the floor, Dick grabbed Jeanne's leg braces and slid each leg through the splints and into the tiny back shoes attached. Jeanne shimmied her legs into position, adjusting the braces on either side of her knees. With her crutches in hand, she gingerly slipped off the edge of the bed, placing both feet onto the hardwood and finding her balance.

Her feet barely touched the ground before she turned to her brother and whispered, "Let's go!"

Dick raced from the room, heading toward the stairs. Jeanne faltered behind, grabbing onto furniture as she hobbled out of the room. At the top of the steps, she lowered to her bottom, sliding down the stairs one at a time, feet first until she reached ground level.

"Wait for me," she hissed, but Dick was already out of sight.

Rounding the corner to the kitchen, Jeanne found Mother at the counter, buttering a piece of toast for each of them.

Madeline, normal height with soft curves and short curly hair, wore an apron around her waist, a dish towel thrown over her shoulder. She placed the crispy brown bread on a small saucer next to a child's size glass of orange juice.

Their father, Raymond, sat at the little wooden table, newspaper in hand. He folded it as the children entered the room.

"Good morning, Jeanne," Madeline said with a smile. "Morning, Dick. Ready for your first day? It's a big one for you, Jeanne." She bent to help her daughter into a chair, pushing it close to the table.

Jeanne nodded, her toothy grin a testament to her excitement. Raymond gave Jeanne a blank stare before returning to his paper, never uttering more than a mumble. Madeline glared at her husband, her eyes burning through the paper. Her annoyance went unnoticed by him, although he wouldn't have cared anyway.

"C'mon, you two," she said, returning her attention to the children. "Eat up. I don't want you late on the first day."

The children ate their toast in silence, Jeanne guzzling her juice and finishing before Dick. With too much in her mouth, a squirt of juice dribbled down her face, leaving a bright orange trail on her soft pink dress.

"Jeanne!" Madeline scolded, hurrying to blot the stain before it set into the fabric. "Now you look like Gravel Gertie." The phrase was a reference to the ragamuffin children in town, whose torn clothes were a clear indication of their social standing. The Gildea family didn't have much money, but Madeline insisted her children appear put together.

"Sorry, Mother," Jeanne said in a quiet voice. Then, with a surge of optimism, "I can just wear my sweater over top!" Madeline chuckled under her breath. Always full of life, her daughter, regardless of what obstacles threatened to block her path. Unfortunately, a sweater wasn't appropriate on a seventy-five-degree day in August.

"I think I got it all," Madeline said, giving the dress a final wipe. A large water mark settled on the front, and Jeanne could feel the cool moisture on her skin. "It'll dry before you get to school."

"Don't worry, Jeanne, I'm sure the kids will still like you," Dick assured his little sister. Once Dick finished his breakfast, Madeline helped Jeanne off the chair and outside, down the narrow porch steps of 703 Blair Street.

Still in the kitchen, Raymond laid a heavy hand on Dick's shoulder. "You're in charge of Jeanne on the way to and from school, Dick," Raymond said, his tone firm and insistent. "Take care of her. You know she's fragile. You must always protect your little sister."

It was the most his father had spoken to him in over a week. Raymond was an inward man, so the children knew that when he did speak, it warranted their full attention. Dick nodded in acknowledgement. He liked the sense of responsibility that Jeanne's entering school bestowed upon him. He'd be her caretaker, of sorts. Her guardian. At least for the short walk to school. Besides the fact that he loved his sister, he felt a greater desire to make his father proud.

So with another slight nod in Raymond's direction, Dick grabbed his school sack and bounded out the door, catching up to Madeline and Jeanne near the sidewalk. Their mother had placed Jeanne in the small wagon, a rolled-up blanket propped behind her back for comfort. The girl's braced legs stuck straight out in front of her and the skirt of her dress pressed flat in her lap.

"Ready, Jeanne?" Dick asked, circling around to the front of the wagon and reaching down to grab the metal handle.

"Yep!" She clasped her fingers around the sides of the red wagon. "Bye, Mother!" She waved enthusiastically.

And with that, they took off toward school, eight blocks away. Dick pulled her along, chattering about what to expect, the ins and outs of being a kindergartener.

"What if no one likes me?" Jeanne asked.

"Of course they'll like you," Dick assured her. "Why wouldn't they?"

From a young age, Jeanne understood she was different. Her family normalized her condition as best as possible, but Jeanne was wary of how she would be treated by strangers. Even as a toddler, she'd seen the stares when the family was out in public.

Only a few feet into their journey, Jeanne glanced over her shoulder. Mother and Daddy were back inside the small white house. She imagined Mother cleaning up the breakfast dishes and getting her little brothers ready for the day. Jeanne was about to turn around to continue her conversation with Dick when she noticed a slight movement in the window. Squinting a bit more, she saw her Daddy's face peering through a slit in the curtains. Her protector: he was always safeguarding, always concerned about her. Knowing this made her heart happy.

* * *

Jeanne was just a baby when she contracted polio—eighteen months old to be exact. It started with a cough and some flu-like symptoms before rapidly progressing to the point that her extremities began deteriorating. The year was 1928, over two decades before the development of the polio vaccine that would abolish the disease and save countless lives.

By this point in the United States, Americans were under a state of cautious paranoia. The epidemic of 1916, one of the most devastating outbreaks in history, was still not quite a distant memory for many. Over 27,000 cases of polio were diagnosed that year, resulting in over 6,000 deaths—the large majority were children under the age of five. Centered in New York, it wasn't very far from Jeanne's home in central Pennsylvania. Hollidaysburg, a small, rural town that would later be known as the home of the "Slinky," sat about fifty miles southwest of State College.

Polio caused mass hysteria. The nation was terrified. Parents confined children to their homes in an effort to avoid contact with infected peers. By the time Jeanne was toddling around the house, panic across the country had mildly subsided, particularly outside major cities. Yet polio was still in the consciousness of parents everywhere, even in small towns like Hollidaysburg with a population of under 4,000.

Children were forbidden to swim in the Juniata River that ran through town. On the hottest days, local officials turned on the fire hydrants, allowing the kids to run through the spraying water and splash in the cool puddles. Yet even that was nerve-wracking for parents.

When Jeanne displayed early symptoms, a high fever that lasted nearly a week and a fussy temperament which the toddler could only explain by clutching and shaking her legs, Madeline was distraught. Polio was easy to identify and diagnose, especially after the pandemic. Not one to engage in an outward display of emotion, she remained stoic, saving her weeping for private moments when she felt safe enough to let her guard down. When her despair threatened to bubble over her unflappable exterior, Madeline excused herself to the bathroom, where she would shut the door behind her, lean over the sink, and watch her tears run down the basin.

Raymond, on the other hand, was determined. Despite his rough surface, often misinterpreted as disinterest in his own children, he vowed to get his little girl the best care possible, regardless of his social standing or financial means.

"You know we can't afford that sort of treatment, Raymond," Madeline lamented in hushed tones after Dick and Jeanne went to bed. She looked down at Joe, an infant swaddled in the crook of her arm.

"Well," Raymond replied evenly, "we have to at least try." He may have been a stern father and a distant husband, but Raymond's world view centered around responsibility. Providing and caring for his family was his duty.

"But how?"

They stared at each other, neither able to formulate a reasonable plan of action.

"I'll go to Shriner's. The children's hospital in Altoona," Raymond announced. "They're specialists. Maybe I can talk to a doctor."

The following day Raymond did just that. With his chin held high, he pleaded for his daughter's life. It went against everything he stood for to ask for a handout. As his upbringing, and later his parenting philosophy dictated: if you wanted something in life, you worked for it. Earned it.

Nothing was given out for free.

So it wasn't easy, being at the mercy of someone else. A proud man, Raymond put dignity aside for the sake of Jeanne. Hat in hand, he asked for help.

* * *

Raymond Gildea was born in 1893 in the bedroom of a small house in Hollidaysburg, Pennsylvania. The eldest of eight children in a devout Catholic family commanded by his father, Harry, he developed a keen sense of independence from a young age. As his mother's attention shifted to the younger children and new babies, Raymond was often left to his own devices.

A smart, scrappy boy, he liked to tinker with toys and tools, and was always curious about how things worked—a skill that would become central to his career as a yard engineer on the Pennsylvania railroad. His upbringing wasn't entirely terrible—bright moments of delight sprinkled in—yet it was far from pleasant. Little parental affection and a "do or die" attitude greatly shaped the way Raymond understood the harsh realities of the world.

Much like other parents of their generation, Harry and Mary Gildea were not the warm and cuddly type. This rough suit of armor intensified after Raymond's deployments to France and Germany during the First World War. Akin to many of his brothers in arms, Raymond was hardened by the things he witnessed abroad. These traumas manifested in self-imposed distance on good days, blatant meanness on the worst. It would take decades to soften him at all.

Working the railroad put Raymond's ingenuity to good use, shifting the cars in the yard and orchestrating their placements. He was busy, focused—work ethic something he valued above all else. He also came to enjoy his fair share of after-hours activities when the work day was done.

"Hey Ray! Join us for a drink after your shift?" Eddie, a buddy from the line, asked one Friday afternoon. It was 1923—the peak of Prohibition—but people still found ways to track down their coveted alcohol.

"Yeah, sure. Why not," Raymond replied, cranking a heavy steel gear. He pulled a bandana from his back pocket and wiped the sweat from his brow.

An hour later, the whistle blew, signaling the end of the day. Raymond, Eddie, and a few other men walked from the rail yard into town, each step leaving another work week behind. They passed the U.S. Hotel Tavern, a mainstay in the little town since the 1830s. A favorite bar among the younger crowd, the tavern— once a prominent spot for food and entertainment—was now all but shut down thanks to the Volstead Act.

The group continued on. Raymond, the oldest of the gang at thirty-one, led the way, his natural swagger rubbing off on the men nearly a decade his junior. A few blocks down, they came to a discreet door along a side wall between two buildings. There was no marking, no address numbers to account for its location. A solitary metal knocker hung in the center of its frame.

Raymond rapped the knocker twice and a few seconds later, a muffled voice penetrated through the wooden door.

"What's the password?" a man's gruff voice asked.

"Nice teeth," Raymond said, turning and winking to his buddies.

The door swung open and the men slipped inside. The speakeasy was busy that evening, groups and couples packing the secret saloon for a taste of happy hour. Women swapped their house frocks for something fancier, the men freshened up and clean shaven after a long week of work.

At five-foot-ten Raymond wasn't particularly tall, so he stood on his tiptoes, scanning the bar to see who else was there and locate an open stool. That night, in addition to a place to sit, he was looking for a certain someone in particular: Helen. The daughter of the local pharmacist, she was his latest romantic fling. They'd been out on a few dates, nothing serious, and while he enjoyed having a pretty little thing on his arm, he didn't envision it going much further.

Raymond glanced around the room, searching for her auburn hair, but he came up empty. She wasn't there tonight. He felt disappointment, followed quickly by relief. Whereas the women he dated were prone to falling hard and fast, Raymond wasn't interested in anything too serious.

Too much time together could send the wrong message. He was a bachelor, and planned to stay that way.

Raymond returned his attention to his railroad pals who had gathered at a table near the back. The men ordered beers and clinked glasses.

"You know," Eddie said, in between sips, "I'm thinking about asking Ruth to marry me." His eyes darted from friend to friend, waiting for a reaction.

"You're what?" Raymond replied, his nose scrunching and eyebrows furling in repulsion. "Why in God's name would you want to go and do that?"

"I love her, Ray. I mean, she's a good woman. Good to me. Not bad on the eyes either."

"Love, huh? Well, I don't know why you'd want to get yourself tied down like that. But go ahead, Ed, if ya think that's what ya want." He took a long gulp of his beer. The others at the table offered congratulations. "Way to go, Eddie," someone cracked.

They raised their glasses and toasted to Eddie and Ruth's future. But all the while, Raymond couldn't help but question whether he'd ever feel the same. He'd been single for so long, free to do what he wanted, when he wanted. Most of the boys he went to school with were long married with children. Maybe marriage wasn't part of his fate.

While his friends saluted Eddie, Raymond shifted his focus to the other patrons, out enjoying the evening. There were many familiar faces in the room, a result of living in a small town. Several people made eye contact and gave a wave or a nod in his direction. Still, once in a blue moon a newcomer would show up, giving the locals a new subject about whom to gossip.

Raymond peered around the room toward the door. That's when he saw Madeline.

She breezed through the entrance with a girlfriend, their arms linked. They had a sense of carefree ease in their body language, light and cheerful, the way one feels after the first glass of champagne. She wore a pale blue cotton dress with a dropped waist and long Chelsea collar—not the fanciest in the room, but enough to catch Raymond's eye. Upon closer inspection, he saw her brown Charleston heels were scuffed at the toes.

Still, he couldn't avert his gaze. It wasn't her lack of fashion statement that drew Raymond off his chair to approach her table, but rather her big smile and the glint in her eyes. Moving closer, he noticed how her cropped chestnut hair framed her round face in a way that gave her a youthful look. She seemed approachable. As he neared the table, his confidence grew.

"Can I buy you a drink," he dared, catching her off guard. He stood to her left, hands in his pockets. Madeline snapped her head toward him and then back to her friend across the table, a coy smile on her face.

289

"Yes," she replied, looking up through her eyelashes. "Sure you can." She blushed as he turned to get them a drink, returning a moment later and pulling a chair over to join her group. Minutes turned into hours and before they knew it, the barman announced last call. Leaving the speakeasy that evening, Raymond knew Helen had been replaced—Madeline was the new object of his desires.

They spent the next three months together, savoring frequent dinners, the occasional night of dancing, and plenty of hours passing the time the way young lovers do. He learned she was a Catholic grade school teacher and had come from Newry, a small town about fifteen minutes outside of Hollidaysburg. He noticed her lips were always chapped, and she'd pick at them as they talked late into the night, peeling off thin layers of lipstick-stained skin. Raymond found the quirk surprisingly endearing.

She told him her father was a pig farmer. A drunk and moody man, Madeline was anxious to escape her home life. Raymond enjoyed Madeline's company—she was sweet, and they had fun. Things were light and easy. Just how he liked it. That is until one Sunday afternoon when they met for lunch and he was startled by the ashen look on her face.

Her hands trembling, her voice shaking, she couldn't look him in the eyes.

"I'm pregnant," she whispered. Her thumb nervously scraped against the nails on her other fingers. "What are we going to do?"

Jennifer Craven holds degrees in fashion merchandising and textiles from Mercyhurst University and North Carolina State University. Her writing began with parenting essays and reported pieces for numerous national outlets before writing her debut novel, "A Long Way From Blair Street." A lover of words and chocolate, she lives in northwest Pennsylvania with her husband and three children.

Made in the USA
Middletown, DE
10 June 2021